IAAC

IMPERIAL AMERIKAN AIR CORP.

STEAM POWERED TALES OF AWESOMENESS!

by Brian D Thomas & Raymond J Witte,
edited by Greg Schauer, Illustrated by Brian D Thomas

Steampowered Tales of Awesomeness, Volume 1
First Edition

www.steampulptales.com

ISBN-10:0615721524

ISBN-13:978-0-615-72152-1

Dedication-Raymond J Witte

Thank you Mom and Dad, for the nearly 20 years of Catholic education that I'm putting to good use writing about sky pirates and sea monsters.

Thank you Brian, for being my friend, my brother, and my mentor. And for forcing me to learn a new set of skills every time you drag us all into a new fandom.

Thank you Brendan, Billy, Troy, and Richie for being there everytime I needed you guys.

Thank you Grandma and Poppy.

I dedicate this book to my beloved wife Amanda, who suffered through many lonely evenings while I helped bring this monster to life. I love you, babydoll.

Dedication-Brian D Thomas

Thanks to the IAAC crew for helping me craft this universe, and spending your time and money FOR THREE YEARS in traveling around promoting the book and the brand. Ray, Billy, Troy, Bev, Jules, Amanda, Denise,Nathan, Flounder and Richie your dedication and time are much appreciated.

Thanks to my cowriter Ray for being the brother-son thing you've become, and for your patience in being a creative partner to someone who still needs to learn how to share his toys.
Thanks to our editor and guide Greg Schauer without whom this whole thing would have been misspelled and written in crayons.

Thanks to my loving wife Beverly without whos patience and support I would never have finsihed this book. Her stipulation that I actually FINISH this before being distracted by something elses on pain of a pillow over the head in my sleep helped me keep my creative focus...oh, look a bird!

To Mom for her encouragement, and to Dad...I wish you could have lived long enough to see that your instruction as an English teacher, your encouragment in my writing and your insistance that I polish my skills actually paid off.
To Dad.

TABLE OF CONTENTS

IAAC

IMPERIAL AMERIKAN AIR CORP.

FOREWORD

By Raymond J. Witte

Comments by Brian D. Thomas

Steampunk sucks!

Then why did we bother to write this book? Shut up and keep reading.

Actually, it really doesn't. Since Brian and I became actively involved in the fandom through a series of booze fueled brain storming sessions during the fall and winter of 2008 (we had both been quiet admirers of the aesthetic since the 1990s), we have made many friends in the Steampunk Community and have had the opportunity to experience some wonderful art in a host of mediums. With brass and leather, silks and cotton, the stage and the human body, film, and print there are a host of talented creators out there doing fantastic things to express and share their artistic visions with the world. It truly is *lovely*.

Ray says "lovely". I say "awesome"-thus the title of the book-just to be clear!

But it doesn't have enough guns. Or sword fights. Or Martian dinosaurs. Or women in short skirts.

...and these are pretty much things we love to read about-especially short skirts-what? We like em!

Being fans of the pulp authors of the early 20th century, as we dove into Steampunk we found ourselves asking, 'Where the hell are all the damned adventure stories?'

Mind you, we truly respect women, especially those that can pull off a good short skirt...or can sword fight. Women that can do both...okay but back to adventure stories.

That sparked the idea.

But back to that word, '*lovely*.' Steampunk is very lovely.

...and awesome...

Apart from being fans of Burroughs, Doyle, Mundy, Merritt, and Lovecraft, Brian and I are also history enthusiasts. And as any history enthusiast will tell you, the period between the end of the American Civil War and the start of the first World War was only lovely for a couple thousand people in cosmopolitan cities across America and Europe. For most of the world, it was marked by pollution, jingoism, racism, sexism, colonialism, social Darwinism, and predatory capitalism run amok, all against the backdrop of a world that was changing technologically at a terrifying pace. And, by and large, this was being ignored in Steampunk, or waved away, when addressed at all.

What he said...!

That fanned the flames.

From that fire, we forged what we took to calling the 'Girth-verse' which eventually became the volume you hold in your grubby little phalanges, *Steampowered Tales of Awesomeness, Vol. 1*. It is universe that diverged from our own in 1066, where distant lands (and strange, alien worlds) are linked by mysterious skylocks that allow instant travel and where physics-bending technologies make gargantuan airships feasible.

'Cause if you want believable science go read a text book-there are no short skirts in textbooks, my friends.

It's the universe of Imperial Norse Amerika that Horace P Thornton, Anton Gray, Wilhelmina Wigglebottom, Major Girth, the I.A.A.C. and the Cavalcade of Fancy Ladies all call home. It's the universe that Brian and I wallow in. We take the bad and make it awful. We dredge up the worst excesses of the period and haul them into the spotlight. Not because we condone them, but because they're conflict. And conflict makes a good story. That's why we wrote this book. To tell some good stories, particularly stories we didn't think were going to get told other places.

Okay, sometimes we have a socially responsible message too but frankly it's purely secondary to short skirts.

So, sit back, crack open a beverage of your choosing and enjoy. Try not to take our universe too seriously. God knows we don't.

A moose once bit my sister...

PROLOGUE—HOLES IN THE SKY

By Brian D. Thomas

All across the globe the skylocks hang in the sky. Those shimmering whirlpools of light that allow instant travel from one point to another and in some cases one world to another. In the blink of an eye airships travel hundreds, even thousands of miles by flying through the skylocks that dot the world's sky, crossing oceans and mountains, connecting nations and continents. Through the skylocks man has even set foot on other worlds like Mars, Venus, and Ultima Thule, and new skylocks are constantly being discovered on these far off worlds leading to ever-new lands. Who can imagine what life would be like without our world-spanning skylocks?

From the beginning man's eyes were drawn upward to those glimmering circles of light in the sky. In every age and in every land men and women peered up in wonder at the swirling pools of light that hung just out of reach, beckoning them to sprout wings and fly up to embrace their mysteries. Mankind grew hungry for the power of flight if only to fly high enough to gaze through these celestial marvels and perhaps glimpse paradise beyond.

Throughout history mankind named them. The pharaohs of Egypt called them "The Eyes of the Gods" and built towering pyramids to try and reach them. The people of China tied prayers to doves then released them to fly up to the "Celestial Gates" in hopes that their prayers would be carried to heaven. The Aztecs built towering temples and burned pyres of burning human hearts sending smoke through "The Cloud Mouths" to appease the flying serpent god Quetzalcoatl.

Poets dreamed of paradise, adventurers dreamed of treasure and priests dreamed of gods, but all men began to dream of flying up to the tantalizing circles of light in the sky. Clever men began to dream of how they might fly. Wise men began to study birds, insects and nature in hopes of unlocking the power of flight just as they scrutinized the sky circles themselves.

One man, neither wise nor clever insisted that he fly. Nero, the emperor of mighty Rome ordered his wisest and cleverest advisors to build him a chariot that could carry him into the sky so that he could "gaze into the eyes of a fellow god" and it was Roman alchemists who first discovered *Liftium* and invented the balloon. As an angry Rome finally rose up against her tyrant, Nero escaped in a great gilded balloon and sailed away above a bloodthirsty mob, disappearing forever through the whirlpool of light that hung above the Tibre.

Man had finally reached the clouds but the mystery of the skylocks remained. If they were indeed gates in the sky, where did they lead? It was a simple hunter who unlocked the first clue.

Every year hunters waited for geese to fly overhead on their way to their winter homes or to return in spring, fat from far off winter feedings. Hunters would find the sky suddenly full of flying foul on their way to seasonal nests when moments before the sky had been empty.

The hunters learned.

Migrating geese and ducks were flying *through* the circles of light. The geese and ducks were winging someplace earthly and common if their roasting flesh was any proof. Eventually men tried to follow. Eventually they succeeded.

Where The Heck...

WHERE THE HELL ARE ALL THE VIKINGS?

By Brian D. Thomas

THEN:

William Duke of Normandy was having a very bad day.

He was wet, sandy and probably about to lose his army. His ships had crossed the stormy channel and finally landed at Pevensey, but instead of finding an empty Sussex beach he and his men faced a waiting army.

The filthy English had even had time to build a sturdy wooden castle at a nearby village called Hastings. King Harold of England had an entire army of Saxon thegns, huscarls, heavy horse and levies of spear and archers just sitting on the beach waiting for William's Normans to land.

"They were all supposed to be up in the north," railed William. "Hardrada and his bloody Vikings should have hit the northern coast days ago. Our spies saw their invasion ships assembled in Norway. That bloody handed Viking has been gathering troops and supplies for months!"

William's tirade was cut off as the first volley of Saxon arrows began raining death upon the English beach and the Norman soldiers.

"This army shouldn't even be here!" cried William, "They should be in York getting slaughtered by Hardrada and Tostig! So where the Hell are all the Vikings?"

BEFORE THEN:

Harald Hardrada waited on the shores of the fjord like a little boy waiting for Christmas day. All his plans, all his schemes and all his dreams were now on the balance scales waiting for the weights to be dropped.

For the hundredth time today and the millionth time in his life his eyes rose up and locked on the glimmering circle of light in the sky. His eyes were not the first

WHERE THE HELL ARE ALL THE VIKINGS? 19

to try and see through those shimmering mysteries.

His grandfathers had called them the "Gates Of the Rainbow Bridge" and believed the hovering circles of light to be the gates to the halls of Odin. In Egypt they were called the "Eyes of the Gods". The silk traders called them Celestial Gates, and the Slavs called them "The Sky Mouths". Men from every land were fascinated with the mysterious circles of light that hovered just out of reach over the rivers and shores on every continent of the world.

Harald had been fixated with those circles of light from the time he was a boy- from the day he had been hunting with his uncles and seen an entire flock of geese fly though one of the "Rainbow Gates" on their way south for winter. His uncle's huntsmen swore that in the spring the flock would return through the same gate, and vowed to bring the boy back so he could shoot "…the ones Odin didn't eat".

The boy, who would eventually become King of Norway, would never forget the sight of the geese returning in the spring or the taste of their flesh at the spring feast. They didn't taste any different than any other goose. They did not taste divine. So where did they fly to every fall when they flew through the rainbow gates?

Harald Hardrada fought hard to make his dreams of a Viking kingdom come true. But Harald was more than just a dreamer and a war leader. He was an educated man, and had studied in the great city of Constantinople…when he wasn't killing the enemies of the Byzantine court. He'd read for himself the histories of Rome and the story of how Emperor Nero had fled an angry mob by flying up into the sky in a boat that sailed the clouds, disappearing through one of the Rainbow Gates. Harald also found buried in those ancient scrolls beneath the golden city of the Byzantines the secrets of Nero's Roman cloud boat.

When King Harald had emptied his vaults to buy blood coal, his sometime ally Tostig the Saxon, had called him mad!

After beating his ally into bruised silence Harald had shown him what he'd learned from those old roman scrolls. Smiths used blood coal when they forged certain metals but Harald showed his battered Saxon friend what happened when you submerged the lumpy red rocks in vinegar. He watched Tostig's eyes widen as an old wineskin attached to a child's toy wooden boat puffed up like a fishing bladder and floated up to the ceiling of his great hall.

King Harald of Norway, greatest King of the Vikings, showed his conspirator in conquest how he planned to make a fleet of longships that would sail both the ocean and the sky.

Sitting and waiting on the fjord Harald mused that he was probably now the poorest King Norway ever had. He had hired hunters from Frisia to Iceland to bring him skins. Seals, otters and even whales went under the knives of Harald, and the great wooden sewing halls he'd built buzzed with the voices of hundreds of busy women. He'd stripped the land just to feed this horde and the 300 specially built longships crewed by the best warriors his dwindling money could buy.

Now everything waited on the single ship he'd sent up through the Rainbow Gate to scout the way. He'd bullied and shamed Tostig into leading twenty of Harald's bravest warriors on a journey that made most men faint with fright. If his bravest didn't return the others would fade away into the night taking both Harald's boats and his gold.

Harald's heart stopped as he saw the dark shape emerge from the gate. It slammed back into beat when his eyes made out the shape of the dragon prow and the tiny figure waving down at him. Harald shoved his way through the cheering crowd to reach the slowly descending skyboat. The huge bladder that lifted the boat threw a dark shadow over the waiting crowd and some muttered charms against the ominous shadow.

Harald had no fear as he spied his pet Saxon's stupid grin. Tostig leapt the last few feet to the ground and the waiting warriors made space for the two lords to meet.

Harald had one hundred questions but his pride willed his mouth shut as he waited for his scout to report. Tostig the Saxon, never losing that stupid grin simply held out his hands.

Gripped in his left he held a freshly cut pine branch, a pinecone still attached. In his right he held a freshly killed goose.

THEN:

One after another the three hundred dragon ships glided through the Rainbow Gate. Harald still held the pine branch his Saxon ally had given him.

Tostig had said that it seemed no time had passed when they sailed through the gate. One moment they were over the coast of Norway and the next they were over a new coastline.

Harald looked down on the new coastline the way a man looks down upon a new bride on his wedding night. Unconsciously Harald wiped his mouth on his sleeve.

From a view usually reserved for eagles, he could see the wide murky river winding far to the west and the deep green coastline disappearing to both the north and south. This new land was vast!

Like dark brooding swans the dragon boats dropped down into the river mouth, and immediately the crews began to pull for shore. Harald had planned this expedition for years and every detail was hammered into the heads of his commanders. Every man knew his task and every crew was hungry for conquest.

Gone was the fear of falling or intruding on some dark god's domain. They had ripped out their fears and burned them on a warrior's fire.

Harald brought skalds on the journey and they were shouting out new sagas praising the courage of Hardrada's skylords even as the skyboats landed in the water.

Harald also brought master mapmakers and he knew without looking that their hands were flying charcoal over skin as their trained eyes took in details only birds ever saw.

Harald's thegns had also seen a village of some kind near the banks of the river, and his own skydragon drove like a thrusting spear towards the first Viking raid of this new land.

Harald Hardrada smiled as the wind whipped his beard and blew his cloak behind him like flapping raven's wings. This was not simply another Viking raid. The lands of his fathers were overcrowded, and his warriors were constantly spoiling for conquest and plunder.

Harald brought his Vikings to this new land to stay.

WELCOME TO THE MODERN AGE!

1903
The Age Of Awesomeness

WHERE THE HELL ARE ALL THE VIKINGS?

¢10

THE HARRISFYORD HERALD

May 30 1906   Harrisfyord Pennsyltucky

OUR AMERICKAN EMPIRE CELEBRATES 840TH BIRTHDAY!

Our beloved city of Harrisfyord joins cities across the nation in celebrating the birth of Imperial Amerika on July 1st 1906! The city fathers have planned a rousing day of parades, inspirational speeches and wholesome patriotic activities. Attendees are encouraged to bring a hearty appetite to this years Greeble™ Eating Contest and a strong arm to the popular annual "Pitch A Stone At A Foreigner" competition. The day's festivities will be capped off by an amazing historical reenactment of the famous "First Landing" by King Harald Hardrada and his Viking pioneers, the founders of our Norse Amerikan Empire. This year's reenactment will be performed by The *Harrisfyrod Imperial Ladies Auxiliary* and led by our own Imperial darling the lovely Ms. Willamina Wigglebottom. Everyone will agree that no one can fill out a chainmail hauberk like our Ms.Wigglebottom, and we look forward to her portrayal of King Harald with heaving anticipation! The role of the Skrealing natives will be played by various Pennsyltucky death row inmates, so come out and cheer on our founding fathers as they literally carve out our Empire! Join our beloved Empress in celebrating 840 years of Amerikan prosperity, colonization and exploration! Fireworks to follow!

WHERE THE HELL ARE ALL THE VIKINGS?   25

The Five Sisters

THE FIVE SISTERS
By Brian D. Thomas

In the current age, all the world wished it were Sicilian. The people of the Kingdom Of Sicily were per capita the wealthiest in the world. They grew no crops, mined no metals, nor created any goods to speak of. The Citizens of Sicily owed their prosperity to their very soil, and the support of their patrons, the Five Sisters.

Nestled between the Tyrrhenian Sea, the Ionian Sea and the Mediterranean Ocean this little island nation had always been a hub of trade, but once man looked up and solved the puzzle of the skylocks the little Island became a true crossroad of commerce. Those wondrous holes in the sky that allowed instant passage from one point to another on our world enabled early explorers to discover new lands and nations and exploit their bounties.

Skylocks lay scattered all across the world. Some linked points several miles apart while others spanned passage across mountains and oceans. Some locks even led to new worlds, offering mankind brand new materials, territories and possibilities.

Only Sicily boasted a concentration of these mysterious yet profitable passages. Five of the Sicilian skylocks allowed instant travel to distant locations. These five locks were a hub of worldwide travel and commerce and became known as the Five Sisters.

Like five beautiful wealthy sisters, the Sicilian locks had many suitors who wished to possess their "virtues'. Pirates plied her skies and waters, and nations fought wars to claim control over the locks and the strategically placed island.

Finally in 1842 the power hungry nations of the world decided the Five Sisters made better spinsters than brides.

The major nations of the world (and some of the minor ones as well) met for the historic Conference of Civilized Conflict in Geneva Switzerland, and the world's sky locks were part of the reason. While every self important nation felt totally within its rights to utilize the sky passages to explore, exploit, colonize and generally profit from their magic, they were finding the prospect of enemies suddenly appearing in sovereign skies distracting in the extreme. Borders could be crossed instantly and trade partners could become competitors overnight. While every nation clamored to expand, constant undisciplined warfare was threatening both sovereignties and profits.

The Conference of Civilized Conflict forged an extensive set of rules and protocols allowing mankind to continue to trade and explore whilst simultaneously slaughtering each other in a civilized manner. Not only did the CCC create rules of engagement they also recognized the need to keep commerce flowing. The CCC created the writ of "free states"-places where every nation benefited as long as their rivals were not in control. The Kingdom of Sicily was the first to be granted "Free State" status as recognized and enforced by the nations of the age. Thus the independence of the Five Sisters was confirmed.

Sicilians had a long history of piracy and turned those skills into an art. They taxed every ship, naval and air for passage and port, and turned virtually every inch of the island's rocky hills into air births and warehouses. Airships brought trade from Africa to Asia, and the Americas to the Mediterranean, and the Sicilians took their cut and more.

Every coastal nook became a port and every home became a tavern. Foreign merchants had to engage Sicilian porters to steward goods, Sicilian warehouses to store goods and Sicilian mercenaries to guard goods. The bounty of a thousand lands funneled through the rocky little kingdom and often things "fell out of the funnel". Pirates still preyed on the weak and the unwary, and often the pirates bore a striking resemblance to those same porters, innkeepers and mercenaries.

No airship could haul the tonnage of cargo a true naval vessel could, so only high cost luxury goods traveled far by air. In all the world two types of airships flew the skies, "geese" and "pigeons".

A "goose" was a craft that spent most of it's time in the water-basically a boat with balloons. These craft would claw their way up into the sky just to cross through a sky lock before returning to the water on the other side. Geese had the luxury of using naval ports for loading and unloading but could not stay aloft for extended periods of time once loaded. Their hot air and liftium bags could only lift so much.

"Pigeons" were true airships and landed on solid ground or birthed at air towers lowering their cargoes on ropes or cranes. Pigeons required that far more of their mass be dedicated to their lift bags. They carried smaller cargoes and crews than their wet cousins but could fly farther, longer and higher.

Sicily provided nests for both geese and pigeons, plucking each whenever possible. Goods were transferred from airship to naval craft and back again all across Sicily. In some cases even sworn enemies were able to conduct trade using Sicilian intermediaries or even craft flying the Sicilian flag. Pirates also rarely targeted Sicilian ships...mainly because Sicilian captains couldn't fire on their own ships!

To ensure that trade flowed smoothly a no-fire zone over the island and twelve miles around her was established. To enforce this edict the Kingdom Of Sicily created a navy to patrol her waters and raised a ring of heavy stationary gun balloons to guard her skies. Any ship, either sea or air that violated the peace was targeted and blasted out of existence. Every nation that utilized the locks was obliged to not only abide by this rule but was also obligated to help enforce the punishment of violators regardless of treaty or alliance. By the grace of The Five Sisters men were safe and free to become wealthy.

****

Major Girth stared at his cards and wondered why the Five Sisters were withholding their favors from him. He had pulled several strings to ensure his airship the *Irascible Wind* was granted a two-week station over Sicily. In theory his airship was here to ensure the protection of Imperial Amerikan trade vessels as they traveled to and from the free zone. In reality he and his crew had two weeks to collect bounties and booty from his nation's enemies according to his warship's letters of Marque. He had two weeks to prowl the edge of the no fire zone looking for prey before he was bumped by another Imperial warship. To date he had nothing to show but an empty hold and a disgruntled crew.

In a sky of geese and pigeons the *Irascible Wind* was a hawk. An Imperial Amerikan Warhawk Airship, or "War Luft" was arguably the most dangerous craft in the sky thanks to Imperial Amerika's monopoly of Phlogistern.

It was simply a question of lift.

Phlogistern had three times the lift potential of Liftium and only Amerikan military vessels had Phlogistern. The source and nature of Amerikan Phlogistern was possibly the most sought after mystery and best-kept secret of the modern world. All that was widely known was that Phlogistern reacted to electrical current to provide lift. Phlogistern allowed The Imperial Amerikan Air Corp to field airships with stronger engines, thicker armor, larger crews and bigger guns. Imperial Warhawks were not the biggest airships in the skies they were just the deadliest, and the *Irascible Wind* was renowned as a killer amongst killers.

All of which had played against her finding favor with the Five Sisters. No Air pirate was willing to tangle with the *Irascible* alone, and her nation's enemies knew her deadly silhouette. Potential targets flew across the island or delayed in port preferring to outlast the *Irascible*'s tour of duty rather than risk her guns.

Major Girth could not plunder just any vessel either. His nation drew a distinct line between profiteering and piracy…at least when the eyes of other nations were watching.

The *Irascible* hovered just off the coast over Palermo like a hungry spider in a cloudy web. There just weren't any flies.

Not only was the Major NOT getting wealthy from bounties or prize ships he was now even losing money to his deck officers at cards. He took it for granted that his fellow crewmen were cheating. They were all cheating. He just couldn't figure out how they were doing it better than he was.

Part of the problem was the shapely leg that was draped over his shoulder. He never questioned why his gun commander preferred to perch high up on the back of his chair with one smoothly curved leg thrown over his shoulder. After all she was just watching the game, and far be it for him to deny her comfort while she was off duty. Her bouncing foot was throwing off his concentration however, and her lovely knee was blocking his reach to the cheese tray. He adjusted her silky thigh without actually removing it and stared at his cards again while he snatched at a wedge of Swiss.

Lt. Stout, the ship's navigator and morals officer had that little infuriating smile that meant either he had an excellent hand or he was sure the Major wouldn't call his bluff. Ensign Witt was glaring at his cards so hard Girth expected them to burst into flames at any second and Sgt. Major Peaches was mumbling something vulgar in Iroquois.

Pilot Airmen Lovechild was practically beaming, which Girth knew meant nothing since the big man-pretty flight leader still didn't even understand the Loki-be-damned rules. How he kept winning was almost as infuriating as his happy demeanor when he lost.

The Major was tempted to reach across the table and punch his flight lieutenant in the eye just to stop him from smiling so much, but since Mr. Lovechild was also the official poster boy of the IAAC…literally… Girth would find himself explaining to the War Ministry why their latest photographs looked like the results of a lost prizefight.

Besides, Mr. Lovechild might decide to hit back!

Girth realized he had been staring at Airmen Lovechild during this whole thought process when the big grinning Dane gave him a friendly wave and laid a straight flush on the table. "Is this good?" the big pilot politely asked.

As Mr. Lovechild raked in yet another pot Major Girth scanned the rest of the bridge crew. While he himself was hardly phased by the creamy white thigh draped across his chest the watch officer couldn't tear his eyes off it.

"Airman, you are supposed to be watching for choice targets OUTSIDE!" shouted Girth. Somewhere just above his head Girth could hear his gunnery officer giggle.

The watch officer mumbled his apologies, then pulled his magocculars down from their hanging perch and jammed them on his blushing face.

After several seconds the watch officer spoke again. "Sir, we have a pack heading out toward the Tyrrhenian."

"It looks like seven geese and a pair of gun pigeons," Lt. Stout grimaced and complained, "Great, another military luft to compete for targets."

The *Irascible* was hardly the only hunter on the prowl in this part of the sky. Two Spanish gun frigates and a massive British man-o-war hung within a mile of the Amerikans. The big Brit bothered the crew of the *Irascible* the most. Her prow proclaimed her as *The Lady Bertha* and she was easily twice as large as the *Irascible Wind*. Of course she would have to be since she lacked the Phlogistern bag of the Amerikan Vessel and had to instead rely on a massive central Liftium sack and two guidance hot air bags.

The *Lady Bertha* mounted an impressive broadside of ten; eight-inch guns plus bow and stern chasers. It was unlikely she could match the speed of the *Irascible* or the reach of the *Irascible*'s four main twelve-inch Thunderer guns, but she would certainly contest any prey that came along. Neither Major Girth nor his crew minded a little healthy competition, just as long as the odds were stacked in their favor ahead of time.

"Watch Officer, read off their flags, and Mr. Witt consult the Hostility Index for this month." Major Girth knew he needed to follow protocol. With the constantly changing politics of the current age it was crucial that crews were kept abreast of their nation's relationships with other world powers. Field officers were issued constant Hostility Index updates via courier telegraph rating every known nation's current political stance. Field commanders were expected to stay abreast of the friends and enemies of the Empire and conduct their command accordingly least they jeopardize some important trade agreements or negotiations by shooting a currently friendly ally.

Of course they were also expected to shoot enemies or unfriendly former business partners on sight, so it was important to stay up to date on the ebb and flow of national friendships.

"We have a couple Italian Free City traders, a Dutch and Flemish merchantman and ...an unmarked sky cog."

Girth untangled himself from his gun commander's perch and pulled down his own magocculars. "The unflagged looks eastern," remarked the Major. While it wasn't uncommon for ships to go flagless within the free zone it was a mark of piracy and grounds for immediate action out in open sky.

"The Brit is moving out too," announced Mr. Stout. He had abandoned his seat at the card table and taken his place at the ship's wheel.

"Sir! The Dutchman and the Flemmy are firing on each other!"

Girth swung his magoccular rig around to follow this new action. "Where are the zone markers Mr. Stout?" snapped Girth.

"We are still four miles inside the no fire zone," replied Stout. "Somebody went and jumped the gun" murmured Sergeant Peaches. "They better hope those gun balloon crews are having a wine break…"

"Marker Round! Marker Round!" interrupted Lt. Stout. "They've been spotted!"

Girth saw the first Sicilian round slam home into the Dutchman's starboard side, ripping her gunwale apart in a spray of smoke and splinters. He averted his eyes just before the round's marker secondary flash charges detonated.

"Both the Dutchman and the Flemmy goose have been marked, Sir," announced the watch officer. Girth readjusted his magocculars, and confirmed that both ships now trailed billows of bright orange smoke and flashing firecracker sparks.

Sicilian Free State policy was very clear. Sicilian guns would not only fire upon any ship violating the no fire zone but would also be marked as targets for any and all nearby ships. Every ship within range was obliged to open fire on a marked violator or face stiff fines. The Sicilians would now be keeping a watchful eye on who responded to the marker flares.

One of the speaking tubes attached to Girth's command throne squawked, "Thunderer main gun commander requesting permission to open fire on marked ships."

Girth pulled his eyes from his magoccular rig and watched as Airman Gams, his broadside gun commander nearly vibrated in place. Her eyes were shut, her fingers were crossed and she was doing a little hopping dance in place on the command bridge.

Girth turned his head and spoke into his speaking tube. "No, main gun. We will let the six shooters have this one I think."

The leggy gun officer shrieked in unbridled pleasure and made little clapping motions with her hands before leaping for the huge brass pole that pierced the command deck. She jumped on the pole and locked her long shapely legs around the shining brass. She leaned backward until she was hanging upside down, and then flashing the bridge crew a "v" with her left hand, she plunged down the pole headfirst disappearing through the hole in the floor. Girth rushed to the gun deck pole and shouted down after her, "Only one cylinder each Mr. Gams!"

The *Irascible's* broadside gun crews were all female and they took enormous pleasure in their jobs. *Irascible* mounted six Colt "six shooters" per broadside. These six-inch guns resembled oversized versions of the famous Colt sidearm with a six shot cylinder. Each gun was mounted in a gun cage, that once extended, could rotate in any direction giving the gunner a 360 degree arc of fire. This meant the gunner needed to actually be strapped into her seat to keep from falling out.

The ships' gun harridans would spend hours shrieking with delight, suspended in their gun rigs spinning in circles, the trigger column squeezed between their thighs throbbing with every shot. Sometimes it took several minutes to pry the female gunners out of their stations. Male six shooter gunners often threw up, and walked funny for hours after an engagement. Female gunners just smoked a lot.

"All ahead half, Mr. Stout, if you please, and sound general quarters," commanded Girth. "Mr. Witt mark each luft, and call them as they come." The atmosphere on the bridge changed instantly from casual malaise to barely bridled chaos.

"Sir!" barked Ensign Witt. "The Flemmy and the Dutchman are still slugging it out, and there's a Chinese sky junk and Orange State clipper-luft swinging starboard off the quarter."

"The Spaniards are opening fire," interrupted Stout.

Girth swung his command magocular column around in time to see the smoking Dutchman take multiple hits to her lift bags and port side. Additional strikes on both the Dutchman and the Flemmish luft indicated that the Italian ships had added their guns to the required retribution for free zone violations. Girth knew that Flanders and Holland shared a long and bitter rivalry, and he was not at all surprised that the two lufts continued to fire on each other rather than return fire on any of the other ships.

The Sicilian marker rounds had created a billowing orange cloud of smoke, and it was getting difficult to see the details of the two marked lufts. Girth hooted and laughed uncontrollably when the Chinese sky junk loosed a brace of rockets at the criminal pair of dueling lufts and missed entirely. The sputtering rockets passed by both and dropped down onto the Sicilian countryside to detonate across the approaching beach. "That's gonna' cost them," muttered Girth, and he smiled when he realized the junk didn't appear willing to fire a second time.

The South African Orange State clipper was far more accurate with her gunnery though. Her Boer gunners fired paired eight inch bow guns through the colorful cloud with devastating effect into the Flemmish merchant's port props, sending wood splinters ripping through the hull and lift bags. A squat little Portuguese sky sloop hung at extreme range and continually popped shots from her single 4 incher. It reminded the Major of a little dog barking while a pack of big dogs fought. "One Mile to the outer marker Major," reminded Mr. Stout.

Girth groped blinding for his speaking tube and flipped the channel lever to speak to his broadside gunners. "One cylinder each Mr. Gams. It's time for us to pay our due to our Sicilian hosts." Girth adjusted his magocculars, and waited to watch his own gun's effects.

Both of the marked ships were now running full steam for the outer markers and the end of the Sicilian free zone. If they could reach open waters they would no longer be subject to Sicilian law and could claim exemption from further attacks. They might even be able to bribe one of the other ships for assistance.

The *Irascible Wind* ended that dream for the ship from Flanders as she fulfilled her host's requirement of enforcement. The heavy six-shooters of the Amerikan warluft fired six rounds in twelve seconds each. They shredded the lift bag of the Flemmish merchant still several hundred feet above the Sicilian beach, and the crippled craft plummeted to plow nose first into the rock and sand.

"Sir! The Brit!" As if in answer to the devastation wrought by her Amerikan rival the British *Lady Bertha* loosed a full broadside into the crippled Dutchman. The Dutch airship didn't just crash. It disintegrated in mid air and rained debris across the same stretch of beach that was now the final resting place of the downed Flanders craft.

As if the big British war luft had fired a starter gun every other ship in the immediate sky sprinted for the border and angled in a different direction.

"They're all scattering Major," announced Lt Stout rather smugly. "I don't think anyone else is waiting around to see who's who."

Ensign Witt slammed his fist on the bulkhead, and growled in frustration, "We can't claim any marked ships for salvage and the rest are on the do-not-shoot list!"

"I'm not so sure of that Mr. Witt," whispered Girth in response. "Where did that flagless eastern cog get to I wonder?" Girth swiveled his magocular rig in a slow circle as he scanned the sky ahead. "Aha! There she is, twenty degrees off the port bow at nine o'clock, and she's at a full run."

Girth spun the dials on his viewing rig as he tried to bring the fleeing craft into tighter focus, "Mr. Lovechild, check the daily update from the Ministry of Commerce and Conflict, and tell me who is on the Hostility Index updates." The big jovial fighter pilot was overjoyed to be finally included in the excitement and snatched up the roll of teletape from its spool on the vaguely piano-looking teleprinter.

"Ah, well it says we are in *restrained combat* with Austria, *heightened belligerence* with Metztecca, *non-exclusive loathing* with France of course, *prejudiced conflict* with the Ottoman Empire..."

"That's It!" cried Girth still glued to his manoculars. "All that gaudy gold leaf, and those oniony domes...she's a royal Turk skycog!"

"According to the update we've been in *prejudiced conflict* with the Turk for exactly four hours Sir," supplied airman Lovechild. "Long enough to count!" shouted Girth.

"What exactly does *prejudiced conflict* mean...exactly Sir?" asked the big man-pretty pilot.

"It means," growled ensign Witt, "since we are past the free zone markers now the commander can attack if he frakking well feels like it!" The ensign was gripping his own magocular rig in white-knuckled hands and was fairly drooling at the prospect of combat.

"...and if that fat Turk is as rich as she looks he frakking well feels like it," supplied Major Girth in a husky whisper. "All turbines full speed ahead Mr. Stout, and tell Mr. Umsipha EEEEK!" Girth's last command transformed into a girlish squeal as *The Lady Bertha* cut across the Amerikan luft's bow and blocked her view of the Turkish skycog. "Get that damned fat bagged blimp outta' my sky!"

Lt. Stout was already spinning his ships wheel and pulling various levers on his complex control column. "She's purposely blocking our path Major! I'll have to angle the secondary turbines to get around her. That means we are going to lose speed."

"I know what it means Mr. Stout," snapped Girth. "What I want to know is what the Neffelheim the Brits are doing blocking us!"

A shapely female airman called out in a calm voice "The British ship is signally us Sir." The pretty airman was watching a blinking semaphore on the British ship and quickly writing down the translation. "Well what do they have to say for themselves airman Bootae?" growled Girth.

"Piss off!" The female airman blushed slightly and smiled at her commanding office, "The *Lady Bertha* just told us to piss off...Sir." Girth snapped his head around to glare at airmen Lovechild, who knew exactly what his commanding officer wanted. "The Hostility Index lists Britain as *beloved trading partner* with the Ottomans and *best, allied friends* with us."

Girth roared, "That Loki-damned Brit is body guarding my prize!"

Girth was desperately trying to angle his magocular around the large rear end of the British war luft in order to gauge the distance to his target. The problem was that The *Lady Bertha* was easily twice as big as The *Irascible Wind*, and her oversized silhouette was effectively blocking the smaller ship's view and aim.

The *Irascible Wind* mounted two large rear drive turbines and four omni-direction turbines used for both thrust and maneuverability . The "guide turbines" could be angled to allow the *Irascible* to slide sideways, up, down, spin and even reverse direction, and combined with her more traditional rudder and tail wings she could out maneuver any other luft in the sky. It was simply a question of lift. The *Irascible* got all the lift she needed from her Phlogistern tank and didn't need to use her tail wings or turbines to raise or descend like other airships. With all six turbines driving her forward she was dazzlingly fast but the big Brit blocking her forced her to sacrifice speed in order to maneuver around the moving obstacle. Lt

Stout expertly guided the *Irascible* around the *Lady Bertha*, but the maneuvers took time and as the two big warships jockeyed for position the Turk drew further and further away.

"They're getting further and further away!" shouted Girth.

"Permission to open fire on the Brit," growled Ensign Witt.

Girth growled back. "Permission denied! We can't fire on a *beloved ally*, especially not after we were seen by no less than four other nations! Now shut up if you don't have anything constructive to say or I'll have you counting spent shells again." The chastised ensign gritted his teeth and sulked at his duty station.

"I thought they were *best allied friends*," supplied airmen Lovechild helpfully. Both the Major and Ensign Witt glared at the smiling pilot as if they were trying to strangle him with their eyes.

The *Irascible* was now past the *Lady Bertha*, but even the big Amerikan guns could no longer reach the Turk. "All ahead full," commanded Girth, and the chase was on. The Ottoman ship had a healthy lead and the free Italian cities to the north promised the same protection as Sicily. If the Turkish ship could cross the Tyrrhenian and reach Naples or Salerno she would be safe from attack. Both cities enforced their own free zone policies.

The Turk was a fast ship, and so apparently was the *Lady Bertha*. Girth assumed he would be able to outrun both easily but he was only gaining ground on the Turk slowly and the British ship was doing a surprisingly good job keeping up. The three-ship race dragged on for hours, with each ship using every trick they had to coax just a little more speed from their craft. "The Bertha just took a...she just dumped her ballast water," Ensign Witt amended.

"She may have just lightened her load but she won't be able to ascend fast now," supplied Lt Stout. Even as he commented the Lieutenant never looked away from his view port or command console. His eyes darted over a host of dials and gauges as he read the wind, air pressure, engine speeds and every other element that might affect the speed or performance of the *Irascible Wind.* Major Girth may be in command of the luft but Lt Stout was her pilot, and he knew every inch of his ship.

"We're getting signaled by the *Lady Bertha* again," announced the communications officer.

"Now what do they want," asked a Girth distractedly.

"Bugger off or we will ram your rear!" This time the pretty communications officer blushed heavily as she relayed the message to her commander. "Do you want me to respond?"

Major Girth swung his magocular rig around to view the trailing British warluft. She was indeed keeping pace and for the life of him Girth could not figure how. He had heard rumors that the British were experimenting with new engines and he had a bad feeling he was seeing them in action now.

If the larger Brit did indeed ram the *Irascible* they could always claim it was an accident and if Girth lost his tail rudder he would have to cut his speed in half, guaranteeing the Turk's escape. If Girth fired on the Brit there could be no mistaking that as an accident and the Major doubted his career nor his head would survive the repercussions. Nor was it any good to simply shoot the Turk out of the sky with his Thunderers. They had been in range for some minutes now but Girth wanted a prize and not a kill. He needed to take the Turk intact and the Brit was certainly not going to just stand by and let that happen.

"We need them to turn," mused the Major out loud. "How far are we from the Italian shore, Mr. Stout?"

"Only a few miles," replied Stout," but we're still several miles from a free city."

Girth snatched at his speaking tube. "Main guns, load case and fire four rounds to the Turks port side, but DON"T try and hit her! I want her to think our gunners need spectacles, and not that we missed on purpose." Everyone on the bridge could hear the gunner's shout of "Spectacles!" over the speaking tube, but several seconds later the bow Thunderers opened fire. Girth smiled as he watched the fleeing Turkish luft respond to four rounds of screaming case shot whipping by her port side. The Turk turned to starboard and the Italian coastline.

"Mr. Stout hard to starboard, tail and rudder only! Mr. Gams, run out the port side six-shooters. Keep the starboard gun carriages tucked in and don't show our teeth to the Brit. Ensign Witt give me a distance on the *Bertha*." Girth shouted his commands without ever removing his face from the magocular rig suspended above him. He kept his eyes locked on the Turkish luft.

"The *Bertha* is still closing at five hundred yards sir," called out Ensign Witt. "..and they are starting to turn with us. Sir, if they loose a broadside into our tail…!"

"Main guns, load that special ammo we acquired in Palermo and target the Turks decks," Girth commanded, ignoring his deck officer's broadside warning. Girth finally took his eyes off the Turkish luft long enough to switch a lever on his speaking tube console. "Bridge to Engine room, be ready to shock the sack on my order!"

Lt Stout half turned from his wheel, but the question he was about to ask died in his mouth when he saw the look in his commander's eyes. Instead the Lieutenant calmly brought his own speaking tube to his mouth and announced, "All hands rig for violent ascent." While the steady increase of voltage to the Phlogistern tank would cause the *Irascible* to ascend, "shocking the sack" or sending a voltage surge through the tanks would…

"Bertha at two hundred yards and closing," called Witt.

"The Turk just unbuttoned her guns," snarled Girth in response. "Main guns, open fire!" The twelve-inch guns of The *Irascible Wind* lived up to their name as they thundered their fury at the Ottoman luft. The Amerikan gunners were right on target and orange smoke clouds erupted across the Turk's deck.

"Keep firing," cried Girth, and the Sicilian marker rounds drilled into the Turk's hull driving the blinding smoke into her bowels. The Ottoman Turk luft disappeared in a billowing orange cloud. "Now Umsipha! Shock the sack!"

The crew of the *Irascible Wind* was driven to their knees as the Phlogistern tank reacted to the sudden surge of electricity. The ship surged straight up like an elevator lift, and it was only Lt Stout's warning that allowed the crew to be prepared for the sudden crushing direction change. The *Lady Bertha's* crew could only try and pull up to match this new maneuver. If they hadn't already vented their ballast they might be able to ascend quicker but they could never hope to match the *Irascible's* rate of ascent.

The Turkish broadside that erupted from the billowing orange cloud caught the *Bertha* full in the nose as she rose. The Turk had fired blindly at where their pursuer had been…the last time they could actually see. The Ottoman luft carried a respectable broadside of four, eight-inch guns and her gun crews fired two more broadsides that slammed into the *Lady Bertha's* hull and lift sacks.

Girth hung in the *Irascible Wind* several hundred feet above the exchange and laughed maniacally. The bridge of the Amerikan luft erupted in cheers and catcalls as they watched the big Brit stagger in mid air, then start to drop nose first for the waters of the Tyrrhenian.

The crew of The *Lady Bertha* was not amused. Even as they struggled to regain control over their stricken ship her gunners retaliated to the Turks treachery.

The *Lady Bertha* peppered the dispersing orange cloud with eight-inch fury, and Girth could see several hits score across the Turk. The Bertha also fired a second broadside. Of course the British captain knew what had happened, but Girth knew no British captain would admit being made the fool nor would he allow even an accidental attack go unanswered. Better to claim the treacherous Turk had turned on her protector for some unscrupulous Oriental reason, rather than accuse a *best allied friend* of instigating a conflict that could never actually be proven anyway. The Ottoman luft limped clear of the cloud as the *Lady Bertha* attempted an emergency water landing in the Tyrrhenian.

"Oh, that's not going to go well," commented Lt Stout as he tracked the *Bertha* down. "If they can't keep her bags filled they'll collapse and smother the hull.."

Girth wasn't paying attention though, "Mr. Gams, target the Turk gun ports and deck. I want both swept clear and I don't care how many cylinders you ladies need to do it!" Girth spun on his heels and pointed at Witt. "Ensign, ready a boarding party. I want fifty redneck marines on that luft in ten minutes and I want your signal that you've taken her in twenty. Pick a prize crew and be ready to fly that prize to Naples before supper."

Girth spun again and snapped his arm in line with his second flight lieutenant. "Mr. Lovechild, get your Bumble squadron in the air and provide support for the *Bertha*. Drop floats and emergency kits and stand ready to start towing any lifeboats to shore. Keep a tally of how many kits you drop and boats you tow. I plan on sending our *best allied friends* a bill." Girth slowly gazed around the bridge of his luft. "Well, don't just stand there. Snap to it!"

Girth was smiling like the cat who'd just eaten the family bird as his crew hurried to their duties. He knew the Italians would quietly purchase the prize ship and support any story the Amerikans spun as long as it didn't interfere with their profit on the sale. The Brit crew would support his story of a treacherous Turk, probably ending Britain's temporary trade agreement with the Ottomans. That little nugget would give Major Girth a whole new set of strings he could pull at his leisure. The Five Sisters had finally shown their favor to Girth.

The Major smiled and gave one final order to his busy crew.

"Somebody get me another cheese plate!"

Blood Above The Clouds

Blood Above The Clouds
By Raymond J. Witte

Shang Xiao Liao's Tianlong-class heavy cruiser rocked as her port rocket batteries unleashed their fury. A shrieking cavalcade of high explosives flashed from the launchers in a wave, shrouding the side of the ship in acrid smoke. Their target, an Imperial German Manticore, disappeared briefly under the impacts of dozens of rockets. The Tianlong's rockets were small and inaccurate- what passed for aiming was pointing the launcher in the general direction of the target and a short prayer to one's ancestors- but the big ship carried hundreds of them.

The Shang Xiao allowed himself the tiniest of smiles.

That took care of the barbarian interloper, he thought, their fleet might give chase, but none can catch us.

The *Roaring Lion* was nearly as fast as the German Manticore class destroyers, despite being nearly three times their weight. The Grossdeutschland class dreadnaughts had no hope of pursuit.

The fools, what good is tens of tons of armor and guns when it is never where you need it to be?

Shang Xiao Liao was happy indeed. The raid on the Amerikan camp had been a masterpiece of deception. His swift, agile supporting forces sent the Western barbarians chasing ghosts in all directions while he himself waited for the perfect moment to pounce. His own attack had been direct and brutal. With the *Roaring Lion* providing fire support, a wave of his marines has swept through the Amerikan camp and quickly secured the target, a mysterious crate, which was not to be opened on pain of torture. Long before the Amerikan fleet could respond, his cruiser had ascended back into the Venusian sky and was making best speed to Chinese territory, where a battlegroup of her sister ships waited.

It had been a matter of poor luck that they had run into the German airship.

If the *Roaring Lion* had previously discharged her rocket batteries, the mission might have turned disastrous. While allowing her to close to rocket range, the *Lion* had taken several hits from the German's fore guns, and there were undoubtedly casualties. The German destroyer punched well above her weight and could have slowed the Chinese ship down long enough for effective pursuit.

That won't happen now, Liao thought as the German ship, smoking and shedding debris from the rocket salvo, began to lose speed and altitude.

Liao barked orders to his crew, commanding them to bring the *Lion* to cruising speed and to raise the ship up to its lift ceiling. At this elevation, the Venutian sky was streaked with pale green clouds.

That is good, they will make excellent cover, Liao thought as he told the helmsman to skirt the clouds. The Chinese cruiser hugged a particularly dense cloud bank, the light vapor enveloping the ship as she came to the proper speed and altitude. Suddenly, the lookouts in the foredeck called a warning. The clouds to starboard had began to darken ominously.

The weather here is as fickle as fortune's hand, thought Liao as he ordered the *Lion* slightly to port, away from the disturbance in the clouds. The Venusian weather could change at a moment's notice, and the very characteristics that had made the Tianlong so suitable for this mission would work against her if the weather turned. The Chinese cruiser was too lightly built to handle gales of a Venusian storm.

As the *Lion* came about to port, the cloud formation began to swirl and part. Liao felt his stomach sink. Even on Venus, when clouds moved like that, it only meant one thing- there was something hiding in there.

The heavy clouds slid away from a enormously armored hull and flight sack, both dotted with a seemingly impossible number of guns. The black and red shape of a Grossdeutschland class dreadnaught loomed from the mists. On the bridge of the *Lion* there was a moment of stunned silence. At ranges this close, the full size of the German ship was utterly imposing, a fortress of armored plate and gun mounts. But the shock only lasted for a moment.

Liao screamed for the starboard rocket batteries to fire. The voice of the captain spurred the rest of the crew back into action. A ragged volley of rockets screamed from the *Lion*, smashing into the German ship, briefly hiding it once more under smoke and shrapnel. Liao ordered his ship to flank speed. He could not outfight the German at this range, but he might be able to slow the massive ship down enough so he could effect an escape.

Liao peered through the smoke, hoping to see some signs of damage on the hull of the dreadnaught. It steamed through the smoke with dozens of scorch marks and rents in its armor, but the massive ship showed no signs of slowing. As one, two score of gun ports slid open. Liao was almost able to bark out orders for the crew to brace for impact when he, and the rest of the bridge crew, were thrown to the deck.

The German's guns roared, nearly forcing the Chinese ship to keel over as their eight inch shells smashed their way into its bowels. A moment later, alarm bells and whistles began to shriek as the crew of the *Roaring Lion* started to assess the damage from the German's salvo. Liao struggled to his feet and shouted orders for the ship to turn away from its antagonist and accelerate to all ahead full.

The helmsman spun the wheel and pushed the throttle as far as it would go. The *Lion's* shuddered as her engines screamed to full power and attempted to pull away from the lethal threat of the German's guns, but the ship made no headway.

What could be wrong? Why won't my ship move? Captain Liao received his answer an instant later, as the panicked call of "Grapples!" was passed up from the lower decks.

Korporal Meinschidt peered down, as much as he was able, through the grate that made up the floor of the drop room on *Veljahelm*. The dreadnaught's heavy grapples, fired from adapted eight inchers, had struck deep and true, and the Chinese cruiser was going nowhere. Now it was the Manticore class *Veljahelm's* turn to work. As the dreadnaught used its bulk to pin the Chinese ship in place, the *Veljahelm* climbed and maneuvered until it rested directly above it's target. Meinschidt watched as the top of the target's airsack came into view. As the *Veljahelm* slowed, Meinschidt heard the locking pins disengage. Then he began to fall, his tether unsplooling behind him.

Captain Liao screamed again at his crew. *What is taking those fools so long to cut those cables? Why must I be surrounded by incompetence!* Liao cursed and slammed his fist on the deck rail. Suddenly, there were a series of thumps on the ceiling of the flight deck. Then came the tearing of wood and metal heralding the arrival of a dozen German troopers in boarding armor dropping onto the command deck. Liao drew his pistol and drew a bead on the nearest trooper, as the Germans began to rip into the deck crew with their boarding claws. He emptied chambers his weapon and began to reload, hands shaking, as one of the German troopers advanced and tore his face off.

The *Roaring Lion* burned as the German ships pulled away. The crate was secured and soon the ships would pass back through the lock and then the prize would be delivered to Berlin, where the best scientists of the German Empire waited to turn it into a weapon that would shock the world.

BLOOD IN THE SKIES

EXPLORERS!
SKYLOCKS LEAD TO EXOTIC NEW LANDS AND STRANGE NEW PLANETS!

1903
The Age Of Exploration

SKYLOCKS TO OTHER WORLDS!

VENUS FOR MILO

VENUS FOR MILO

By Brian D. Thomas

Milo peered over the side of the Amerikan air ship, down into the murky green Venusian jungle, and wondered for the hundredth time what he was doing here. In the course of a week he'd gone from adjunct professor of Egyptology and hieroglyphic writings at the University of Pennsyltucky to a draftee in the Imperial Amerikan Air Corp. Seven days ago he was gazing out a third floor window at some attractive co-eds and now he was staring down several hundred feet into a dark and mysterious alien rainforest. Milo did not like this new view. The slight, mousey academian was startled by a sudden smack on his back that threatened to hurl him over the airship railing.

"Venus," shouted the big overweight Amerikan officer. "A thousand shades of green, and a million ways to die! Wait until you see it up close, son!"

Milo griped the railing in white knuckled hands and turned to stare in horror at his new commanding officer Major Girth.

Major B.T. Girth was the commander of the Imperial Amerikan warluft *The Irascible Wind*, and held letters of marque and conquest from his beloved Empress of Amerika. He was a high-ranking officer of the Empire, and in military matters had power and authority to rival an Imperial senator.

Major Girth had marched into Milo's classroom interrupting a lecture on the similarities of ancient Egyptian writings and the newly discovered Venusian hieroglyphics, and announced, "...that's exactly what I wanted to discuss with you!"

Girth then produced a blank warrant of Imperial Service, and Milo had watched helplessly as the rotund Major filled in Milo's name enlisting him into the Imperial Air Corp as a "civilian advisor". The Major had pointedly left the "duration of service" line blank. As an officer of the Imperial Service Major Girth had the authority to draft any Free Resident of Amerika into service, and Milo was years away from earning Imperial Citizenship and the privileged protections citizenship granted.

Milo was ordered to collect all his research materials on Egyptian and Venusian Hieroglyphs, and was then escorted by two armed and goggled airmen to a waiting battle luft parked on the campus lawn. "We're gonna' put that sharp mind of yours to work my boy," Girth confided. "Besides, service grants citizenship. You'll earn your Citizen's Imperial Eagle in half the time it would take in some dingy classroom! You'll fly her Majesty's skies, breath clean air and probably even live to talk about it. Praise the Empress you're a lucky boy!"

Four days later, The *Irascible Wind* had crossed through the Mississippi/ Venus skylock, and now flew through purple tinted skies over vast jade jungles. Directly below, Milo could see one of the famous massive pyramids of Venus. As he boarded one of the smaller landing lufts, he gazed down at the grey stoned pyramid and began to suspect why he had been virtually kidnapped to this humid green hell.

The dark stone pyramid though similar to those found in Egypt was easily twice as large as even the Khufu structure at Giza. It rose out of the jungle canopy like a dark iceberg on a deep green sea. The ship's smaller launch descended down through a hole in the dense canopy, and Milo could now see that the gap had been literally blasted out of the jungle.

The trees on Venus were massive and created a dense leafy dome nearly eight hundred feet high. If what Milo was seeing was true then the only way to penetrate the canopy was to blow a hole in it. The entire area around the eastern face of the gigantic pyramid was burned black, and the little battle luft landed on the jungle floor with a cindery crunch.

Major Girth stomped down the gangplank followed by Milo and at least a dozen armed Imperial airmen. The Major briefly stopped to survey the area, and then to Milo's surprise and mild horror signaled the luft back into the air.

"Can't be to careful son," explained Girth. "Things tend to crawl onboard the launches if they stay grounded very long."

Milo nervously began glancing at the ground around his feet. That's when he noticed the bones scattered across the burned field. The ground was carpeted in bones in some spots and Milo gasped as something big moved underneath them.

A female trooper standing next to Milo quickly drew her sidearm and began blasting away at the mysterious moving hump in the ground. "Mice" was her only comment. No one else seemed to react.

The group started moving toward the pyramid and Milo stumbled to keep up, trying to watch the ground, the bones, the jungle edge and the looming structure all at the same time. A chorus of strange hoots, whistles and growls sounded from the deep green, and Milo kept catching glimpses of "things" at the jungles edge moving through the underbrush or flitting through the trees. He tried to watch the jungle but his eyes began to water and his head ached from the green glare. It was as if the light was too bright or the jungle…too green.

As they rounded the edge of the pyramid's eastern face Milo's attention was caught by a loud metallic crunch. He snapped his head up from his search for "things that crawl on board" to see what appeared to be some kind of steam tractor. It seemed to be driving repeatedly into a large pile of coal. Milo could not see the driver, but as the group approached it spun about amazingly fast, honked loudly and brought a large multi-barreled gatling to bear.

Milo froze in place, but the big Major threw his arms out wide and yelled "Rascal!" The honking iron machine churned up the ground and rocketed forward on a collision course with Girth. None of the other troopers reacted to the machine as it sped towards their leader, so Milo took a few hesitant steps forward. The tractor-thing came to an abrupt stop in front of the Imperial officer and the big Major put his hands on either side of a large central glass sphere and shouting loudly …kissed it.

"Has my good boy been waiting for daddy and guarding the door like a he was told? Did my Rascal miss his daddy? Did my Rascal miss his daddy?"

Milo was getting used to being confused by the Air Corp, but this…he stepped around so he could see the machine better. The machine was roughly five feet high, and looked vaguely like a cannon carriage with two large front wheels and a long backward pointing brace mounting a third smaller wheel. The body was barrel-like with a large central smokestack and a top mounted gatling gun. There did not seem to be any seats for a driver, and Milo couldn't see the honking horn. The front-the part Girth was holding in his hands looked like a hinged steam shovel bucket, and there was a glass globe perched on top.

As he looked closer Milo realized he could see inside the globe. Floating in the sphere was a brain and a pair of eyes! The eyes tracked the Major as he patted the globe and stroked the shovel, and the machine thing honked every time the Major patted it.

"It's his dog," explained one of the goggled airman.

"Waaa…" stammered Milo.

The airman nodded and continued. "It's a dog, or at least it used to be-that is the brain and eyes were a dog. I think there may be some other dog parts inside too cause' it needs to eat meat as well as take in coal for it's boilers" the airman continued. "That's probably where all the bones came from! The Major left it here to guard the entrance until he could fetch back an expert to read the hi-ro-glyfs inside that there pyr-a-mid. I guess that'd be you."

Appalled, Milo turned to see Girth carefully pulling a large bone out of the open shovel-mouth of his mechanical pet. Milo could see inside the thing's maw and took a step back. The open shovel exposed multiple sets of whirring and grinding teeth like some horrible mobile abattoir.

"Puppy needs to chew his food better," scolded Girth as he waved the bone in front of the construct. The machine was waging its entire back end as the floating eyes tracked the bone in Girth's hand. The Major took a dramatic step backward and then threw the bone out into the charred field. The dog-tractor gave a final loud "HONK" and chased after the thrown bone. Milo watched open mouthed as the huge mechanical-dog-monster snuffled through the burned field of alien bones looking for the one its master had tossed.

"Let's go, Son. It's time to see if you really know your stuff," announced Girth. Milo followed the Major and one other airman through the stone doorway leading into the great pyramid.

Girth glanced back and said, "This is Mr. Umsipha our officer of engineering. He's three fourths Zulu so don't borrow money from him unless you're sure you can pay it back." Milo smiled weakly at the big muscular officer.

Everyone knew the reputation of the First Bank of Zululand, arguably the most powerful bank in the world. While gold and diamonds had made the Zulu nation rich it was still a nation of warriors and its bank officials were no exception. Clients who defaulted on loan payments were run down through city streets like prey animals. The fact that the big negro walking beside him also wore the Silver Eagle of Imperial Citizenship meant he must have seen at least a dozen years of active combat service, and the easy way he glided down the stone hall made a chill creep up Milo's spine. It was like being followed by a uniformed panther.

"Are you sure you can read the Venusian writings?" rumbled Umsipha. "We've spent a lot of time and effort collecting you and bringing you here. I don't like wasting time and effort."

"No, no," replied Milo. "It's quite simple really if you know your demotic. The symbols are close enough to suggest a common alpha..."

"Good," interrupted Umsipha, "then read that."

'That' was a massive wall of characters and pictures carved into a wall of the chamber they had just entered. The wall was separated into chapter-like sections, and immediately Milo could see each chapter seemed to be a set of detailed directions. Fascinated, Milo forgot the big, intimidating Zulu Amerikan, the maniacal Major and his monster dog and all the creeping jungle things, and sat down to open his reference books.

"It seems that each section gives the directions to another temple," explained Milo. He had spent several hours working on the translations, checking and rechecking his decryptions before sharing them with Major Girth. "The writings describe these other temples as burial shrines, and seem to have been the final resting places for hundreds of …people." Milo continued, "There are markers in the jungle that point the way to each temple and each section describes the path to a marker, but there seems to be something missing." Milo turned to face Girth. "The hieroglyphs keep referring to 'a key' and give instructions that reference it."

Smiling, Girth brought his hand from behind his back. In it he held a book sized stone tablet. Milo could see the tablet had a bowl-like depression at one end and two sets of ringed glyphs surrounding the bowl. Holding the tablet level, Girth pulled a water bottle from his belt and poured a small amount of water into the bowl. Umsipha stepped closer holding a small metal needle piercing a piece of cork. Carefully Mr. Umsipha floated the needle cork in the water filled bowl and the needle began to slowly spin in place. After a moment it settled in one direction and as the Major slowly turned the bowl the needle retained it's direction.

Recognition lit Milo's face. "It's a compass! These sections here must be coordinates!" Milo pushed at the outer ring surround the bowl and found it rotated easily. "This is what the wall picts refer to. They detail how to set this outer ring and the distances to each subsequent marker. You just follow the directions from each marker to the next until you get to the burial temple."

Major Girth leaned close to the wall to scrutinize the strange hieroglyphs, and then smiled back at Milo. "And you can read both the directions and the distances?" he asked.

"Yes," replied Milo confidently. "If you just give me a moment I will write down the directions for you, and give you a list of translations for when you arrive at the first direction marker. It…"

"Don't bother," Girth interrupted.,"You'll be right there to provide any translations we might need."

Milo waited in the burned clearing with the other troopers and watched Major Girth make faces at the jungle. The longer he was in the rotund Major's company the more sure he was that the man wasn't quite right in the head. Girth was shouting loudly in what sounded almost like baby talk, and kept wiggling his fingers in front of his face while he scanned the tree line.

Suddenly someone…or some *thing*…stepped out of the trees in front of Girth. It looked like a man…a blue man…a skinless blue man…a naked skinless blue man. It was several feet away but Milo could clearly see the muscle bundles and major veins on its arms, legs and chest. Its head is what kept Milo's attention though.

The "man" had a bald head, huge eyes, and it looked for all the world like he was trying to swallow a squid! Where the creature's mouth should be was a writhing mass of tentacles. The blue-skinned squid-faced creature walked steadily up to Girth and raised a hand in Imperial salute. Girth returned the salute and then placed his hand under his chin and wiggled his fingers, shouting "Bllrrbitty Blurpblurp!" The creature's face tentacles waved back and a sound like "Blupblurp blurbyblurp" came bubbling out of its throat.

"What is he doing?" murmured Milo.

"He's hiring porters and guides," replied Umsipha. "These are native Venusians, and the Major has worked with Pink Spots before."

Milo realized that yes, the creature standing in front of Girth also had bright pink spots dusting his chest and shoulders. Even as Girth and the native continued to converse more of the alien natives stepped out from the tree line.

Girth gestured to his troopers, and a marine stepped forward holding a flowered hatbox. With a deliberate dramatic flair Girth removed the lid and lifted out a shinny black top hat and held it out to the native. The creature's face tentacles spasmed wildly and the blue native made little clapping motions with its hands.

Girth returned the top hat to the hatbox, and handed it back to his trooper making the universal 'no no no' finger wave at the Venusian as he did so. Girth and the native then seemed to go into intense negotiations as the Imperial switched between shouting in Imperial Anglish, and making baby noises while wiggling his fingers under his chins. The negotiations ended quickly and PinkSpots waved a half dozen of his fellows forward.

"I don't understand why I have to go," whined Milo, "If the Major speaks their language why doesn't he hire them to guide you?"

The natives began separating the various Imperial packs and crates that were stacked in the clearing.

"First," replied Umsipha, "he doesn't speak their language, at least as far as anyone can tell. They understand Anglish fine, but they just don't have the right mouth parts to speak it. They get their point across using sign language and such."

"So what language is Girth speaking to them?" asked Milo.

"Nonsense babble," replied Umsipha quietly. "He *thinks* he's speaking Venusian, and the native just don't want to hurt his feelings!"

Professor Milo blinked in confusion. "That still doesn't explain why you don't use natives to follow the hieroglyphs," fussed Milo.

"Oh that's simple," rumbled the dusky officer. "They can't read."

"Stay!" Major Girth stood at the edge of the jungle clearing waving his finger at the dark metal monstrosity that had once been his dog. "You be a good boy Rascal, and wait here." The mechanical creature hung its head dejectedly and sounded a long low "hooooooooonk".

"Let's get a move on Sergeant!" A bald, blond bearded noncom marched to the front of the group and started barking orders.

"Alright A Squad, sling shot cannons, and B Squad grab Blitzens. Squidys grab the packs and I want two of you wiggle faces up front chopping trail!"

If the natives minded the tone or terms the sergeant used they didn't show it as they shouldered their burdens. Each of the natives also had crossbows slung over their chest and carried what appeared to be bone swords at their hips along with bolt quivers, pouches and other less identifiable oddities.

Milo saw that PinkSpots also carried an Imperial issue saber similar to Girth's strapped about his waist.

The Imperial Marines were separated into two groups, what Milo assumed was A and B squads. While he had certainly seen female crewmen on the *Irascible Wind*, Milo was surprised to see female combat marines in both squads. He remembered the female marine that had calmly opened fire on the mysterious "mouse' at the landing field, and decided he didn't really care about the gender of anyone who was that fast on the draw.

Milo didn't really know anything about guns, but the Imperial Marines certainly seemed to have big ones, and a lot of them. Half of the troopers were carrying what looked like oversized shotguns, and Milo reasoned this was A Squad. The other half carried what looked like moderately sized rifles, though they seemed to be comprised of quite a bit of "stuff" with tubes, pipes and gauges sticking out all over the weapons.

In addition all the marines carried sidearms, knives, short swords and a variety of bulky looking pouches. As he surveyed the group Milo found it interesting that the Major seemed to be the lightest armed member of the troop. Looking at the overweight officer he reasoned the Major probably didn't want to lug around one of the heavier weapons, instead carrying only a sword and a sidearm. Over all it was a fairly intimidating looking group, at least to Milo's untrained eyes.

"Professor, if you will do the honors." Girth said to Milo.

It took a moment for him to realize that everyone was waiting for him, and he glanced down at the alien compass to get his bearings. "Ah, that way," and with a hesitant point of the finger the Imperial troop, their native porters and one mildly anxious Egyptologist set off into the Vensuian jungle.

Once they had their initial bearing Milo was free to inspect his surroundings as the party marched. Mr. Umsipha compared Milo's alien compass with his own Imperial issue model, and once he confirmed the march direction, the dark skinned officer seemed to forget Milo was even there.

The native trail blazers worked like buzz saws clearing a path with their bone swords, so that aside from an occasional branch Milo found the going fairly easy. Milo was an educated man and he reasoned that the huge trees and dense canopy limited the amount of undergrowth that could grow in the diminished light.

Indeed, Milo found that it was actually getting quite murky the deeper into the jungle they traveled. The troopers marched in a double line with natives capping both ends of the column.

One of the native porters was marching next to Milo. This particular fellow had bright lime green stripes on its shoulders, and up close Milo could see it did indeed have skin. It seemed the native Venusians were covered in a thin layer of slime or oil. Milo found it a little disconcerting to be able to see the creature's muscles expand and contract as it walked and moved, and he could even see fluid…alien blood…flowing through the big veins in the native's arms.

Milo realized he was staring at the creature and he brought his eyes up to meet those of the Venusian he was studying. The native seemed to have a curious look on it's face, as if studying the strange human in return, and wondering what the little pink skinned creature thought it was doing in *his* jungle.

The Venusian narrowed its eyes, quirked it's mouth into what could almost have been a smile…and disappeared. "AWK!" shouted Milo and he stumbled in amazement.

The native porter had disappeared right before his eyes…but the pack, crossbow and sword were still bobbing along next to him! Just as quickly the Venusian reappeared, quickly materializing like a man stepping from a fog. Keeping that same almost-smile the porter then faded in and out of Milo's view, and the little professor realized the native was like a chameleon. It was changing its slime… skin…to match the jungle behind it.

One of the marines behind Milo chuckled, "Now you know why they don't wear any clothes!"

"Yes," admitted Milo, "but then why do they seem to want hats?"

After almost an hour of marching Milo thought the jungle seemed to be getting denser, and the marching pace definitely seemed to slow. The trailblazers began leading the file around obstacles rather than chopping through them and Milo was called to the front of the column several times to confirm their direction.

Milo was tired and kept hoping the Major would call for a rest, but the fat man maintained the pace. Milo actually heard him complaining about the lack of progress.

"I want to get to the next marker by midday boys!' shouted Girth. "We do NOT want to be marching through Venus at night boys, cause' Venus can be a tricky vixen at night!"

Girth pushed the trailblazers forward and called for two more of his troopers to help clear the path. The column picked up pace for a while until the trailblazers suddenly stopped.

Milo was intently watching the stone compass and didn't notice the pause, and so marched right past the natives into the jungle. A sharp rattling sound caused him to lift his head, just as Girth shouted, "I smell asparagus!"

At first Milo was confused. Why was he alone? What was that insistent rattling noise? What was Girth yelling about now? Something moved in front of Milo and finally he stopped. The bush directly in front of him seemed to expand as several large "fruit" rose up out of the thicket. Milo could see that the melons…were they melons?…were shaking, and that was the source of the rattling noise.

The melon shapes started to sway and weave as they stretched closer to Milo's face. Milo watched hypnotized as the closest melon slowly split open to reveal a toothy mouth. The alien plant no longer resembled a melon but rather a bigheaded snake swaying and weaving inches from Milo's noise. The mouth kept opening wider and wider and part of Milo's stunned mind realized the thing could now easily swallow his head.

Just as the toothy plant reared back to strike, a hand clamped on Milo's shoulder and yanked him backwards to land with a thump on the ground. Major Girth loomed over the professor, his bulk blocking the little man from the toothy plant. With far more speed than Milo expected the Major drew his sidearm and fired.

Milo expected the loud band of a handgun. What he didn't expect was the massive fireball that exploded from barrel of the weapon and engulfed the killer plant. The toothy pod was instantly burned to a cinder and Milo remembered the scorched earth around the alien pyramid.

Girth swung his massive arm to the side and sent several balls of blinding fire into the offending bush. Each blast was like a miniature sun, and they blazed a fiery path through the jungle before exploding into a burning cloud of flames and smoke deeper into the green.

Girth reached down and lifted Milo off the ground. "They kinda' smell like asparagus to me. Do they smell like roasted asparagus to you?"

Milo was too stunned by his close call to answer Girth, but the Major already seemed to forget the little man. Girth was plucking the leaves off one of the plants that hadn't been completely engulfed in his fireballs. Milo watched with stunned fascination as the Major sniffed, then nibbled one of the killer plant leaves.

"Yes, quite like roasted asparagus," declared Girth and he began stuffing several of the singed leaves into a pouch.

The column began moving again, and Mr. Umsipha pulled a small brass device from a pouch on his belt. "If the professor's translation of distance is correct we should be near the first marker."

Milo checked his notes and called out the number he'd translated from the pyramid.

"Yup," replied Major Girth as he conferred with his hulking brown officer. "We should be within several yards of it. Everybody keep your eyes peeled."

"What exactly are we peeled for?" asked one of the marines.

"Something stony," replied Girth.

"Loki's luck!" cried the bald Marine sergeant, "Is this stony enough fer ya Major?"

The sergeant was standing next to a wide stone square-sided monolith. One side was covered in huge hieroglyphics. As Milo approached, he could see that this was indeed what the party was looking for. Milo stared hard at the carvings, and pushed the fog of fatigue from his brain. The direction change was simple enough as was the distance indicated, and Milo didn't even need to crack a book to translate the course change.

Making the necessary adjustment to the stone compass ring Milo raised a confident finger and pointed. "This way gentlemen!"

The more Milo thought about this whole venture the more excited he got. Not only was he verifying his theory that the glyphs on Venus shared a common root as those in Egypt, but a more base desire settled in his brain. This military troop wouldn't be tramping through a hostile jungle to prove a hieroglyphs theory. It was far more likely that the Major was pursuing a more elemental goal...treasure! Egypt had long been a source of fabulous riches and even now archeologists and treasure seekers were digging up the desert in hopes of finding a lost cache of wealth.

Venus was a recent find, and it was likely that no human foot had traveled the path they now followed. Even the natives were ignorant of the language in the pyramid and so were unlikely to have disturbed the hidden burial temples. It explained Milo's virtual kidnapping, and the Imperial officer's insistence on haste. Milo was leading the column to a treasure trove and if he just cooperated he was sure the Major would allow him both a share in the spoils and credit for its finding. After all the Major seemed like a reasonable man...mostly.

The trees were getting smaller, the vegetation thicker, and it felt to Milo like the jungle was actually trying to bar their way. The noises and furtive movements were creeping closer, and several times Milo was sure he was being watched with hungry eyes.

It was with vast relief when the Imperial column broke into a clearing. It was better than a clearing. It was a path, wide and flat like a road, and best of all it ran in the exact direction the compass indicated!

Pinkspots immediately began waving and burbling at Major Girth, making stopping motions with his hands and shaking his head in a definite "no". Girth simply patted the native on the arm and waved his men forward onto the path. They were making excellent time now, but Milo couldn't help but notice the native porters seemed anxious. They kept burbling at each other and pointing down the path. Milo studied the ground under his feet as he walked. The ground was pounded flat and Milo assumed it was some kind of native road. The trees to either side had been crudely knocked down, and Milo wondered what kind of engines the natives employed to fell such large trees.

So far he'd only seen their simple crossbows and blades and though the trailblazers had been very good at clearing a path he doubted they could accomplish such a feat with simple bone hand blades. Of course who ever built the massive stone pyramid could also easily build such a crude road.

In fact…and Milo turned to question the native he had been walking beside-the chameleon with the lime colored stripes, when he realized LimeStripes was gone again. This time there was no pack or crossbow either. The porter just wasn't there anymore.

Milo turned to alert the Major that one of his natives had nicked the luggage when a loud snort sounded from the path ahead.

For the second time in a day Milo's heart stopped as a gigantic…something… stepped onto the path ahead of the column. It was huge, nearly as wide as the path, and was covered in armor plates and serrated horns and spikes. Its wedge shaped head looked like a cattle catcher on the front of a steam train, and it had at least three sets of short powerful legs.

Milo couldn't see any eyes but the thing had huge nostrils that quivered and snorted as the behemoth pawed the ground. Milo could also see a second stone marker pillar just past the huge beast.

"Well," purred Umsipha, "looks like we found the road crew."

As if in response the massive beast tossed it's armored head to one side and snapped a tree in half.

"This must be a game trail. I think it's his game trail, and I think he wants us off his trail," continued Umsipha. The Zulu Amerikan was backing up and waving the rest to do the same.

"Nonsense!" declared Girth. "It's just a big cow."

Then the beast lowered its head and charged.

Milo followed the marines as they dove off the trail and into the jungle. The monster trumpeted and snorted as it thundered down the path. Milo looked back to see not three but five sets of stomping legs further flattening the game path, and he could see that the beast's thrashing had also widened the path in spots.

After several yards the beast stopped and turned around ready to start its charge again.

"By Odin's eye, I'll be damned if some alien cow is gonna' make an officer of the Empire hide in the frakking bushes!" swore Girth. "B Squad shoulder arms!"

On command and without hesitation the six marines of B Squad stepped back onto the path, rifles at the ready. The behemoth either saw or smelled them because it immediately lowered its head and charged again.

"Fire at will!"

Milo didn't know much about guns, and so was once again shocked by the ferocity of Imperial firearms. It was as if Thor himself had deemed the alien cow an annoyance, and so smote it with his magical hammer. Blazing bolts of lightning streaked from each rifle and slammed into the charging beast stopping it cold. The air was suddenly charged with ozone and the smell of roasting meat as the men and women of B Squad demonstrated the power and might of the Imperial Blitzen arc rifle.

Milo had to shield his eyes from the actinic glare, and the crackling buzz of the man-made lightning was almost deafening. The huge creature gave a strangled scream, then toppled dead onto the smoldering path. Milo slowly got to his feet and followed a now visible LimeStripes into the clearing. The men and women of B Squad were laughing and joking as the Major joined then to celebrate.

"Smells like Sunday brisket," commented the Sergeant, and Girth nodded his head slowly as he marched closer to the dead monster.

"Yes, Sergeant. Actually it smells very much like Sunday brisket." Girth made a little smacking noise with his mouth. "I wonder what it would taste like with some roasted asparagus?"

"Sergeant, call a meal break!"

After an admittedly delicious lunch of electric roasted...whatever...Milo was back in line marching through the Venusian jungle. The directions on the second marker were easily translated and the little professor was feeling rather smug. The elation he felt from his survival on the 'stomper path' soon faded though. The further the company pushed into the deep green the more sinister their surroundings became. The hoots and snarls from the deepening underbrush grew louder. Things rustled in the treetops and shapes flitted at the edges of Milo's vision. Even the native guides seemed anxious as they tightened their grips on crossbows and knives. For every step the company took the volume of the alien jungle increased. The marines had to shout to be heard over the din and the march slowly ground to a halt.

Girth Bellowed at the jungle. "Nope, wrong I'm not having this! I have a schedule to keep and I'm not letting a bunch of noisy foreign fauna delay that!"

"Airmen, ready hand bombs!"

The Imperial Airmen's cheers startled Milo as the bald Sergeant began distributing dark metal balls from one of the porter's packs. The Sergeant called "FORM SQUARE," and the marines quickly formed a human block around Milo and the two Imperial officers.

"Light'em up!" Milo watched as each trooper thumbed a flint wheel on top of his ball to light a sputtering fuse.

"LOOSE!" As one, the troopers threw their hand bombs into the jungle. The multiple detonations were deafening and to Milo's horror all the troopers readied a second bomb.

"LOOSE!" Again the Imperials threw their bombs, this time deeper into the heart of the jungle. The alien rainforest erupted in noise, movement and fire as every creature and even some of the plants struggled to flee the massive explosions.

"Troopers form column, loose at will!" The column reformed and began marching again. The troopers threw their hand bombs in every direction, driving the jungle denizens back.

Milo heard something big crashing away from the column through the trees screaming like a giant scalded cat as it fled.

Girth drew his hand flamer again, and sent searing balls of fire down their intended path. Milo watched something that looked remarkedly like a dinosaur on fire stumbled into the brush and collapse behind a stand of strange looking trees. The trees immediately pulled up their roots and shuffled away from the burning saurian.

When the troopers exhausted their supply of hand bombs they brandished their firearms. Every few paces a trooper would loose a blast from a shot cannon or send a burst of man-made lightning into the jungle. The Imperial column was literally bludgeoning its way through the Venusian jungle. Milo's ears were ringing and his nose burned from the smell of gunpowder and ozone.

The marines laughed and joked as they marched, calling targets to one another and making bets on their shots. The marines opened fire on anything that moved or even anything they thought might move. They were all practically running now as they powered through the greenery, the trailblazers struggling to clear the way fast enough for those following behind.

Girth slammed a meaty hand on Milo's shoulder and pointed at the stone compass, not bothering to try and shout over the weapons fire. Milo numbly pointed forward and Girth smacked him on the back in a painful display of camaraderie.

Milo tried to block out the noise and smells and focused his thoughts on the potential riches at the end of their trip. It couldn't be much further now. The little professor lost all sense of time as the Imperial column chewed it's way through the jungle.

Milo translated two more marker pillars. The last pillar was the most difficult to translate because one of the marines had accidentally blown the top off while shooting at a very, very large bug. Milo had to scrape gooey splattered insect remains off the hieroglyphs in order to read them. Thankfully the Major had decided not to taste them.

The first hint that the party was close to their final destination were the huge stone blocks littering a clearing. The jungle had settled into a sullen silence, as if coming to an understanding with the trigger-happy marines. The clearing was scattered with stone wall sections and fallen statuary. It was hard to tell what the statues had once depicted. The sudden quiet and the broken masonry gave the clearing a graveyard-like feeling, and Milo rechecked his translations to verify their arrival.

Whether in a sign of reverence or superstition the Imperials moved silently through the ruins. The tumbled walls and huge stone idols created many places for things to hide and the dwindling light that heralded the end of a Venusian day allowed shadows to blossom and deepen. It was probably their sudden silence that saved the lives of Girth and his command.

Mr. Umsipha was moving low along a fallen pillar when he suddenly stiffened and shot his fist into the air. Every one of the Imperial marines dropped into a crouch and Milo was practically knocked to the ground by the Sergeant. The bald Amerikan noncom clamped his hand over Milo's mouth before a complaint could be sounded, and Milo's heart leaped into his throat.

Girth was crouching next to the big African Amerikan, and their body language told Milo what his ears couldn't-something was wrong. Milo eased the Sergeant's hand off his face and slowly crawled toward the two Air Corp officers.

"Is it another one of those big stomper beasts?" whispered Milo.

"Oh no," replied Girth quietly. "It's much more annoying. It's the French".

Girth allowed Milo to peer over the stone pillar they all hid behind. Through the rubble Milo could see the temple, and he could also see it was surrounded by tents, lanterns and French soldiers. In front of the temple Milo saw a stack of pickaxes, shovels and other digging gear. Milo had seen such equipment dozens of times on his trips to Egypt. The entrance to the temple lay blocked by a massive stone door, and the little professor could only assume that the Frenchmen planned on opening the temple themselves.

"Those filthy frogs plan on taking the treasure for themselves!" Milo didn't realize he'd spoken out loud, and the look he got from Major Girth was calculating.

"Indeed professor, that's something we simply cannot allow." Girth made a series of complex hand signals to his men. They stared back at him dumbly.

"Circle around, Loki damn you," Girth hissed and his marines ashamedly began moving from cover to cover towards the temple. Milo realized he could no longer see any of the native porters.

"We have to get closer to use the Blitzens," rumbled Umsipha. "I told you we should have brought some standard rifles too. The shot cannons are even shorter ranged than the damn…"

"Enough of your spleen Mr. Umsipha," snapped Girth. "We're Amerikans for Odin's sake! Wait for my order to open fire!"

One of the marines must have heard Girth say the words "open fire" because a second later the entire troop began shooting at the French. Man-made lightning leaped out at the French encampment, and heavy shot sprayed French blood across Venusian stone. For several seconds the battle seemed to be completely one-sided as the Imperial Amerikan Air Corp poured hell into the French camp.

Then a new sound joined the symphony of death. Milo heard a mechanical ratcheting sound and then a loud ripping like heavy cloth being torn. He was about to poke his nose over the pillar for a look when Girth yanked him back to the ground.

The top of the pillar erupted in stone chips and dust, and a sound like a hailstorm exploded from the other side. It took a moment for Milo's ears to register the same sounds coming from all around him.

"Damn Bavards!"

"French Chatterbox repeating rifles," Girth swore. "We are not going to let these filthy frogs and their wind-up guns take this temple!"

Milo could see other Imperial marines under cover trying to poke their heads up long enough to return fire, but the storm of French bullets had the troopers pinned in place. Then, one by one the IAAC marines stopped shooting.

"Keep firing men," shouted Girth.

The female trooper crouching beside Milo simply shrugged. "Sorry Major, I'm out."

"I'm dry too sir," hissed a marine hiding behind a rather ugly statue to Milo's right. One after another the imperial guns fell silent. The IAAC was out of ammo.

"You're soldiers!" cried Milo, "Didn't you bring extra bullets? What was in all those packs?"

"Of course we brought extra ammo," snapped the female trooper beside Milo. "We used it all in the jungle!"

"We used it all?" whispered Girth in a confused little voice.

"Well, B Squad used a full capacitor each on the stomper," said Umsipha. "... And you wanted to see if those tree squids tasted like calamari. Then there were all those shifty looking flowers with the eyeballs..."

Girth gave a resigned little sigh. "Well, I guess its side arms and sabers boys! Prepare to charge that position on my command!"

"You mean you intend to charge into THAT!" Milo gasped in disbelief and waved his hand at the continuing bullet storm that pounded their meager cover.

Girth's response was fierce. "Of course! They will never expect a frontal attack! We're Amerikans! We always attack!"

Milo sat stunned and watched helplessly as the troopers readied their handguns and drew their blades. The curvy trooper behind Milo…and part of Milo's brain registered that she was *very* curvy…handed him a knife. Milo simple stared at the wickedly sharp blade, and wondered what exactly the curvy, crazy women intended he do with it.

Major Girth grabbed Milo by the collar and growled "On my mark troopers. 3…2…"

HONK!

The sudden honking explosion of metal and gunfire that erupted behind them startled everyone, including Girth. Milo was blinded by the muzzle blast of a cannon only a few feet away and his ears rang painfully. As he blinked back tears and tried to make sense of this new threat, he saw… Girth's mechanical monster dog had followed the column. The metal beast smashed it's way into the rock strewn clearing, sounding it's earsplitting horn and loosing it's own storm of destructive fury.

Milo saw through tear-blurred eyes that what he originally assumed was a smoke stack was in fact some kind of big gun. The barrel was now pointed forward and it loosed a barrage of hellstorm into the French campsite. The gatling gun on the construct's back twitched and tracked targets like a hound's nose sniffing quail.

The French swung their fire onto this new horrible target, but Milo watched bullets ricochet from its iron hide. A metal dome dropped like a visor down over the vulnerable brain bowl, and Milo could still see the floating eyes through a slit in the shell as they followed their prey.

"Rascal's got em' running boys! Over the top and at 'em!" Girth shouted the command and the Imperial Marines leaped from cover and charged the French camp.

Milo stayed exactly where he was. He was too shocked and confused to move. Girth's metal monster seemed unstoppable. Milo watched as it crashed through a stone wall and ran directly into a group of French soldiers. The creature didn't stop. It rammed bodily into them, and Milo heard it *chew* its way through the soldiers!

Milo heard the blood curdling screams of the French soldiers over the incessant honking and deafening weapons fire of Girth's gruesome pet. Milo slid down behind the refuge of the pillar and tried to block out the sounds of combat and slaughter. He didn't care about the treasure anymore. He didn't care about Venusian hieroglyphics or Imperial citizenship either. He was sick of this horrible jungle, this horrible world and that very, very horrible man! All Milo wanted was to be back in his comfortable little office where nothing wanted to kill him. Above all else, Milo desperately wanted to be far away from Major Girth.

"I found him!"

Milo was pulled to his feet by a familiar curvy female marine. He didn't know how long he'd been hiding, and he suspected that at some point he'd actually passed out. It was nighttime on Venus and the French lanterns were lit, throwing the carnage of the French camp into flickering relief. Girth stood near the temple door, absently stroking the brain bowl of his mechanical horror.

"Glad you're still with us professor," commented Girth. "After coming so far I wouldn't want you to miss this!" Girth took several steps back from the temple.

Rascal dropped its big gun in line with the stone door and opened fire. The stone portal was reduced to so much rubble, and Girth, Umsipha and Milo proceeded into the alien temple.

Mr. Umsipha carried a lantern in each hand. The flickering light revealed a large central chamber. The walls of the cavernous room were lined with burial niches and Milo could see the withered, desiccated feet of hundreds of dead Venusians poking out. Girth strode directly to the closest corpse and pulled it from its niche.

"You see Mr. Umsipha, mummified just like the ones we found in the main pyramid! Aren't they just gorgeous!"

"Yes, commander," replied the big African. "They look excellent!"

Milo wasn't paying particular attention to the conversation. His eyes were busy scanning the massive chamber for signs of treasure, artifacts or gems. He wasn't seeing any. In fact he didn't see *anything* in the chamber except dead alien mummies!

"Where is it?" whispered Milo.

"Where's what?" answered Girth smiling.

"Where is ...whatever it is that made this trip worth it?" Milo was shouting now, and if anything Girth and Umsipha were smiling even harder.

"Why boy, you're looking at it!" Girth waved at the walls lining the chamber, walls holding hundreds of mummified Venusians. Milo stared at the rotund Major in complete and utter confusion now.

"Mummies..." stammered Milo. "We came all this way for mummies?"

Umsipha stepped closer to the stammering professor. "The British first discovered it in Egypt. They raided every Egyptian tomb they could find for treasure, and ended up with a surplus of mummies as a result so they just started burning them in the locomotives as fuel."

"They found out that mummies burn well...very, very well." Girth continued, "Pretty soon they were using them in their airships too. Mummies are lighter than coal and burn ten times hotter, at least once they are cured a bit."

"Wait," interrupted Milo, "They cure mummies?"

Girth ignored Milo's question and continued. "It got so you couldn't get good mummies anymore. The price on the Egyptian ones skyrocketed and the ones from Peru are kinda...soggy. The ones we found here on Venus though are excellent, and we are not letting anyone else get their filthy foreign hands on them! Venusian mummies are gonna' power Amerikan engines through the skies of a dozen worlds, or my name ain't Girth!"

Several troopers who had been listening at the temple door began to clap and cheer, and Girth gave a modest little bow to his men.

"Signal the *Irascible Wind*, Mr. Umsipha and tell your crews to start loading the mummies into the number four hold. Also tell em' to take Rascal up too! I miss my dog and he did a damn fine day's work today, besides we need him to keep guard on that damn pyramid."

"Why?" Milo was still reeling from the realization that there was no treasure, no gems and no payoff.

"My boy," purred Girth. "There are directions to at least a dozen other burial temples in there. We can't just leave that kind of information unguarded! You are going to be one busy little man translating those directions and guiding all those acquisition parties."

" Waaa…"stammered Milo!

"In fact," continued Girth "I think we should just go ahead and make your enlistment official. Why after a few months here on Venus you'll be an absolute veteran, and besides service grants citizenship! Sergeant, let's get Airman Milo a uniform…and some guns! Yes son, you are gonna' love being part of the Corp!"

Airman Milo of the IAAC was speechless.

MARS HO!

TIRED of life on Earth? No job prospects? Sooty coal clouds making it hard to breathe? Not enough room in your district to stretch out? Come to **MARS!**

Free passage available for qualified colonists and IMPERIAL CITIZENSHIP granted after only fifteen years of residency!

MARS! The exciting and **PERFECTLY SAFE** land of opportunity! Free Residents and Citizens of all ages are leaving each week for the **SPLENDOR** and **EXCITEMENT** of the **RED PLANET.**

Able bodied men and women are needed for blood-coal mining, **SQUIDLING FARMING**, canal patrol, fungal harvesting, and to quarry the majestic **THARSIS BULGE**. Enjoy clear **PINK SKIES**, crystal blue canals, **MAJESTIC RED CLIFFS** and wide open spaces!
Join the adventure, and hop the next airship to **THE RED PLANET!** Your **FORTUNE** awaits!

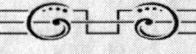

A Special Message from the Imperial Ministry of Inquisition-
The recent disappearance of Martian fishing fleets has been attributed to excessively high tides and instances of swamp gases. There are not, and have never been, any of the following on Mars: locomotive sized apex predators, advanced alien civilizations, dust storms that blot out the sun for weeks at a time, man-sized annelids that can dissolve steel and eat human flesh, or titanic cephalopods large enough to wipe a mining town off the map in a minutes. Any information to the contrary is the result of treasonous rumors spread by jealous foreign nationals. God save the Empress!

A GOOD DAY FOR GIGASQUID

A GOOD DAY FOR GIGASQUID

By Raymond J. Witte

The city-state of Ur Nehenkara was celebrating.

After three generations, the great work was complete. Part temple, part enormous ramp, the massive structure stretched high into the sky, and would finally allow the people of the city, those chosen by the Gods, to step through the Threshold of Heaven and into Paradise. Over sixty summers ago, the priests had spotted the flying Nephilim that had crossed through the shimmering Threshold, circled the city thrice, then returned to the realm of the gods.

Obviously, it had been a sign. The people of Ur Nehenkara were select, holy and sacred to the Gods, who had sent their Nephilim messenger to invite them to leave the corruption of this world. Their priests told them they were to join the Gods in their realm beyond the sky, where there was no want or pain. Construction had begun almost immediately. For three score years, the focus of the city had been the spiraling tower, that slowly rose from the ground. Fields had been torn up to plant more straw for mud bricks. The city itself had been cannibalized to speed up the project- rich and poor alike had given up the very roofs over their heads to see the project finished. And now it was done.

Three times three days, the priests had burned sacred incense and offered chants of praise as the final bridge was extended to the Threshold. All that was left was to ascend the great stairs and step into paradise. It was time. The first to cross the Threshold were the city's herds and flocks- a fitting gift for their divine hosts. Once the animals were herded through, the people of the city followed. First the priests, then the cities nobles, then the people. All crossed the sky bridge to paradise, from the oldest to the youngest.

The Martian Gigasquid was having the best day of its life. The enormous multifaceted eye high on its mantle flashed a brilliant purple as its dozens of arms lashed out, harvesting the food-from-the-sky and stuffing each morsel into its giant maw.

Initially, the Gigasquid had been disturbed by the food-from-the-sky. First, it fell from the sky instead of swimming in the sea. Second, it made much more noise than the Gigasquid's usual fare and it was soft and pinkish instead of hard and scaly. But the food-from-the-sky was delicious, and the titanic creature let out a deep purr of delight as it swallowed another mouthful.

Yes, today was a good day for Gigasquid.

A GOOD DAY FOR GIGASQUID

EAGLE FOR A SON

EAGLE FOR A SON

By Brian D. Thomas

Sergeant Major Ulfric Sleeping Bear Ulfricson, known through out the Imperial Air Corp as Sergeant Major Peaches, took another long drink from his honorary ale horn and tried to look happy. By all rights he should be happy for today was a special day.

Today was the end of his second enlistment tour and the receipt of his second Imperial Eagle.

The coin-sized silver emblem of the Imperial Amerikan Eagle in his breast pocket was reward for his twenty fourth year of service in the Imperial Amerikan Air Corp, and men and women toiled and died throughout the empire to earn the privileges the little silver metal bestowed on it's owner.

Sergeant Major Peaches sat in a Martian bar, surrounded by cheering comrades the owner of not one but TWO imperial eagles, and it was all he could do not to hurl his ale horn at the wall in frustration. He always thought being a full citizen of the Empire would solve all his problems, but now he knew better.

While "Free Residents" of the Empire led a fairly good life only full Imperial citizens enjoyed all the privileges arguably the mightiest nation on earth could provide. Only citizens could own property, own businesses, serve in the government, travel freely and in general reap the full rewards of their labors, and there were only a few ways to achieve citizenship. Citizenship could not be bought nor was it automatically granted at birth. Imperial Amerikan citizenship had to be earned through service to the Empire. Few paths were open to the Free Resident who sought full citizenship, and military service was the quickest and most popular option. The fact that the Empire of Amerika was almost constantly in conflict with SOMEONE …often several someones, ensured a constant need for military recruits. With few other options and dreams of a privileged caste a young Algonquin-Swede with a peach fuzz beard joined the IAAC to earn his eagle.

Ulfric, "Peaches" Ulfricson had entered Imperial service at sixteen and earned his first eagle at the age of twenty-eight. He'd fought in four wars on six continents and two different worlds. He'd traveled through more skylocks than a northern goose, docked at more foreign harbors than a Chinese sky junk, and after twelve hard years he'd been rewarded for his service. Imperial citizenship allowed him to continue his military career as a non-commissioned officer, granted him the right to own property and increased his pay enough to afford finding a wife.

Now that same bearded Algonquin-Swede had a second eagle and for the life of him did not know what to do with it. In his pocket he held the key to his only son's future. With this second eagle he could guarantee a better education and far more opportunities for his little boy than he himself ever had. While citizenship could not be sold, an Imperial Eagle could legally be passed from parent to child, and Peaches was not the only marine who fought through a second tour of duty to ensure a future for their child.

An eagle could however be "sold back" to the Empire. The price for twelve years of service was five hundred gold sovereigns, and while many complained about the bounty, as the only entity allowed to purchase an eagle, the Empire could set the buy back price to what ever he thought fair. This was Sergeant Peaches' dilemma. While he wanted to provide a future for his son he needed to provide a home for him now, and that was the problem.

While the Empire extolled the virtues and privileges of citizenship to encourage the masses in their labors they failed to mention the responsibilities that came with it, namely…taxes. An Imperial Amerikan citizen had over twice the tax responsibility of a free resident and failure to pay the required tithes was not only grounds for citizenship loss but seizure of all monies and properties.

An Air Corps sergeant's pay was not enough to afford the home, taxes and lifestyle sergeant Peaches' wife and child demanded. A sick baby accrued a mountain of medical bills and both Peaches and his wife had insisted on only the best doctors for their ailing infant. His now healthy boy ate like a horse and it seemed he grew out of his clothes almost daily. Peaches' wife Helgafrey still had another eight years of service in the munitions factory before she earned her eagle, nor did his wife's employer offer "additional enlistment". Once she had earned her own citizenship eagle there would not be a second opportunity.

In any case Sergeant Peaches did not think they would be able to hold out that long. By then his son would be too old to enroll in a citizen's primary school and would be lucky to be accepted to even a minor trade guild.

They also needed money now to pay debts and outstanding taxes, or they would loose their home. The sergeant had his bunk on the *Irascible Wind* but Imperial airships did not allow family members to bunk onboard, and Peaches didn't want to see his boy grow up in the harsh environment of public Free Resident housing.

If he took the Imperial bounty in exchange for his newly won eagle he could pay off all his debts and provide a small nest egg for his wife and child to live on. He hadn't even begun to think about what he was going to do with himself now that he could technically muster out of Imperial service.

The Air Corp was all he knew and frankly he was rather good at taking orders and killing things. The idea of waiting another twelve years for a third eagle made the ale in his stomach turn sour and he was sure that in any minute he was going to spoil his uniform with vomit.

The bottle that broke over his head and bar fight that erupted around him was actually a welcomed distraction to his troubles.

Peaches' comrades knew their sergeant's dilemma and had been focused on helping him forget his troubles, or at least drown them a bit in cheap Martian ale. The first any of them realized they were in the middle of a fight was when the little brown man landed squarely in the middle of their table, sending their mugs and horns of cheap Martian ale crashing to the floor.

To be fair, the little Indian looked as surprised to be lying on the marine's table, as they were to have him there. He gasped and sputtered apologies even as he tried to crawl out from the spoiled party. The big turbaned man who threw the little Indian into the Amerikans pushed through a crowd of fighting bar patrons. He followed up the Indian toss with a bottle to the back of Sergeant Peaches' head, and the game was on.

Peaches' brain blanked out all his troubled thoughts and trained reactions took over. He spun around blindly and slammed his drinking horn point first into the face of his turbaned assailant. The big man with the turban let loose a high-pitched scream and fell backwards with his hands pressed to his ruined face. Peaches didn't stop moving and grabbed his chair as he spun around. As soon as his head cleared from the bottle blow he smashed the chair down onto the fallen man silencing the screams. Bar patrons were shouting and swinging all around him and without thinking Peaches waded into the fight.

The four other Amerikan Marines at the table exploded into action. With an ear-splitting battle cry an eye patched female marine grabbed the sputtering Indian who had just spilled her drink with his hurled body, and threw him back into the bar crowd.

Two of Peaches drinking companions each grabbed a leg of the table, and together lifted the heavy bar furniture in front of themselves like a shield. With a shout they rammed the table like a battering ram into the crowd and drove several brawlers into a wall. The fourth Imperial marine simply grabbed the nearest patron and head-butted him into unconsciousness.

Sergeant Peaches didn't know what started the bar room brawl nor did he care. He and his fellow marines only cared that they were in yet another fight, and as in any fight they fought to win. They also didn't concern themselves with the niceties of not fighting dirty. Even miners and longshoremen weren't tough enough to stand against a pack of motivated Imperial marines, and Peaches' depression had made him and his comrades very motivated to fight.

By the time the constables had bothered to show up the bar fight was over and the marines were gone. The Martian town of Paradise Canals was a mining and skylock town, so the authorities were used to brawls and "public displays". The local law officers found it easier to just let these little dust-ups burn themselves out and then roll in to fine everyone who survived for the damages. Even if the constables had seen the marines they wouldn't have tried to handle them alone, instead calling for provosts to deal with the trained Imperial killers.

Peaches and his drinking companions were in no hurry to tangle with Imperial provosts since they were as well trained as the marines, and had the authority to shoot their troublesome brothers-in-arms if they couldn't be bludgeoned into submission. Instead Peaches and his comrades had battled their way to the door and finding it blocked by brawling patrons had sent several miners crashing through the main window to create a new exit. When the local constables finally arrived the four marines were already blocks away sharing a bottle they had acquired during the fight and comparing battle tactics.

Sergeant Dzbanki laughed and adjusted her eye patch as she handed Peaches the whiskey bottle she'd stolen from the bar during the fight. Technically she hadn't stolen it. She had stopped the miner who tried to hit her with it by breaking his kneecap and caught the dropped bottle before it hit the floor. Not wanting to see a good bottle of whiskey go to waste she'd tucked it down her shirt before kicking the crying miner in the face.

Dzbanki felt sorry for her brother sergeant, and understood his dilemma. "What you need is some side money," she told the slowly sobering Peaches. "We have two week's leave here on this red dirtball, and you just need to pick up a little side work before we ship out again," she explained. "There's always some little job that needs doing in these frontier towns, and me and the boys would be happy to help you out…for a small cut," added Dzbanki.

Peaches took the offered bottle. The sulking sergeant then gestured at the buildings built into the canyon walls behind and above him.

"Where am I supposed to find two week's work that pays as much as cashing out an Imperial eagle?" grumbled Sergeant Peaches.

"I don't know how much that is, Sahib, but I could pay you quite well to keep me alive for two weeks," replied a voice from the shadows.

The little Indian from the bar walked slowly into view. He was battered and bleeding and Peaches could still smell the ale that had covered the man when he'd literally crashed their party.

Many of the newly independent "Princely States" of India had claims on Mars, and the Indian Nawab governors hired out workers to foreign held districts to ensure friendly relations with their neighbors. This man did not have the look of a mineworker or canal sailor though. Even battered and bloody he had the bearing of a gentleman and his abused state did not speak well of his physical abilities in even a casual conflict. He wore a traditional Indian dark blue embroidered sherwani jacket and the disheveled pagri wrap on his head looked to be made of fine silk.

"Is it my understanding that you gentlemen…and lady are seeking temporary employment?" the Indian asked. "Allow me to properly introduce myself. My name is Suresh Rawat. I am a pundit…a surveyor, and it seems I am in rather immediate need of bodyguards. You will remember that when we first met I was being harried by some rather unpleasant persons."

"You were being thrown around like a little brown sack of flour," smirked Peaches.

Peaches didn't particularly like Indians. Like most Amerikans Peaches didn't particularly like any foreigners, but he was least fond of…brown foreigners. Peaches was typical of "old family" Amerikan bloodlines that combined

Scandinavian Viking colonists with native skrealing tribesmen, but again like most Amerikans he considered himself "pink" and not brown. The fact that his own Arapaho blood made his skin a ruddy tone did little to dampen his mistrust or dislike of "browns".

"Why were those other turbans trying to beat you like an old rug?" smirked Peaches. "You try and skip out on your beef and beer tab?"

"They don't eat beef you trolls-ass!" snapped Dzbanki. "Now shut up and let the man talk!"

Anger seared from the small man's eyes but he kept his tone civil. "As I said, there are some unpleasant people who want information I have, and they are willing to go to very extreme lengths to get it from me. Once they have that information, they will no doubt wish me permanently silenced so that I cannot share it with others. I saw how...effective...you and your companions were in the tavern and I also could not help but overhear that you are in need of money. I believe our needs are mutually conducive to business."

"He followed us sergeant," growled the marine named HammerCloud. HammerCloud had a penchant for head butting, but he was still remarkably sharp witted. The big bearded marine looked like someone had dressed a grizzly bear in a uniform and he often behaved that way when angered. Sergeant Dzbanki could see he was definitely getting angry. "So he followed us," snapped the female marine. "I care more about how much he thinks guarding his body is worth."

The pundit drew a small pouch from inside his jacket and shook the contents into his palm. The light from the gas streetlamps glittered off the facets of the little gems in the brown man's hand. The five marine's eyes widened as Suresh pushed the little gems around with his finger. "These are Martian fire rubies, my...friends. The violent men chasing me want to find the source of these little beauties, and I need my own violent men ...and lady... to stop them while I collect the rest."

"How many more are there?" purred Dzbanki. The female marine never took her good eye off the shiny jewels as she spoke.

"I'm not sure," replied Suresh. "I have registered a claim with the Nawab governor, but the claim is only temporary, and the site will revert to the district governor at the end of next week. I have until then to prospect the area for more such gems, and news of my find has somehow leaked out."

"Why did the governor give you a temporary prospectors claim?" challenged Peaches. "I've never heard of such a thing even on this stupid red dirtball of a world."

Suresh paused for a moment before answering, then seemed to make up his mind about his reply. "Because I did not tell the governor's office about the gems," he finally answered. "They believe I am doing soil surveys for liftium, and because it is hardly rare here on Mars they were willing to grant me a temporary permit before the territory changes hands. They probably hope to increase their asking price by including my report in the land survey. That is after all what they hired me to do."

The marines crowded around the Indian pundit and his palm full of tiny rubies. "My offer is this," continued Suresh, "I will give you half of what I hold in my hand and one quarter of what I find in the coming days, and in return you will act as my personal guards and help me pan for stones."

"Half!" corrected Sergeant Dzbanki before any of the others could speak. "And you pay for the camp supplies."

"One third," countered the pundit, "and you must help me prospect the site." The female sergeant locked eyes with her male counterpart. "He's got about a thousand sovereigns worth of gems in his hand, and your cut should be enough to at least take a chunk out of your problems," she added. "Even if we don't find any more it's still worth skipping a couple weeks of getting drunk and beating up Martians."

"Besides," she added looking back at the gems "It sounds like the Martians may be coming to us to get beat up."

Sergeant Peaches and the three male marines stayed with Suresh while Sergeant Dzbanki returned to The *Irascible Wind* to collect their weapons. While Imperial Air Corp marines were never actually unarmed, they were discouraged from taking heavy firearms on shore leave.

The six met outside the town just as the sun was breaking dawn in the Martian sky. Suresh had purchased ponies and a small wagon filled with tents and supplies. Dzbanki arrived leading a pack mule heavily burdened with implements of death, and two more marines.

"How did you get Vickers?" asked a surprised Peaches as he pulled the heavy automatic rifle from a canvas bag on the mule. Dzbanki quickly grabbed the wind-up repeater from her brother-sergeant's hands and stuffed it back out of sight in the sack. "Ensign Witt owes me a favor," hissed Dzbanki. She snapped her head toward Suresh. "And you owe Mr. Witt ten gold sovereigns for looking the other way while I requisitioned all this gear," she added to her new Indian employer.

"You also owe us," added one of the two new comers. Two female marines walked beside the pack mule. Both women had extremely long rifles strapped across their backs. "I would have thought five of you were sufficient for this job, but if you wish to share your portion...," Suresh commented. He looked over to Sergeant Peaches for a response.

Peaches knew both of the new marines. They were both Longarm marksmen, Imperial marine snipers. The massive scoped weapons on their backs, when wielded by a professional, could hit targets at over a mile away, which was handy when airship combat was measured in miles and not yards like ground combat. He also knew that no one could requisition a Longarm rifle. The rifles and elaborate scopes were permanently assigned to a specific sniper and those marines never loaned out their beloved weapons.

He gave each of the women a casual salute, letting them know they were both welcome. Sergeant Peaches knew the short brunette as airman Goolia, and he also knew the cherubic little woman could be volatile when she drank. She was a remarkably good shot as all marine Longarmsmen were though, and Peaches was happy to have her along.

The other woman gave the Sergeant pause. She was airman Seota'e, a full-blooded Cheyenne and new member of the *Irascible* crew. Her people had only recently joined the Empire after over a hundred years of open warfare around the Missouri river and the Dakotas. Rumor was that Seota'e learned her skills with the rifle at a young age by shooting Imperial "blue coat" pony soldiers out of their saddles at eight hundred yards.

Rumor also whispered the raven haired young woman had turned down placement in the Imperial army because she couldn't get into an all-skrealing unit, and didn't trust her new "pinkskin" Imperial brothers and sisters not to attempt a little payback during some long secluded patrol. Seota'e meant *"ghost woman"* in the Cheyenne Algonquian language, and the haunted look in her eyes bothered Peaches enough to make him hesitant to welcome her as a sister-in-arms. Peaches knew rumors aside, airmen Seota'e was by far the best Longarm marksman on The *Irascible Wind*, and he suspected he might need such skills in the high cliff canyons, and long winding canals of Mars.

Various gun barrels and blades poked out from the bundles and sacks on the mule. "Are those hand bombs?" whispered Hammer Cloud. His voice had the soft hint of a child at Yule opening a particularly special present as he caressed the dull black metal globes. Sergeant Peaches sighed and waved his squad, including the two new marksmen toward the waiting wagon and ponies.

Suresh led the wagon and string of ponies along the shore of the Paradise Canal toward a dock. He waved the squad onto a flat-bottomed canal barge, and though the steam driven paddleboat seemed large at first glance the wagon, ponies, mule and marines quickly crowded the craft. Dzbanki grabbed the Indian by the arm as he made his way to the pilot's wheel. "Here put these on," she barked and shoved a jacket and hat into his arms. Suresh held up a short jacket the same color and fabric as the airmen's uniforms in one hand and a tan kepi in the other. "I am quite happy with my own…," he replied.

"You stick out in that fancy jacket and head wrap like a turd at a tea party," snapped Dzbanki. "With these on anyone looking will see a full squad of IAAC airmen on a simple canal ride."

Suresh was about to argue further when HammerCloud punched his own open palm with a loud smack that sounded like a pistol shot. Obviously the lady sergeant had given an order and just as obviously the little Indian was expected to obey it.

Reluctantly, Suresh handed his sherwani and pagri to the female marine sergeant and put on the short amber jacket and kepi. Neither had any patches or emblems, so Suresh assumed he wasn't breaking any military rules by wearing them. As almost an afterthought Dzbanki handed him a gun belt and pistol. As Suresh put on the unfamiliar weapon he glanced back at airman HammerCloud with slightly more confidence.

HammerCloud simply smiled and punched his palm again.

Suresh moved to the front of the canal barge and shouted for Peaches to engage the engine. The barge was a simple affair; a high walled wooden box with a little steam engine and firebox attached to a rear mounted paddle wheel. Two coal bins sat full of black lumpy fuel for the firebox, and Peaches doubted water was an issue when traveling along a canal. He stoked the furnace and after building a head of steam engaged the paddle wheel. Suresh steered from the front as Peaches maintained the steam engine at the rear.

The barge moved quickly down the canal, and Peaches watched the cliff face town of Paradise Canals slide by. Like most towns on Mars people built their homes in the canyon walls of the canal rather than up on the high wind blown plateaus. Nothing lived up on the plateaus but herds of massive grazing buffalopes, leaping camazells and the giant Martian predators that ate them.

Peaches looked down warily at the placid canal water. Supposedly, there were equally dangerous predators living in the deep canals and sea-sized lakes that waited for thirsty grazers that wandered down one of the earthen ramps that connected the canal floors with the plateau tops, but you could never trust frontier rumors. Still Peaches wondered as he looked back up the canyon wall at the town.

The town of Paradise Canals was built on the ruins of a much older Martian cliff city, one not built by Amerikans, Indians or the British. Supposedly the ruins of Mars were old even when men first discovered the skylocks and flew balloons from earth to dig gold and liftium out of her red sandy cliffs. The earthen ramps were certainly too regular and well located to be natural and the canals looked far more cut out than any river or gorge on earth. The seven marines watched the cliff face buildings, plateau edge and narrowing canal beach for signs of pursuit, but no one at Paradise Canals took notice of a squad of IAAC airmen going for a boat ride.

The company traveled for several hours, as Suresh expertly navigated the interlocking spider web of Martian canals. Peaches couldn't see much from the back of the barge, but he could see Dzbanki sitting on top of the wagon taking notes every time the barge made a turn or crossed a canal intersection. The mines and towns on Mars were scattered and without a map Peaches doubted his little crew would be able to find their way back through the maze of waterways to Paradise Canals and their waiting airship, assuming their Indian was no longer with them.

The steady chugging of the steam engine was starting to lull sergeant Peaches to sleep, so it was through half closed lids that he noticed something looking at him from the water. It took a moment for his napping brain to register the yellow eyeball regarding him from just a few feet to his left.

Peaches own eyes snapped open and he watched as something that looked like a cross between a pig and an alligator return his gaze. The creature swimming beside the barge was easily ten feet long with a huge gator-like tail lazily propelling it along. The skin looked like pink wet leather and a bristly shock of black course hair ran from the thing's snout to the tip of its long thick tail. The creature was not looking ahead as it swam though. It was looking sergeant Peaches directly in the eye, and it took several seconds for the sergeant to find his voice.

Peaches glanced toward the front of the barge and yelled loud to be heard over the chugging steam engine and splashing paddlewheel. He waved frantically at airman Gerade, the wide shouldered marine from Yersy, but when he looked to see what had agitated his sergeant, there was nothing there. Peaches searched the water to either side of the barge but the sly eyed canal monster had disappeared. Peaches spent the rest of the canal ride wide-awake.

Finally, Suresh relayed the message back to Peaches to slow the engine. The Indian Pundit had maneuvered the barge toward a sandy stretch of beach near a tall dark cave-like split in the canyon wall. He directed the marines to off-load the wagon and ponies, and then showed them how to tie the barge to anchor stakes he unpacked from the supply wagon. Once the barge was secure, Suresh led the wagon and his bodyguards into the cave.

The canals of Mars crisscrossed the world and their walls rose several hundred feet on either side to level out into flat rolling plateaus. The narrow cleft Suresh led the company through cut completely across one such plateau like a giant crack. Peaches rode one of the ponies and looked up the cave wall to see sunlight poking through the ceiling several hundred feet above. The cave was more of a small dry gorge with walls several hundred feet high but only several feet apart. There was just enough room for the small wagon and Peaches realized the pundit must have known that and so picked a wagon that he knew would fit down the path.

Suresh explained as they rode that the heavy rains during the monsoon season washed the sandy soil from the walls and floor leaving only the harder rock behind. As they rode he pointed at little specks of yellow exposed in the wall. Even the marines knew gold when they saw it.

"The rain exposes all the deep metals and gems in this cleft," lectured Suresh. "The heavy rain washes everything out the other end of this gorge, and if we were here during a monsoon we would be washed out too!"

"I don't think any other human has ever walked this gorge, but you can see hundreds of buffalope hooves have stamped the ground flat. I think they use it to get to the canal."

After a mile or so the company exited out on to the wide valley floor of another canal, and Peaches noted the wide red stain of the cleft-wash at his feet. A dry streambed led from the cleft mouth down toward the canal bed. This canal section had a sandy beach over a hundred yards wide and Peaches could see the canal made a sharp turn to the right just ahead. The beach was studded with short ruddy trees, thorny Martian sting bushes and thousands of small and medium rocks. There was more gravel here than Peaches had ever seen on a canal beach and Suresh was impressed he'd noticed.

"That's the whole point!" explained Suresh excitedly. "That cleft was hundreds of feet high so the strata we saw exposed was old and mineral rich. The yearly rains knock everything loose from the walls and it all washes out here at our feet!"

Suresh lept off his pony and grabbed a handful of the pebbly red wash dirt. He let the sandy soil run between his fingers exposing various little rocks and nuggets. He plucked one nugget out of his hand and held it up for Peaches to see. Tiny flecks of gold were sprinkled through the rock.

"I panned just one section of this wash for several days and found those stones I gave you as well as a sizeable number of small gold nuggets and chips. Imagine what eight of us could find in two weeks!" Suresh opened his arms and turned slowly in place to emphasize just how large the washout actually was. "You saw the gold in the walls, and I'm sure we could even find at least a small vein near those flecks if we had more time. There is something else I want to show you."

Suresh led Peaches to a dry little pond near the canal edge. The dry ditch ran from the cleft mouth and ended at the dry pond. "Everything that doesn't get left up on the wash ends up down there," Suresh continued excitedly.

Peaches could see they were still over fifty yards from the canal. Suresh saw the sergeant measuring the distance with his eyes. "That's right, the canal doesn't flood this high even in the rainy season, so anything washed into that dry pond stays there."

Peaches looked closer at the excited little pundit's "dry pond". If this was a pond then Peaches was a schoolgirl. He had been in the military long enough to know a bomb crater when he saw one. Looking back at the canyon wall he could see how the entire area around the cleft opening looked crumbled and fallen, unlike the crisp flat canyon wall across the canal. While the damage to the land looked very old Peaches didn't doubt this was the scene of some serious ordinance play. Still, the little Indian's theory about the run-off collecting in the crater seemed sound.

Peaches could see the man had been busy proving it too.

A small steam engine sat next to the edge of the crater connected to a jury-rigged conveyor belt. It looked like the pundit had stripped the paddle wheel and engine from a canal barge to bring earth up from the crater bed. A long wooden trough on a chest-high stand ran back along the dry ditch, and what looked like an old wine cask was perched on a tower at one end. Suresh was practically beaming as Peaches turned toward him for an explanation.

"I stripped a canal barge for the parts I needed, and built the earth lifter. I also connected a pump to the barge engine to pull water from the canal and fill my water tower," explained Suresh as he pointed at the canvas hose that ran between the canal and the wine cask on the rickety wood frame. He then reached up and opened a valve letting water cascade down from the big cask into the long wooden trough.

"This is a sluice. You bring dirt up from the crater and dump it into the sluice box, then start the water. The water pushes everything down the sluice over these stepped riffles at the bottom of the trough. The heavier gems and nuggets get caught against the riffles while the lighter sands washes out the other end. We can also use the water at the end to hand pan the cleft wash, though I think the real finds will be in the floor of this pond."

"What about the gold we saw in the cave walls?" asked Peaches.

"Unfortunately there is not enough time to properly mine the walls, and besides I believe the crater as you call it will prove a rich source of…riches!" replied Suresh.

The rest of the marines had crowded around during the pundits little lecture. Sergeant Peaches locked eyes with the rest of his now gold-fevered crew. "First things first marines. We need to set camp."

"I brought tents enough to set up here in the valley if you don't mind sharing…" Suresh added as he indicated the supply wagon.

"Trollshit!" barked Peaches. "We are NOT going to camp out in the open of a Loki-damned valley under Loki-damned cliffs next to a Loki-damned canal with who knows what kind of Loki-damned critters swimming in it!" swore the now shouting sergeant. "We have a perfectly good dry cave with a back exit, good visibility of the valley and cover from most angles. We set up camp inside the cleft."

Sergeant Peaches began barking orders. "Sergeant Dzbanki, unload the supply wagon then get the boys to push it back into the cleft trail a couple hundred feet. Tie the ponies up there too. We'll bring em' out for water and feed but I don't want any nosey so-and-so doing a fly-over and counting mounts."

He turned and pointed at airman Seota'e. "Marksman, scramble up that tumble and see if you can dig out an over-watch nest." The Cheyenne woman looked up at the crumbled cliff face then turned back to the sergeant and smiled. She gave a sharp noise that sounded like a dog bark then sprinted off toward the tumbled rocks.

"What do you want us to do Sarg?" asked airmen Rolf and Gerade almost simultaneously. Peaches smiled and pointed back at the cave mouth. "Start gathering rocks, boys."

By nightfall the Imperial Marines had built a horseshoe-shaped wall of rocks chest high across the mouth of the cleft. It was hard tiring work, but it never occurred to the marines that they were technically still on leave and did not have to take orders or do manual labor like this. Training was ingrained in every Imperial soldier from every branch of service dating back to the Roman legionnaires they were modeled after. Building a secure camp was at the top of the must-do list for every soldier of the Empire regardless of the situation.

Peaches had ordered his marines to rub red Martian canal silt into the bright white canvas until it was a similar ruddy color as the canyon walls before allowing them to pitch a section across the cleft opening like a great canvas door flap. He also had them rig canvas covers over the sluice run, water tower and steam engine, though this was more to provide camouflage from the air rather than shade for his part time prospectors.

Goolia and Seota'e found a promising ledge half way up the cliff face and dug out a sniper's blind, borrowing some of the stained canvas for a sun cover. Rolf and Gerade lashed a pair of poles together and raised a small Imperial Flag in the center of the camp. Even Peaches didn't argue with this obvious sign of Imperial presence. He was after all a citizen.

Dzbanki had been overjoyed when she found a small case of dynamite sticks in the supply wagon. She'd sent HammerCloud back down the path to set a surprise for anyone coming up the cleft uninvited.

"How will you avoid harming the innocent?" protested Suresh when he saw what the marines intended with his mining explosives.

Peaches pulled the wooden lid off a box of Greeble tins and quickly scrawled a note using a bit of charcoal from the campfire. "Here, prop this up a few feet past your snares." Suresh watched wordlessly as sergeant Peaches handed Hammer Cloud a crude sign that read "Knock First!"

With their camp firmly established the company of bodyguard prospectors got to work early the next morning. Sergeant Dzbanki, airmen Goolia, and airmen Gerade worked the sluice, watching the muddy flow that washed down the trough and picking at the bits left in the riffles. Hammer Cloud and Rolf panned the wash, scooping spade full's of the red cleft wash dirt into tin pans, swirling run off water from the trough around their pans hoping to see the glint of gold or sparkle of gems exposed in the bottom of their pans. Seota'e sat perched in her cliff face nest with her longarm watching over the crew like a mother hawk.

Suresh ran from the crater floor to the sluice run and the panning team offering instructions and tips on refining the prospecting teams techniques. Sergeant Peaches stayed in the crater shoveling dirt into the earth lifter, wondering if any of this was going to benefit his son.

Suresh could see the smoldering anxiety in the sergeant's face each time he rammed his shovel into the dirt or slammed another load onto the conveyor belt. The Indian pundit was an intelligent man and could see the marine sergeant was still wrestling with his troubles, and so tried to distract him with conversation. Peaches' responses were surly but the little Indian pressed on undaunted. He forced Peaches to tell him about his family, his military career and tried to distract the troubled marine with his own stories of travel and exploration throughout the canals and plateaus of Mars. The team worked like this for days, and soon Peaches found himself infected with the pundit's enthusiasm and optimism. He also found himself beginning to like the little brown foreigner, despite his 'foreignness' and 'brownness'.

Everyone's spirits rose when the sluice started producing gold. Early the third day Dzbanki and her team starting plucking tiny rice-sized grains of gold trapped in the sluice riffles. The eye-patched female sergeant teased airman Hammer Cloud for not finding anything in his pan but dirt, and the big Dane began tearing through the cleft wash like an angry oversized badger. Taunts and threats were tossed back and forth between the two teams of prospecting marines and Peaches had to calm a worried Suresh.

"It's just the way marines play," explained Peaches. "I doubt they will really start shooting, and beside down here in the crater they won't hit us, so don't worry!"

The atmosphere of the camp went from optimistic to ecstatic when airman HammerCloud found a rough ruby the size of a walnut at the bottom of his pan. He was so excited he rushed to the sluice and picked Dzbanki up, spinning her around and roaring in her face like a berserk grizzly bear. Suresh thought the two had finally taken their taunts seriously, and it took several seconds to get HammerCloud to release the female sergeant long enough to explain his find.

"Praise be," whispered Suresh. "This stone is worth…thousands! We could fund an entire proper mining operation here on just this stone."

"Yeah, if we were staying here, which we aren't after next week so put in the box and let's get back to work," replied Peaches coolly.

They had all agreed to put everything they found in a metal ammo box. No one was to "pocket" anything, and they would share everything, as first agreed. Dzbanki found a loose rock in the cleft cave and dug a little nook out behind it. The treasure box was kept there, just in case any visitors happened by or any of the crew developed "temporary gold fever fingers". There was no thought of leaving the site early, even after HammerCloud's find. Everyone had the bug now. Everyone wanted just one more find, just one more strike, just one more drop in the treasure box.

It was on the evening of the eighth day that Peaches really started to believe that there was a light at the end of his own dark tunnel. There was a healthy sum building in the ammo box, and all of Suresh's theories about the wealth from the cleft were proving true. They had not seen another human since arriving and the only visitors to their camp were two camazells that Seota'e had bagged from her perch, and was roasting over a cook fire. Everyone was happy and he watched as his fellow marines spent the last hours of daylight playing stickball.

Every Amerikan child played stickball. Other countries played it too but never as well as Amerikans. The French called it "la crosse", but like most Amerikans Peaches didn't give a tinker's fart what the French called anything, and beside it had been Peaches own Skrealing ancestors who invented the sport and showed his Viking ancestors how to play it so screw the snail-eating French.

Supposedly the early Viking settlers competed with the native tribes in massive stickball games with hundreds of players. Land rights were the prizes to the victors, and the Vikings quickly learned to play well if they wanted prime land and hunting rights. They also learned to cheat well, and Peaches watched as his marines carried on that proud tradition whacking each other with their amtacha net-sticks, kicking the ball when they though no one was looking and in general blowing off steam like good Imperial citizens.

"Citizens," murmured Peaches out loud. That's what this had all been about and Peaches couldn't stop his thoughts from focusing back on the questions that haunted him. Would his share be enough to satisfy his debts? Would he be able to transfer his second Imperial Eagle to his son and still be able to provide the funds needed to support a citizen family? Peaches shook his head and picked up his own amtacha intent on joining the stickball game. He needed something to distract his thoughts and he didn't really want to get hit in the head with a bottle again. He spent the rest of the evening playing with his brother and sister marines and forgetting his troubles. The next day trouble came knocking with a vengeance.

Sergeant Peaches was in the crater shoveling dirt with Suresh when trouble rode into camp. He heard Seota'e's sharp dog bark call over the chugging steam engine and looked up to see what she wanted. He had almost forgotten why she was perched up on the cliff face. She did not expose herself or her location and so Peaches scrambled up from the crater to look around.

A line of horsemen came trotting down the canal beach in single file from the north. From two hundred yards away Peaches could only see that there were a dozen horsemen, and that they were all wearing Indian turbans. He slid back down into the crater and pulled the Vicker automatic repeater from where it hung by the conveyor belt with the rest of his web gear. He was too busy winding the weapon to stop Suresh from scrambling up the crater to take a look.

One of the horsemen must have seen the little pundit pop out of the ground like some big Martian prairie dog, because Peaches heard a distant shout from the canal. He grabbed Suresh by the leg and pulled him back down into the crater, then poked his own head just above the crater lip to see the horsemen's reaction. He watched as the group spurred their long legged mounts into action and drew saddle rifles from long holsters behind their legs.

"Ut, Ut Ut," shouted Peaches in practiced Imperial marine alarm. The three-word alert sent the other marines diving for cover and reaching for weapons. Peaches watched as the riders spread out even as they spurred thier horses into the prospecting camp. The sharp crack of a Longarm sounded across the little valley as Seota'e plucked the first rider off his horse with a heavy caliber rifle round, and Peaches watched the man tumbled from his saddle, raising a little red cloud of dust as he hit the ground. Peaches' head barely cleared the crater edge but he was still forced to drop back down as the riders sent answering bullets into the camp.

"Stay down!" barked Peaches as he shoved Suresh down onto the crater floor. The pundit had the pistol Dzbanki had given him clutched in his hand and Peaches swatted his arm aside before the little man accidentally shot him. Peaches scrambled up the crater near the conveyor belt using the steam engine as cover and watched as the riders closed on the camp, shooting as they came.

The attackers all handled their mounts like professionals and Peaches saw that the horses were magnificent animals expertly trained. He swung the Vicker barrel up and began cutting down the horses like so much dog food.

TAT TAT TAT TAT barked the wind-up repeater as it sent a steady stream of bullets across the valley floor.

Peaches needed to stop the charge first, and as the other marines targeted the riders he could see they were also following their training. Years of facing Skrealing horse warriors in the hills and plains of Amerika had taught the Imperial marines the best way to stop a horde of skilled riders was to make them wounded walkers, and they knew bringing down a mount brought down the rider too.

"One little, two little, three little Indians..." sang HammerCloud as he ripped the turbaned riders from their saddles with short vicious bursts from his clockwork rifle. He did not flinch even as return fire sparked off the rocks by his head. HammerCloud smiled instead. "I've been shot at by far better than you boys, and Odin hasn't called me home yet!"

The Indian horsemen spurred their horses through the firestorm, returning fire as fast as they could. The screams of horses and men filled the little canal bank and the smile on HammerCloud's face quickly faded.

The horsemen only lasted a few minutes in the open valley, with little cover while facing the rapid fire of dug in marines with automatic repeaters. Dzbanki and her team were using the sluice. HammerCloud and Rolf had dived behind the little rock wall at the cleft mouth and were sweeping the valley with wind-up death. What bothered Peaches the most was that the attackers never broke. They continued to fire from the ground after their mounts were shot out from under them and not one tried to escape back down the beach. They moved like professional soldiers, dropping prone to provide less of a target and pumping out shots as fast as they could. If it weren't for Seota'e and the Vickers, Peaches thought things might have gone quite differently.

Sergeant Peaches crouch-ran to Dzbanki behind the sluice as Seota'e silenced the screaming cries of a dying horse. "Everybody stay where you are," shouted Peaches even as he and Dzbanki broke cover to inspect one of the dead riders. The dead man was Indian, and he was well equipped. As Peaches and Dzbanki quickly searched each fallen raider they noticed the same thing. "They are all equipped the same," commented Dzbanki. "Who ever heard of bandits all having matching gear?"

"Yeah," agreed Peaches, and these jackets almost look like some kind of uniform."

"It is a uniform," agreed Suresh as he crept up to the two Imperial NCOs. "It is the uniform of the governor's private household guards. These men are his and those horses you killed are imported from India just for their use."

"Well, it looks like we know who leaked out your secret mine location," replied Peaches. "I'm guessing the Narwab figured to grab as much as he could from you before he lost this territory."

It all made sense to Peaches now. The Empire was laying claim to whole Martian territories and this was probably one of them. That's why the *Irascible Wind* was in Paradise Canals in the first place. She was hovering over the town to "ease" the transition from independent town to Imperial outpost. The Indian governors were selling their territories to the Empire after having taken them from the British, and the Amerikans were flashing their military muscles to keep everyone honest. Peaches was about to explain his revelation to Suresh and Dzbanki when the engine by the crater exploded in a cloud of steam and shrapnel.

Peaches grabbed Dzbanki and Suresh and dove to the ground as another round blew the wine cask water tower to splinters. "Loki's luck, that's cannon fire!" shouted Peaches.

The three hugged the ground and spun on their bellies to look back at the canal. A canal barge with twin decks was steaming around the bend and they watched helplessly as a deck gun fired another round into the camp. Peaches realized that the cleft was too far away, so the veteran sergeant dragged Suresh and Dzbanki back into the crater.

"That's a three incher," shouted Peaches in a tone that sounded like he was commenting on some machine that was not currently trying to blow them into tiny bits of burning meat. They heard Seota'e fire at the armed barge and a moment later the cliff face just below her perch exploded in a shower of rocks and sand.

"They're not as good with their guns as they are with their horses," commented Dzbanki as she crawled toward the crater edge. "I can't believe they just missed her."

Another round slammed into the cliff face just above the sniper perch and Dzbanki saw her Cheyenne marksman slide down the steep cliff face in an uncontrolled tumble. Dzbanki snarled in Polish and ran to the crater edge sending a steam of bullets at the barge before Peaches pulled her back down again. A three inch shell smashed the crater edge into flying rubble and Peaches punched the female sergeant in the shoulder for giving away their position.

"We need something heavier to hurt that barge and we need to get out of this hole," shouted Peaches. Dzbanki shoved her repeater at Suresh and pulled her amtacha out of her belt.

"You are going to play a game with them?" stammered Suresh as he watched the female marine move toward the crater edge facing the cave with her net stick. Dzbanki put her fingers in her mouth and gave a loud sharp whistle, then raised her arm and made a fist. She pumped her arm twice in the air then readied her net stick.

Peaches grabbed the amtacha out of her hand and pushed her up the crater wall. "I throw farther than you," he growled. "Be ready to run."

A moment later a black globe came sailing out from the cave mouth and Peaches caught it expertly in his net stick. He grabbed the black hand bomb and thumbed its fuse to life then dropped it back into the net of the amtacha.

"GO!" he yelled as he sprinted up the opposite side of the crater and launched the sparking hand bomb at the canal barge.

The barge was nearly eighty yards away, but no one on board was watching the crater. Peaches had been playing this game for thirty some years and he and his fellow marines had turned the ancient game into a weapon many times before. Sergent Peaches snapped his whole upper body forward and the net stick launched the sputtering hand bomb like a catapult. The hand bomb landed next to the deck gun and blew the gunner to shreds. Dzbanki launched herself out of the crater as soon as Peaches let loose. She sprinted for her life towards the cave mouth, and dove over the rock wall with a yell to clear the way. Peaches turned as soon as he saw the hand bomb land and was startled to come nose to nose with Suresh.

"I told you to run!" Peaches screamed and he dragged his Indian charge up out of the crater in frantic haste.

The two men scrambled to their feet and started running toward the cave. Peaches repeated Dzbanki's dive over the wall and it took him a moment to realize Suresh was not beside him. It also took him a moment to register the shot he heard as he dove.

"Crap," muttered HammerCloud, "the little guy didn't make it."

Peaches sprang back to his feet and saw that the Indian pundit was laying several yards away in the middle of the cleft wash. He was rolling on his back and yelling as he grabbed his bleeding thigh with both hands.

It would be heroic to say Peaches didn't think twice before diving back over the wall to save the wounded man…but Peaches did take a moment to think.

All the marines were safely in the cave, and even Seota'e who had been dragged to safety by Hammer Cloud. The gold and gems were within easy reach in the ammo box and the way out the back of the cleft was still open. The Imperial marines could grab the ponies, ride out the other end of the cleft and even set a slow fuse on the remaining dynamite to cover their escape. There was no need for Peaches to risk his life saving a foreigner he had only known a week when he had the answer to all his family's needs so close to hand.

"Cover me damnit!" shouted Peaches as he scrambled back over the rock wall. The Marines crowded the rock wall and emptied their repeaters at the canal barge as Peaches ran and scooped up the bleeding Suresh. The sergeant threw the screaming Indian over his shoulder and pounded back toward the cleft mouth as the marines automatically adjusted their cover fire so as not to riddle the fleeing men with Imperial bullets. Peaches tossed Suresh over the wall then dove in behind him.

"You run good for an old pinkskin," commented Seota'e from the cave floor. She was covered in red dust and blood and her leg seemed to bent at an odd angle. Her beloved Longarm rifle was clutched to her chest like a baby.

"Thanks marine," replied a breathless Peaches. "Looks like I have two of you to carry out of here now," he said with a smirk.

They both glanced over at the other marines who were quickly backing into the cave. Everyone could hear the impacts and pings of rifle rounds striking the cliff face and rock wall outside.

"When they get a new gunner on that…" Rolf started to say when a three-inch shell screamed into the cave an detonated inside the cleft.

Peaches heard the ponies scream in terror and pain and knew they were quickly running out of options. "They have our range now and even these stupid towel heads seem to have figured out which end of the gun is which," snarled Peaches then he threw a guilty look over at Suresh. It was the first time Peaches had ever felt guilty about calling foreigners names, and the disappointed look he got from the man he had just saved felt sharper than the cuts and bruises he was now covered in. Then another noise grabbed everyone's attention.

The cleft amplified the loud hum of airship engines, and the air was rent with the sound of yet another terrific explosion. "That," whispered Dzbanki "was not a three inch gun."

The marines slowly crawled to the cave mouth. They could see what was left of the canal barge smoking on the water, and bits and pieces of burning debris littered the beach. Hanging in the sky over the valley was an Imperial gun luft with the emblem of the Imperial provost proudly emblazoned across her side. The sleek Imperial gunboat settled majestically onto the canal, and the marines slowly moved out from the cave to reclaim their camp.

"We heard the cannon fire and saw your Imperial flag flying in the camp so we figured we'd just play it safe," commented the provost captain as they all gathered in the center of the camp. "This whole region is now Imperial territory, and we have strict orders to keep everyone out of this particular area," continued the Imperial officer then he spied the citizen's eagle on the caps of Peaches and Dzbanki. "Of course if you citizens have a legal claim here I'm sure the new district governor will honor it," he amended politely. The fact that he had just killed who knows how many people on an armed river barge seemed to hardly occur to the man.

"Of course we do," replied Dzbanki smoothly. "Just let us get our gear and we can head back to town to straighten things out," she added.

"Sorry, Madam Sergeant but nothing leaves this valley. The new governor was very specific about that," the provost continued in a more formal tone that brooked no argument. "We will give you a ride back to town and no one will disturb your…camp until the governor reviews your claims," he added knowingly.

The provost officer had been on Mars long enough to know a prospecting camp when he saw one even if it was mostly blown to pieces. The marines and their Indian friend had little choice but to gather their wounded and board the provost luft.

They all knew the ammo box was well hidden in the cave, but it did none of them any good if they could not come back and retrieve it without getting shot by the provosts. The six inch guns on the patrol war luft made the three inch gun of the crooked Nawab and his men look like a pop gun, and Imperial gunners were far better trained, even provosts.

"So all that was for nothing," sighed Peaches. He couldn't believe they had come so close just to fail now, but Imperial rule was clear. Suresh was not an Imperial citizen. He wasn't even a Free Resident, but it didn't matter because only a full citizen could hold property rights. Peaches knew he also couldn't claim to have purchased the property from Suresh, because the little Indian didn't have the right to sell the property and no claim was on file with the marines name on it. Doing it now was too late. They would not be allowed back on the site, and Peaches was fairly sure Suresh's little secret was known to the new governor. Imperial war lufts didn't just fly out to the middle of nowhere and blow up people for no reason…usually.

Dzbanki had been unusually quiet during their ride back to Paradise Canals, and Peaches assumed she was as depressed about the whole affair as he was. When she finally spoke it was not to share in his misery.

"Suresh," she asked slowly "didn't you say over dinner that both your parents were dead?"

Suresh raised his head wearily. "Yes I did, thank you for reminding me that not only am I now a poor man, but now I am also an orphan," he answered sourly.

"Ah, but that's the point isn't it?" she replied as a smile started to bloom on her face.

"Why are you picking on him marine?" snarled Peaches.

Everyone including Suresh looked at the sergeant in surprise.

"What?" he snapped.

Dzbanki was smiling like the proverbial cat who ate the canary now. "For old family you really don't know your Imperial history do you citizen?" purred Dzbanki to Peaches. "A citizen's eagle can only be passed to a blood relative or from parent to child. They do not necessarily have to be the same thing." Everyone was now looking blankly at her.

"In the old days of the Empire, powerful Imperial citizen families recruited wealthy foreigners or influential tribal leaders into their family by adopting them! As long as there were no blood relatives of the adopted person to object they became full and legal members of the Imperial households. Heck, that's how half of the Crow nation became Imperial citizens practically overnight."

Dzbanki became more animated as she spoke. "If you adopt Suresh as your legal son, you can give him your eagle and the governor will have to honor his previous claim on the cleft. We just need an Imperial official to oversee the adoption and record the transfer of your eagle."

"I am not a child," snapped Suresh "besides the governor will see through such an obvious attempt to keep my claim."

"Tough," replied Dzbanki "it's perfectly legal as long as it's signed by another district official."

"I doubt the new governor is going to just sign over the mine because a bunch of grunts say so," added Seota'e from her cot.

"I wasn't thinking of that official..." replied Dzbanki smoothly.

Sergeant Major Ulfric Sleeping Bear Ulfricson, known throughout the Imperial Air Corp as Sergeant Major Peaches took another look at his new son. His commanding officer, Major B.T. Girth, was both an Imperial official and the holder of an Imperial Senatorial seat, not to mention he also commanded the largest and deadliest war luft for hundreds of miles.

Sergeant Dzbanki had convinced Sergeant Peaches and Suresh to explain the full story to the Major, knowing how likely the Major was to help a fellow marine if the price was right. Girth had laughed hysterically for several minutes over the situation and then with watery eyes had agreed to make the adoption scheme legal for a price. The price had surprised everyone, especially Sergeant Major Ulfric Sleeping Bear Ulfricson.

Girth had simply chuckled and slid the reenlistment papers across his polished desk to his sergeant major and offered him a pen.

The marines had reassembled at the Paradise Canals bar to celebrate…again. Girth draped an arm over Peaches' shoulder in a show of camaraderie.

"You're going to be a wealthy man and the head of a wealthy family Peachy old boy." Girth continued, "According to Imperial patriarchal law your new son can't make any family business decisions without your approval, so you control the purse strings. You can afford to hire tutors for your youngest boy, and his older brother can groom him to work in the family mining business."

Girth gestured to the slightly confused looking Indian holding the Imperial citizen eagle loosely in his hand. "Your eldest son will set up the new Ulfricson & Sons Mining Company and thanks to my own small cut you will have an Imperial Provost watching his back until you can hire your own people. I hear Dzbanki has some real head busters in her family you might consider."

Major Girth smiled warmly at his favorite sergeant major and patted him on the back. "Best of all you can continue your duties aboard The *Irascible Wind* with me knowing your family is prospering. If you get killed on this tour your younger son will inherit your eagle early, and he won't have to worry about selling it back to the Emperor. Everybody wins!"

Major Girth threw his other arm around the still-perplexed Suresh and squeezed the two men together in a bone crushing hug. "Now we are all one big happy Imperial family." He released the two men and grabbed at a tray of ale mugs from a passing server.

Peaches exchanged an awkward hug with his new son. "How old are you actually?" Peaches asked Suresh in a small voice.

"I'll be twenty eight in two months," replied Suresh sheepishly.

"Odin's eye," swore the Algonquin-Swede with the new Hindu Indian son. "Let's teach you how to drink like a proper Amerikan."

LADIES!
GENTLEMEN PREFER
HIGH ADVENTURE
BIG BUSTLES
& BARED ANKLES!

1903
The Age Of Opportunity

PROF. SPANGO'S SHOW OF WONDERS

COME! SEE!

BE AMAZED!

Featuring Sara and Sasha,
The Astounding Two Headed Girl!

Watch as this beautiful vixen-and-a-half
tames the ferocious six legged Venusian Swamp Tiger!

LOOK!

See not one but two amazing

CYCLORAMIC PANORAMAS

depicting inglorious COLOR
the Conquest of Venus and the
Battle of Plymouth Rock!

Foreign Grotesques!

Trained Penginunopods!

LIVE AT THE CONEY PIER!

CONEY
By Raymond J. Witte

It was one of those pleasantly hot early summer days when I, following a whim, struck out for Brooklyn, with the goal of reaching Coney Island sometime in the late afternoon. It was close to the turn of the century and Brooklyn, in those days, was a splendid place to be a gentleman of leisure. The prosperity brought about by shipping arms and munitions through the Skylocks for the Europeans, Zulus and Wogs to kill each other with had pushed out the true roughs. The genuine cut-throats and immigrant strong men were gone- either dead or in prison or pursuing legitimate venues for theft and extortion. They did, however, leave their mystique, and a horde of lesser scum, behind them. In those happy years "slumming it" was all the rage amongst the younger set. The spoiled scions of high society flocked to the swarthy neighborhoods, cloaking themselves in the glamour of the borough's more anarchical past.

As someone who had been there in the bad old days, I tell you these calves would have likely been robbed blind and sold in stocks to Singapore traders back then. But, thank God, by that time those heady days were well past us. What was left were a bunch of generally filthy immigrants and tradesmen, with enough whores and pushers to make life interesting. There were maybe a handful of thieves left in the lot, but none brazen enough to take a run at an Imperial Citizen or someone Manhattan might actually give a damn about. It was enough to give the place an aura of danger, without any actual peril, at least not if you had your Eagle or if you were rich.

So that left people like me- wealthy and of good stock but with the experience and callous of a few years of rough living in our younger days- well entrenched at the top of the food chain. So, my plan had been to drink my way down to Coney Island. I would take the steam lines from pub to pub, scaring up what sport might be had on the way, then spend the evening chatting up every pretty thing that crossed my path. Should I grow weary of my planned entertainment, well, there was always the prospect of strong arming some simple mark. I tell you- there is nothing like the thrill of taking that which isn't yours- especially if you're taking it from some fool of a popinjay who makes it so easy that it seems like a crime not to rob them.

So, with my head full of pleasant thoughts of decidedly less than moral activities, I went about my day. When I reached Coney's piers, I was well on my way to intoxication. I was feeling happy, cocky, and utterly contemptuous of the rest of the world- the drinkers amongst you will know the glory of that feeling. On my arm was Caesaretta Kline, a debutant with a pleasing shape who was dogged by scandalous rumors that I felt it was my duty to investigate. I had run into her an hour before and promised her a dinner. She was very taken with me and with the way things seemed to be going, I was looking forward to an evening of thoroughly investigating each of her moral failings. So we ambled along, her tittering vapidly and me playing my reputation as a something of a semi-retired adventurer to the hilt. Things were shaping up nicely- I had her blushing and giggling almost on command as we made our way to the string of eateries on the waterfront.

That was when she saw it. On the outmost pier, someone was fiddling with a contraption of bronze. Attached to the device was a hunk of iron that looked to be an engine of some sort. Now, in those days, nonsense like this was not uncommon. In fact, the Imperial Senate encouraged it. Some fool with a bad idea would con a bigger fool into funding a grand experiment, with both parties hoping to make a fortune from the next steam engine or Colt Revolving Canon or Levitatus turbine. Almost inevitably, the device would shake itself to pieces or catch fire or explode spectacularly. Unfortunately, most accidents failed to kill the pea-brained imbeciles who came up with the failed apparatus, and the fools would move on to their next bad idea, having effectively defrauded their investors. Had it been a purposeful scam, I would have admired them. Sadly, the inventors were as sincere as those whose money they squandered. To this day, I dream of partnering with some crooked drop-out engineer and bilking bright-eyed investors into funding projects that will do nothing but collapse into heads of scrap. We'll spend maybe a third of the money on the worst kinds of pig-iron and rusty boilers and pointless dials and take the rest and...

Sorry, sometimes I get away from myself.

Anyway, someone was about to perform a test of some sort. While I could care less, Caesaretta was all aflutter at the prospect of "Seeing science first hand!" as the brainless creature put it.

Now- to any young men who may be reading this- this moment will come up time and time again in your dealings with women. Invariably they'll be fascinated by some idiocy and they'll wish you to indulge their fancy, batting their lashes and simpering with glee and the promise of unlaced corsets and hoisted skirts to come. And it is always some foolishness that you know full well you should avoid, undoubtedly a recipe for disaster every single time. But, if you're anything like me, you'll charge forward gleefully, despite your better judgment, thinking of nothing but what she'll look like with her knickers around her ankles.

So I indulged the girl and we strolled down the boardwalk towards the final pier. As we approached, I could make out the contraption more clearly. The bronze bit was bell shaped and not the solid bronze I had first suspected- it had cutaways covered by windows of tinted glass dotting the surface, and a central shaft which looked like a support of some kind. It was dotted with gas lanterns along the outside and was maybe nine foot around and four foot tall. A canvas hose connected it to the larger device. The larger device was made of iron and was square and heavy looking. I guessed it was some sort of factory device that had been dragooned for whatever purpose this man had in mind. As we stepped onto the pier for a closer look, a crane barge slid up to the pier, casting lines and tying off next to this man and his machine. A few workers jumped from the barge to the pier and the man began ordering them around.

The man was wearing a lab coat over some sort of tight fitting leather suit. He was heavy but not overly fat, with arms and legs that seemed a few sizes too small for the rest of him. He was balding on top and he had an eager expression on his boyish and pudgy face. He wore a pair of goggles which seemed to be too tight and he fiddled with them constantly, nudging them aside to rub his eyes.

As we approached I waved and called a greeting to him. He finished fiddling with his contraption, then turned to us and smiled broadly.

"Ah, my good fellow! You and your lovely companion are most fortunate, hmmm yes, you are about to witness a new technological marvel being unveiled!"

He was a grating combination of nasal and bombastic. I could see immediately that he fancied himself as much a showman as a scientist. I regretted coming here already. Before I could think of an acceptable excuse to extract myself, the irrepressible Miss Kline opened her mouth.

"Whatever does it do?" she pulled the 'o' out into a long, high coo, which might have been charming in another setting, but given where my mood was quickly heading, it made me want to strangle her. I settled for flashing her a glance that would have splattered her back across the entire length of the boardwalk, if it were that looks could kill. She either didn't notice or decided to ignore me.

"Well Miss..."

"Caesaretta Kline," she supplied, offering him the back of her hand, the tart. He, of course, accepted the invitation and brought her fingers to his lips.

"Well Miss Kline, this device is my patented movable Aquatic Exploratorium. You see it works through the principal of...."

At that point my eyes glazed over and I stopped really paying attention. I half listened while I watched a pair of quite fetching Siamese twins working the marks as a sideshow barker from the corner of my eye. I made a note to myself to pay them a visit after hours. I'd had two women at once before, but never one and a half and those carney folk are always looking for a buck.

While I puzzled over the mysteries of bedding conjoined twins, the inventor prattled on. He called himself Doctor Fizenshiven and supposedly he had enough degrees to wallpaper a large flat. This particular thing was actually two devices. The big locomotive engine looking part was a pump, connected to the bell thing by a canvas hose. The bell was designed to carry a bubble of air, constantly refreshed by the pump, down to the sea floor where the passengers would science things or sweep for treasure or some other nonsense. What he was testing today was a scale model- apparently he planned to build a much larger one, assuming that he didn't drown testing the theory.

"...and so the pressure remains constant. Hmmm,my pardons sir, but aren't you Horace P. Thornton?"

I snapped out of my idle fantasy involving of a romp with the conjoined twins when I heard my name.

"I am sir," I cursed to myself. Nothing good would come of this character recognizing me.

"Well Mr. Thornton, given your previous adventures, I do say you might be interested in the ultimate goal of this project."

That brought on more silent cursing in my mind. Yeah, I was something of an adventurer. Yes, I traded on that reputation constantly. It didn't mean I put my irreplaceable self into danger because it was amusing to me. What amuses me are frisky girls, one sided fights, and having all the ale and wine I can possibly drink, not being uncomfortable, half starving and having spears thrown at me. The dirty secret about my time as an adventurer is that it was basically an unintended side benefit to a part of my life spent as a small time criminal. I didn't set out to fight savages and pirates like the hero of the Amerikan Empire the papers made me into. When I first left York, I had merely intended to trade a crate of Blitzen Casters for hull full of opium and making a tidy profit from the ruin of others. The 'glamorous' parts just kind of happened and I at the time I was thoroughly miserable because of them.

But as I said, I've been trading on that reputation for a few years now. People expect me to jump at whatever lunacy they throw my way with a smile on my face. I could see where this was going. So Fizenshiven plowed ahead and explained how this was part of a plan he had concocted with his benefactors to explore the Hudson Canyon. Apparently he had convinced them that there was something of value down there, and he was set to go explore it. Once again, my mind returned to those sideshow lovelies while he prattled on, while I nodded and made serious sounding murmurs as appropriate.

As I expected, he wanted me to go along on his little expedition. The idea of going a mile down in this piece of junk horrified me. This little fool was trying to drag me down to my doom, and the simpleton on my arm was grinning excitedly at the prospect.

Now it was time for me to pay the price for all the free drinks and open boudoirs my reputation had purchased for me. I couldn't weasel out of this without giving my reputation a fatal blow. Caesaretta was a relentless gossip and if I didn't live up to her expectations, I knew the spiteful creature would be relentless in making it known that I was a has-been. This would be unacceptable. Trading on reputation had saved me from having to actually work to earn a living for the past four years. I had no intention of ever attempting to honestly make money again. That said, I had no intention of letting this man take me to a watery grave either.

I looked at the diving system again. It certainly didn't look safe. In fact, I doubted that it would do anything other than flood, even in these shallow waters. I began to calm myself down. I had an idea.

"Well friend, this plan certainly seems...ah...interesting. I'll make you a deal- you show me it works here, and we'll talk about your little expedition when you get back to the surface."

The idiot beamed. So did I. I had a strange feeling that Doctor Fizenshiven wasn't coming back to the surface in one piece.

Caesaretta and I, along with a small crowd of similarly interested passersby, watched the Doctor make ready for his test. When no one was looking, I pulled a heavy nail from a piling and secreted it in my pocket, while I studied the machine itself. Much of the guts and sprockets of the big pump engine was exposed. A piece of luck, I though. That will make things easier.

The Doctor fiddled with the bell portion of the apparatus while his workers positioned the crane. I scanned the engine for the best place to jam my nail. He fussed and worried over each hose and connection like his type tend to. I swear it's more than half performance for them- a dog and pony show to impress we witless philistines while they exhibit their mechanical expertise. In any case, it makes for a wonderful distraction. While the crowd craned their necks to watch the good doctor, I secreted the nail into a juncture which looked important, pushing it into the one of the sprockets, a place where it was sure to strip enough gears, at least I hoped it would, to ensure something appropriately catastrophic happened.

The Doctor and his crew finished whatever it was they were doing. He shed his lab coat, handing it to one of his assistants while the rest of his crew swung the bell apparatus over the water. Once it was over the water, thin legs slid down from the rim. The design was actually quite clever- the combination of the central shaft and the supports along the rim would actually raise the bell from the seafloor. The bell would trap a bubble of air near the seabed but would be raised enough to allow ingress and egress. The crane lowered the bell until the rim touched the surface of the water. The Doctor stepped to the edge of the peer.

"And now," said he, "I will make scientific history. Wish me luck"

And then he was into the drink. He briefly bobbed outside of the bell before submerging and coming up inside the bell. Peering through one of the windows, he waved to the crane operator and the bell slowly began to sink into the Atlantic.

As the bell sank, the pump on the dock began to huff and chug loudly. The slack left the canvas hose and it grew turgid as the hose slid into the dark water. There was a muffled thump and the crane operator halted his pulley. The crowd on the dock fell into a hushed silence. I waited for some sign of calamity. After a period of time that was brief but far longer than any man can hold his breath, a small bell chime rang out from the top of the diving bell, and the crane began to haul the contraption up.

As it emerged, there was Professor Fizenshiven, grinning like a chimp, sound and whole, from inside his bubble. He rose to the cheers of the crowd while I sullenly clapped along, cursing the fact he hadn't been drowned down there. He swam out from under the bell and clung to the side with one hand, waving to the crowd. Once the bell had cleared the docks, the crane swung it around so Fizenshiven could leap off and greet the now adoring public. And, of course, my hand was the first he wanted to shake.

Still smiling like a simpleton he proudly strode over to me.

"So, Mr. Thorton, will you join me next time?"

What could I do? The last thing I wanted was to go beneath the waves in this man's death trap. Going down into the harbor with it was a bad idea. Taking it to the Hudson Canyon seemed like suicide. But I was conned by this idiot and by my damnable reputation.

"Of course, Professor. When do we leave?"

He laughed and patted me on the shoulder, all bonhomie and good cheer. He handed me a business card and said something about a dinner in two days, before turning away to fool with his equipment. Ceasaretta made her way back to me, all smile and brainless enthusiasm, nestled herself into the crook of my arm and gently began to tug me away, eyes full of wanton longing. Obviously I would not let this chance slip away, in spite of the fear seeping into my very soul and the increasingly sour feeling in my stomach, so I went with her.

But I swear to you, as Ceasaretta hauled me away, I overheard Fizenshiven say to an assistant "You found a nail in the secondary pump's actuator? I was wondering what had balanced the pressure! The bell would have blown out entirely without it!"

Sometimes, life just isn't fair.

Two days later, I found myself standing outside the good Professor's home, stomach still in a knot, gathering my will to go in and listen to this lunatic plan our doom. I had almost convinced myself to simply leave and fake a carriage accident to avoid scandal when a frightfully strong hand clamped on to my shoulder.

"Horace, my boy, is that you?"

My heart leapt into my throat. I would have recognized that deep, booming voice anywhere. And it would have sent me running. Its owner, Hugo Skarson, was a mountain of a man, who I knew from long experience, was everything I was supposed to be.

In the newspapers, that made him a national hero. But the ink-stained wretches that write broadsheets will never have to spend any extended period of time with the man. If they did, those few of that cohort not hopelessly feeble minded would realize in short order that those same qualities that made such salable copy were actually the qualities of a mind that was bloodthirsty and sociopathic in equal measure.

Any man that volunteers for duty as a jump trooper in the Imperial Air Corps is one that would be better off in a dimly-lit padded room and this monstrosity in a sharp uniform had spent 10 years leaping from Warlufts into storms of flack and shot for the chance to massacre crews of foreigners and pirates.

Needless to say, I turned to face Skarson with no small amount of dread. If he was involved in this venture, things were even more grim than I had through. He had changed little since I had last seen him. He was tall and broad, and even beneath his overcoat I could tell that his arms, chest, and shoulders were still banded with muscle. He had gained a bit of lard around the middle, but he was still physically daunting. He smiled broadly at me. I suppose he was trying to be friendly, but I've seen him smile like that while he shoves a knife through a man's ribs or lights a hut on fire, so I had to suppress a shiver.

"It is you, Horace! I should've known you'd be up to your eyeballs in an adventure like this! Don't waste time gawkin'. Dinner's waiting."

I tried to stammer a reply, but it was pointless as this lunatic more or less dragged me up Professor's front stairs, through the door, and into the foyer of the Professor's house.

Fizenshiven was visibly thrilled to see us and at least had the courtesy to order his butler to fetch us drinks. In short order we were seated at his table. We made small conversation during the meal. Fizenshiven was happy to discover that Skarson and I were previously acquainted and pressed us for details. Obviously I was not in a talkative mood, so I allowed Skarson to carry the story, grunting and nodding to confirm this or that detail when appropriate. Skarson was more than happy to run with it. In his own way he's a bigger self-promoter than I am, and has always been eager to talk about himself.

He regaled Fizenshiven with the official version of our story, a winding tale of fighting pirates and Frenchmen and high adventure in the Atlantic skies. He left out the parts about the load of Afghani poppy which had made the trip worth it for the both of us as well as that bit about that hold full of Armenian refugees we traded to Veratula Khan for it. I must say, Skarson was crazy, but he had an eye for profit, if he wasn't in the throes of one of his blood-lusts.

As supper wound down, we adjourned to Fizenshiven's den for more drinks and to discuss the expedition itself. I was well into the Professor's stock of brandy by this point and, consequently, I was more sanguine than I had been since I left the pier two days prior. Or at least I was too drunk to continue counting the ways Fizenshiven might get me killed. I had just refilled my glass yet again when the Professor stood to address us.

"Gentlemen," he began, "I want to thank you for coming. Together, we will make scientific history."

He raised his glass to toast and we echoed.

"As you know, the device that Mr. Thornton saw embark on it's maiden voyage and which I demonstrated to you, Mr. Skarson, just last night is a mere prototype. The actual Exploratorium is far larger. Large enough that I saw fit to commission a barge and a pair of tugs to service it. You see, it had to be large to survive the depths we'll be exploring soon. Though the Aquatic Exploratorium is a scientific marvel, it is not actually the endpoint of my research."

This was interesting. All along, I had assumed that Fizenshiven was in this game as an inventor first, trying to make a name for himself on the qualities of his pet device. It appears, however, that he had a different game.

"The true object of my studies is the Hudson Canyon. Gentlemen, take a look at these."

Fizenshiven retrieved a box from beneath the low table in the center of the room and began laying out a series of objects. They were somewhat reminiscent of the Skraeling artifacts every child is familiar with- somewhat crude but identifiable hand versions of tools and weapons made with unrefined materials. But instead of wood and rock, these seemed to be mostly bone and shell, bound together with what looked like some sort of plant fiber rather than animal sinew. I picked up a piece of what looked like it had been a spear and examined the head of the weapon.

"This is a shark's tooth, is it not?"

"Very observant Mr. Thornton. It is, in fact, the tooth of a Carcharodon carcharias, colloquially known as the White Shark. In fact, the materials for every one of these tools are aquatic in origin. I have studied cultures on all three of the known inhabited worlds, and I believe this particular design of tool to be unique. Every item here was pulled up in the drift nets of boats fishing the Hudson Canyon."

"What exactly are you getting at Professor?"

"It is my belief, good sirs, that there is a civilization of some sort on the ocean floor a mere hundred miles off of our coast. It is our duty, as Imperial Citizens, to investigate its existence and ascertain how it can benefit the Empire."

I had to choke down a laugh at this point. Fizenshiven might be a Citizen and Skarson certainly was one, but despite the common misconception I had never been suckered into that racket. A man who acquires enough favors owed and greases enough palms can damned well make a good life for himself without having spending half of it chasing an Eagle.

But, if Fizenshiven was actually on to something, there was money to be made here. Letters of conquest and marque were licenses to do as you damned please in the name of the Empress while you lined your bank account at the expense of some poor, stupid locals. That is, if you didn't get killed in the process. Fizenshiven's machine was not exactly confidence inspiring. The thought of having to go down some thousand fathoms deep in the contraption sobered me up in a hurry.

With the freshly cleared head that only an impending sense of doom can bring, I watched and listened as Fizenshiven laid out his plans for our expedition. At least, in this, he seemed to be well prepared.

We would each wear a leather suit to protect us from the cold. And thank the gods in heaven and hell we would be armed. Fizenshiven demonstrated a weapon that actually gave me a touch more faith in his ingenuity- a three barreled spear gun powered by the same pumped air that would fill the diving bell. He also showed us a set of helmets that, when secured to the leather suits, would allow us to explore the bottom with a bit more freedom, provided we were tethered back to the diving bell via canvas hose.

Technical questions and planning consumed the rest of the evening. I was still quite unhappy about having been dragooned into this expedition and I was still convinced that Fizenshiven would do nothing but lead us to cold and watery graves, but I'll be damned before I let any chance of survival slip away from me.

Late that night we adjourned. Fizenshiven required the rest of the week to make ready his equipment, so we agreed that we would leave port early the following Monday.

The intervening days passed with me wallowing in self pity and drink. I left my rented room only to seek sustenance and to acquire more spirits and I took no visitors. The time passed all too quickly, and soon I found myself on the Yersey docks before sunrise, staring stupidly at the full sized version of Fizenshiven's device.

It must have cost a fortune in bronze and glass alone, never mind the price of what was a truly monstrous pump mechanism that would keep it full of fresh air. The bell was the size of a parlor, fitted with kerosene lamps along the bulkhead, and attached to a pair of hoses as thick as a man's waist. The device sat on a crane barge. It had to, because there was no other way to get this thing into the water short of a military airship.

Fizenshiven saw me and called for me to climb aboard. I allowed myself one final opportunity to seek an escape. Maybe an unfortunate stumble on the docks and I could dash my head on a piling...

No. These idiots would probably be waiting outside of my hospital room, expecting me to leap at the chance to get myself killed as soon as the doctor gave me the all clear. I went on board and soon we were under way.

The trip would take until the early afternoon, so for want of anything better to occupy myself with, I spent most of my time familiarizing myself with the diving apparatus. Like the smaller version, it was a essentially a dome on stilts. However, the full scale model was tall enough to have a floor area above the stilt portion of the device, with hatches to access the sea floor. Apparently, the diving vessel could be fully enclosed. I found that fact comforting. The roof was crisscrossed with support struts and buttresses and the viewing windows were thick and built of many small panes of glass held in triangular bronze brackets. It was large enough that there was a table in the center of the thing and several low benches near the walls, as well as a few equipment racks, holding our helmets and spear guns as well as some large specimen jars. I noted with approval that the Professor had brought an ample amount of ammunition. If we actually survived the trip to the bottom, at least we would have some protection.

As I had predicted, it was nearly midday by the time our small flotilla came to a halt. Fizenshiven ceded control of the barge to the hired crew, and Skarson emerged from the cabin where, by the looks of it, he had apparently been sleeping off a hangover. Fizenshiven was grinning like a child on Landing Day.

"Gentlemen, I would like to thank you once again for joining me. We are sure to make scientific history today! Below us lies a yet unknown civilization, yearning for the benefices of our glorious Empire. As we descend into the murky depths, we bring with us the light of Amerikan culture and civilization."

Fizenshiven had apparently never seen what "culturing the natives" usually meant. I had to stifle another laugh there. He continued to lay out the plan for our trip. We'd don the leather suits on the surface then board the Exploratorium for the descent. The engines of the barge themselves would function as the pump for our air. Once on the bottom, we would survey the terrain and decide if risking a trip outside of the apparatus was worth it. We would be there for an hour after touchdown, then the crew would begin to haul the apparatus back up to the surface.

I wasn't happy about that, but then I wasn't happy about anything involved in this trip. I prayed to whatever gods would listen as I squeezed into my diving leathers. The Professor was already in his diving suit, looking as cheerful and doughy as ever. Skarson was dressing as I did, but in a move typical of his dubious sanity, had burdened himself with close to a dozen blades and was trying to wiggle into an honest-to-god mail shirt, completely unconcerned about the effects of adding thirty pounds of steel to the human body before entering the water. Personally, I had opted for only two knives, a foot long dagger, worn at my waist, which was a perpetual companion, and my boot knife, a small and slender cutting blade.

When we had made ready, the Fizenshiven opened one of the bottom hatches. "Gentlemen, shall we?"

With a feeling of dread and hopelessness, I forced myself to crawl into the apparatus. Skarson nodded to me, wearing mixed expressions of severity and eager ferocity on his features. Fizenshiven was positively beaming with excitement, motioning for me to sit so we could begin. I found a bench slightly away from them- if I were about to die, I'd rather it be alone and in peace- and the Professor motioned to the man operating the crane.

There was a sickening lurch as the slack was pulled from the line and the diving apparatus began to rise from the deck. Then we began to swing ever so slightly as the crane ponderously turned so maneuver us over the water. Every fiber of my being wanted to start shrieking for them to stop, but somehow I managed to hold it together, grinding my teeth as I felt the color drain from my face. Skarson cracked a joke about me being motion sick, sending he and Fizenshiven into peals of laughter, and had my hands not been clenched on to the bench, I would have grabbed a spear gun and skewered him. I heard a splash from below as the apparatus touched the surface of the sea, and then we began to sink.

Watching the water rise up over the view-ports was a terrible sight, and I was convinced that I was seeing the sky for the final time. Once we were submerged, there was a coughing noise from the attachment points for the hoses then a slightly warm breeze as the air pumps kicked in. Our descent was long, and after a while, I decided that I might not be doomed after all. The apparatus didn't spring any leaks, the line suspending us didn't snap, and the entire thing didn't simply crumple under the pressure of the water. I screwed up the courage to look out the view ports and I was surprised by how barren the sea was. There was little but blue-black and the occasional curious small fish. Outside of the circle of light cast by the kerosene lanterns, it looked like there was nothing at all. It was oddly hypnotizing, and I must have stared at it for some time. Fizenshiven's voice snapped me out of my thoughtless fugue.

"Gentlemen, we are nearly on the ocean floor."

Having returned to my senses, I noticed that there was an abundance of fish, unlike the scarcity of life that had marked our descent. Almost on cue, the apparatus shook slightly as we touched the seabed. As soon as we struck bottom, Fizenshiven started a chronometer set for fifty minutes. I was still in a state of semi-shock. I still couldn't believe that we had actually survived the trip, and I was on the verge of giddiness over it. In fact, I was nearly eager for the rest of the venture.

"Thornton, if you would?" Skarson was motioning that I should help him fasten his helmet to his diving suit. It was awkward, given the amount of armor and weapons the man was wearing, but I managed it. The helmets were leather on a brass frame, with glass windows to provide some illumination. A hose line extended from the rear of each helmet back to the diving apparatus to keep them supplied with air. After his was affixed, it was my turn. Inside the helmet, the world was limited. Sound was muffled and we had to communicate with hand gestures. The placement of the view ports meant that we only had limited vision to the front and sides. It was a little claustrophobic, but I was still intoxicated by the fact that I hadn't died yet, so I didn't mind.

When we were ready, the professor joined us. Apparently he had some practice with this, because he had secured his helmet without help. He handed us each a spear gun and a quiver of ammunition and we prepared to leave the Exploratorium.

We exited through the bottom of the device, our hoses attached to a smaller pump trailing behind us. The water was frigid, but the suits kept the worst of the chill away. However, the suits were not exactly conducive to swimming- they were restricting and the helmets were heavy so instead we began to slog along through the muck on the bottom.

We trudged along through the gloom, kicking up little puffs of mud with each step. We walked in a V-shape, with Fizenshiven in the lead. The schools of fish which swam about darted around us as we passed. Though the Exploratorium had set down on a flat, relatively featureless portion of the seabed, the terrain of the ocean floor quickly became broken and almost hilly, with large rocks and boulders piling up on top of each other, creating tiny caves where I caught fleeting glimpses of slick bodies and many-suckered arms.

Suddenly, Fizenshiven raised his arm for us to stop and pointed. Half behind one of the larger rocks I saw a flash of a humanoid shape before it slipped out of sight. The three of us exchanged glances. We had found what we were looking for.

Half crouched with spear guns raised, we stalked around the rocky outcropping. What we saw on the other side was amazing. The professor was right. There was really was a civilization under the waves. In a sunken hollow, a mere hundred feet away, lay what looked to be a large village, populated by creatures which I had never even heard rumors of.

They were a dark greyish green for the most part, with cream colored bellies. Though some of them swam, many were also walking upright like a man. They had two long, ape like arms, ending in webbed hands with noticeable claws on the tips of each finger and their legs were powerfully muscled. The ones that were walking kept their legs folded like they were bipedal frogs. They had large, bulging eyes like the carp that orientals keep, and their backs had spinney ridges running down their length. There had to be close to a hundred in the area, going back and forth between what looked to be dugout huts or fiddling with objects similar to those the Professor had collected. A dozen or so seemed to be involved in the butchering of a small whale.

We observed them unseen for a while, still and silent, taking in something that had never been seen by man, in a state of near awe. The creatures seemed to be oblivious to us, at least for the moment. Finally, one of the smaller ones seemed to notice us. It turned with obvious curiosity, moving with the subtle awkwardness that is common to the juveniles of every species of animal. It swam towards us at a leisurely place, alighting maybe twenty feet away from where we were standing.

Up close, I noticed that it had gills on both sides of its neck. Its face was lipless and covered, like the rest of its body, in small scales. It looked like a fish crossed with a man, with just enough frog thrown into the mix to make it even more vaguely unsettling. It certainly was an ugly creature, but it seemed friendly enough and reached an open arm out towards us, burbling something that sounded vaguely friendly.

Then Skarson's weapon went off with a barely audible rush of air and a plume of bubbles. The Professor and I stood slack jawed for what seemed like an eternity- granted, my experience with this lunatic gave me no reason to doubt that he would open fire at the first opportunity- but the sheer blood-thirsty bravado was shocking. I snapped out of it when the spear slammed into the chest of the fish thing.

As it fell backwards, it let out a gurgling cry that caused each of the hundred or so heads in the settlement to turn towards us. This might be bad. I surveyed the situation, took a quick count of the fish things, and noted how close they were to us and how far we were from the diving bell.

There was no chance we could make it to the bell quickly enough to escape the fish things if they rushed us. I didn't know if they would, but I wasn't about to take any chances. If they rushed us, we were done. So I picked out the three nearest me and let them have it, my spear-gun letting out an evil sounding hiss with each shot. I started to reload. Skarson, true to form, continued laying into the things with a vengeance, grinning madly as each creature fell.

For the most part the creatures seemed confused, halfway between flight and trying to get organized enough to mob us. That was fine with me- like I said, they probably would have taken us if they had rushed. Instead, they mostly just stood around looking stupid, making themselves into very easy targets. I finished reloading my weapon, picked three more targets, and skewered more of the ugly beasts. I guess the Doctor finally reached the same conclusion that I had, because he decided to join the fight, launching a wave of spears into the murk.

The ocean was starting to cloud- the fish things stirred up the bottom as they flitted about in panic and the blood and viscera from the dead ones were beginning to cut down on visibility. I almost felt bad for the things. Their confusion demonstrated that they had no idea of what was happening to them. Of course, I didn't stop shooting- I just felt sort of sorry for the devils for a moment or two. It passed.

Eventually we ran out of targets. All the creatures were either dead or had gone to ground. The professor began signaling frantically for us to make for the Exploratorium. Thinking quickly, I shuffled out and grabbed the first one we had encountered, tossing it over my shoulder. I was going to sell this thing as soon as we got back and make myself a fortune.

So we made our way back to the Exploratorium as quickly as we could, eyes over our shoulders the entire time, waiting for a wave of fish-savages to overtake us. They didn't. The Professor and Skarson were the first ones into the apparatus.

I heaved my fish-man through the hatch and followed shortly after. As we huffed for breath, the Professor released a buoy, apparently a signal for an early ascent. He closed the hatch, and soon enough the Exploratorium began to rise to the surface.

Meanwhile, Skarson and I were helping each other out of our helmets. I don't know about him, but I was still to shaking from the excitement of murdering a camp full of fish things to do much talking. We both went to inspect my prize. I moved close to examine it, noting the open, sightless eyes, the muscle-corded limbs, the soft scales of the belly and sides, and the cold, slick feel of the creature when suddenly it sprang forward and tried to fix its arms around my throat!

It was frightfully strong. I was larger than it, but it still put up a hell of a fight. Skarson was yelling and waving a bowie knife about. Fizenshiven looked stunned and stupid. The creature screamed and gnashed a mouth full of sharp teeth at me, desperately trying to come to grips. I slammed it's head into the floor of the Exploratorium twice, but its grip only tightened and it pulled closer to me. It was then I realized I only had one option left. I turned my head and bit its arm hard enough to draw blood. The creature shrieked and threw itself away from me. That was all the time Skarson needed to jam his knife into its head. He drew a second one and hacked the thing's head completely off in three quick strokes, but that was probably overkill. At the time, I appreciated his thoroughness.

I found myself gasping for breath, with a mouth full of blood and some strings of flesh. Fizenshiven and Skarson were staring at me.

"What?" I barked. I had nearly been killed by a fish thing. I didn't need their gawking.

"Mr. Thornton, you're chewing."

So I had been, without realizing it. I stopped for a moment, then continued chewing, slowly, concentrating on what was in my mouth. I almost expected slime and rot, maybe rotten fish that had sat in a sewer for a day or two. But the texture was pleasantly dense, almost like a tender cut of pork. And the taste was quite similar to that of a good tuna steak, but with a hint of spice and something that was familiar but unidentifiable. Rather than the vile taste one might expect from something that looked like a nightmare from the deep, the fish thing was actually quite delicious. I finished chewing and swallowed, before wiping my mouth on my sleeve.

"Yes, so I was. And it turns out they're quite tasty."

Skarson raised an eyebrow, but then gingerly sliced off a bit of flesh from the creature's other arm, using his fighting knife like a surgeons scalpel. He examined the piece of flesh for a long moment, pausing to trim a bit of skin and gristle from the cut. He sniffed it cautiously, then popped it in his mouth and chewed. He thought for a moment.

"Actually, he's quite right."

These things were quite delectable. Possibly some of the best meat I'd ever tasted. I started to chuckle quietly to myself, a wide grin spreading across my features. I had a few connections in the restaurant business and I knew several concierges at some of the most exclusive hotels in York. I looked at Skarson, he locked eyes with me, and then we both smiled in understanding. A certain class of person would pay a small fortune to eat a meal this exotic and they would pay even more if it happened to be this delicious. We were about to make a lot of money.

By the end of the day, we had samples of what we were calling "Beef of the Sea" to the best procurers of Fulton Market. By the end of the week we had already gone back thrice. The Professor collected plenty of artifacts and Skarson and I collected many "samples." To this day, I'm not sure if the professor didn't realize or didn't care what we were doing with the fish thing bodies we'd haul up each trip, but he never said anything about it.

Fizenshiven was appointed to a department chair at the Harrisfyrd University of Pennsultucky for his discovery. Skarson and I kept things a two man operation for as long as we could, but eventually worked out a contract with the Greeble works in East York. It made us both a good deal of money. I'm not sure what happened to the fish things or their villages, though I know a thing or two about Greeble processing, and it doesn't bode well for them, but every once in a while I'll buy a can of Ocean Feast Greeble for old time's sake, and raise a forkful to those poor fish things.

IAAC

IMPERIAL AMERIKAN AIR CORP.

YERSEY AND YOU PERFECT TOGETHER!

Come the Imperial District of Yersey!

Come experience exotic foods
like **ROLL-O-PORK** and
breathe the **HEALTHFUL CLEARISH** air!

Friendly People!
Pristine Shoreline!
Majestic Scrub Pine Forests!
...and Miles and Miles of Beautiful Swamp!

YERSEY FRESH

By Raymond J. Witte

Yersey- words generally won't suffice to really capture the essence of the place, but I will make the attempt- it is as if someone found the arsehole of a swamp and decided to build a string of factories and bog farms around it. It is a chancre below cosmopolitan Nyt York, a place that someone with my standing in society typically considers it polite to ignore, never mention in good company, and does their best not to waste thought on it regularly.

So when I found myself on the ferry bound to a town inexplicably named for that frumpiest of English queens, let it suffice to say I was not happy about the situation. However, I had found myself earlier that week nearly stone broke.

Dear reader, you might say that I am not a man who is responsible with money, and you would be entirely accurate. The discovery of those delectable fish things off the coast of Nyt York had made me a moderately wealthy man. But to my eternal woe, my tastes are those of an exceptionally wealthy man.

Before long, women, liquor and gambling had drained my coffers. Selling my residual rights on one particularly whiskey soaked evening had kept me afloat for another few months, but soon even that money had run out, and I found myself broke and with no means of support, scant weeks from facing eviction from my rented room, a circumstance from which my social standing would never recover. Barely a year after making my fortune, I was mere steps from the ranks of the destitute. This would not do.

While I have never really been qualified for any career other than smuggling and small scale piracy, my reputation made people assume that I was competent in a vast array of fields that I had no business dabbling in. Playing on this fortuitous circumstance, I had found myself in the offices of Inns, Mouth, and Harbor, Inc, a powerhouse in the world of industrial finance. During one of my poker sessions, I had heard a rumor that they had gotten Zulu backing for a new project.

Zulu backing meant a flow of cash and specie that would make Solomon blush. Of course, that also meant dealing with Zulus. Zulus make good traveling companions and comrades-in-arms, but as bankers or bosses they're terrifying.

To a Zulu taking off your hand at the wrist is a satisfactory penalty for a late interest payment, and I'm told that their language doesn't have a word for employee. They use the words for "day slave" instead. But, they hewed scrupulously to the terms of their contracts, and it wasn't my name on that roll of doom, so if things went south it wouldn't be me waking up with an Assegai in my back.

The interview was a laughable affair. I was treated like visiting royalty and David Inns and Yuri Mouth fawned over my every word. I had been clever enough to acquire several trade publications from the field of real estate transactions and I came to the interview well armed with a head full of choice phrases and terms of art for me to toss around, which helped, but I'm almost convinced my usual minstrel show might have done the job on it's own. A touch of bluster, just the right amount of professed modesty, and a sprinkling of eagerness later and they were practically falling over themselves to bring me into the operation.

It turns out that Inns, Mouth, and Harbor was bankrolling a string of factories along some of the Delaware River tributaries in the south part of Yersey. The factories were a mix of Greeble canneries, refineries, and munition plants, but that didn't really matter to me, so I stopped paying attention for a while, mentally plotting how I would spend all the loot I would rake in from this operation. I nodded and agreed or disagreed solemnly until they came to the part that involved me.

Apparently the firm had run into some difficulties with the locals. They were buying up acres and acres of property, but a few freeholds were sticking it out, holding to ridiculous and contradictory conditions for sale or outright refusing to even entertain any offers. It would be my job to turn on the old Thornton charm, get the locals to see the light of reason and sell their miserable swampland to my employers so they could drain it and build their factories. Easy enough. And from what I gathered, they didn't even expect me to try and burn the recalcitrant muck farmers from their houses if they wouldn't listen. Even back then, people were going soft on me, which was fine. I had no urgent desire to dodge buckshot from angry swamp dwellers.

Several handshakes and an expensive dinner later, I drunkenly wandered back to my rented room, basking in the familiar feeling of elation that my problems were gone forever and good times were here in perpetuity. As usual, I was spectacularly wrong on both counts. I ought to have realized it as soon as my ferry crossed the river.

Elizabethtown stunk with a unique bouquet of vile odors. Like everything in Yersey that wasn't barren hills, the place had been a wretched pine swamp, and by God it still smelt like it, plus the tar, burnt coal, and sulfur that accompanies heavy industry. And by the looks of it, the visages of the locals reflected the way the place smelled. The crowd on the docks was a good cross-section of the dregs of Amerikan breeding stock. Slouching, filthy, stunted and sulking, they could have comprised a catalog of deformity and medical oddities, if there were any doctors with a hardy enough constitution to stand the place long enough to record their myriad of physical faults.

Even their clothing was off-putting. It was a delusional drunkard's parody of high fashion. They wore pastel shirts with overly tall collars, clinging tightly to bulbous arms and torsos, castoff trousers either far too small or far too large, and strange hats consisting of nothing but a brim were der rigueur, all topped with coif of hair cemented to the scalp by what looked like particularly slimy effluence.

Amid these castoffs stood my liaison, a beleaguered bastion of decent style in a sea of yokels, marks and rubes. He stood there, looking sad and pitiable amid a sea of filthy longshoremen and dockworkers, holding a carefully penned sign bearing my name, dressed impeccably but getting shabbier, as if through osmosis, by the moment.

I thought to myself, No wonder he has had no luck. This man did not look like the type of person you sent to haggle with bog hopping throwbacks. He wore a lovely jacket and well tailored trousers, with subdued vest over a starched white shirt and a kravat around his neck. He was neatly shaven and wore his hair short and tidy. Everything about the man was designed to blend into the background of a building full for neat desks and polished offices, but here it marked him indelibly as not only an outsider but an enemy. The feared banker or taxman, who had come to steal with paper from men who wretched a meager living from the Earth. In fact, the more I thought about it, the more I was surprised he had not taken a knife to the kidneys.

Not wanting to spend more time on the docks than strictly necessary, I waved to him and as soon as the ferry was close enough, I leapt over the rail and on to the pier. It got a few stares, which quickly turned back to studied disinterest.

You see, I had dressed for the part. I wore a pair of workingman's trousers with a simple vest over a four button shirt and modestly covered my hair with a bowler cap. Granted, I looked much better than this crowd of apes, but I would have fit into any similar den of laborers on the Atlantic Seaboard. The look was intentional.

One of man's biggest weaknesses is that we trust our eyes implicitly, a trait I've used to my advantage time and time again. I might have been a moderately foppish wastrel of a socialite, but I had dressed as salt of the Earth yeomanry, and I had spent enough time around the type to know how to match word and deed to look. That was the crux of my plan. I would charm the muck farmers into believing I was one of them and that I really had their best interests at heart. Then buy the land out from under their feet.

I made my way through the crowd to my liaison, and introduced myself.

"Horace Thornton," I said, plastering an eager grin over my features and extending a hand.

"Mr. Thornton, it is a pleasure to meet you. I'm Johann Lenape. I'm the agent in charge of this transaction," he shook my hand limply and briefly. "Shall we head back to my office?"

I agreed, and off we went through the streets of Elizabethtown.

Lenape's "office" was actually a section of blocked off section of catwalk overlooking a truly gargantuan warehouse. Steam-lifters clomped about, ferrying wooden crates and pallets of materiel wrapped in burlap to and fro. As we ascended the scaffolding, a team of workmen were pulling a flat-car into the warehouse from a new-looking rail siding. As soon as the mammoth doors of the warehouse closed, even more workers swarmed over the rail car like ants on a dead cat. It reminded me of nothing so much as the staging ground for the first airlift of arms to Zululand. This wasn't simply building a factory- the I. M. & H. company was preparing for an invasion. The fact that, through a combination of salesmanship, false assumptions, my own greedy and conniving nature, and a willingness to lie, I had been chosen to spearhead this operation was a bit daunting. Naturally I wasn't about to let that show to Lenape. But it made me suspicious immediately.

No one ran an operation on this scale without a good supply of muscle. In fact, for an enterprise this big, hired hitters and heavy thugs almost always performed the exact duties that I had been called in to do. It was much easier for a suspicious fire to persuade a recalcitrant squatter and his immediate family to vacate than it was to have someone try to talk him off of the land. As we worked our way over the gantry to Lenape's office, we passed a table surrounded by that exact type of man- quiet, serious, and looking to all the world like apes in well made suits. I. M. & H. obviously had the muscle to move on the land they needed. What was stopping them?

When we got to Lenape's office, I wanted to broach the subject immediately. But, however related it is to your eventual goals, bringing up arson and manslaughter at the start of a conversion is something of a faux pax, and makes you look like a bloodthirsty madman as well. So I thought I would be social.

"This is a splendid operation you've built here, Mr. Lenape..."

"It's damned expensive, that's what it is. Every day that this stuff sits here costs out mutual employer a small fortune. We must break ground soon, Mr. Thornton. This stoppage is eating into the operations budget for our new factories. If this keeps up for too much longer, we will be unable to afford to run them for a week, if the plants themselves are ever built."

"So why don't you.."

"Already ahead of you," I was starting to see why Lenape was running this operation, as he interrupted me for a second time, "We can't just run them off, because two of them are Citizens. You can't just threaten a full Imperial citizen. If they were only free residents, we could have just burnt them out, and we would have broken ground a month ago." For all his meek appearance, the man seemed to have the predatory mindset of a Venutian Sky Shark. "So that's where you come in, Mr. Thornton. The Manhattan office is apparently convinced that you'll be able to talk them out of their land."

He paused to scoff, as if he was party to a joke that was being played on me.

"God knows how you'll do it. I tried just about every trick I could think of. They wouldn't sell. I offered women, whiskey, adoption to citizenship for three generations out, but they wouldn't budge. Said something about the place being sacred to their religion," he paused to light a cigarillo, "What kind of stupid bastard religion has a sacred place in god be damned Yersey?" He exhaled a cloud of smoke, his frustration evident. "In any case, I'll set you up with a carriage to take you there. You'll leave first thing tomorrow."

The next morning, as promised, a carriage arrived at the hotel where I had overnighted. I was ready and waiting, if a bit worse for wear due to a long evening the night before. While I had been given a stipend at the outset of this little adventure, that was barely adequate to keep me housed, fed, and in drink for the week or so I had expected to be here. The lion's share of my payment had, in what I must grudgingly admit was a wise move, been withheld until the successful completion of my task. If things were as impossible as Lenape made them out to be, there was a good chance I would never see a single Geld of personal profit from this entire trip. Naturally, I got drunk in response to such a dismal prospect.

However, in the depths of my drunken self-pity, I had struck upon an idea. I'll be the first to admit it was a bad one. I have embroiled myself in a number of deceptions, most of which have been reasonably effective. I can play the working man, the solid comrade, the good soldier, or the society gentleman all rather convincingly. But religion? Acting genuinely religious is well beyond me. Oh, I'm good for muttered prayers, making the right gestures, and sitting, standing and kneeling at the right times, but that is as far as it goes.

Still, I was out of ideas and I needed this money, so I decided to give it a try. What, I thought, is the worst that could happen?

This, dear readers, is one of those fatal phrases that spawn nothing but trouble for you. Should you find yourself thinking along those lines, or worse, uttering them, stop immediately and put as many miles between you and the situation in question as you can, as quickly as you are able. The worst that could happen is usually, at the very least, death, probably at the hands of some crazed thug with a length of pipe or by a random bullet in a muddy hell-hole. But death looks right appealing compared to some of the other things I've seen. Don't ask me about the Chinamen the Dowager Empress sends to Mars, what it's like to be a serf on a Russian airship, or what happens to the Arapaho who get caught during a plains sweep. None of those fates bear mentioning, except each one of them makes taking a knife to your own throat seem like the kiss of an expensive whore.

But this is hindsight, and at the time I was considerably more foolish. So, I exchanged the brown pants for black ones and managed to be awake and out of bed early enough to meet my ride. The trip took the better part of the morning, taking us further south and inland, following dirt roads and then barely cleared trails until I guessed we were close enough. I had the driver let me out about a mile away from the steading- better to keep up appearances, I judged- and began to walk, after arranging for him to pick me up two days hence.

It was typical Yersey lands, half marsh, half pine forest. It had been muggy when we left and the weather had only gotten hotter and more humid. I quickly found myself pouring sweat as I trudged down a road that was part packed gravel, part mudhole. I had meant to look a touch disheveled when I got to the small collection of farm homes, but now I really did look a mess. I was covered to my shins in mud, cursing myself for not wearing gators. My shirt was undone to the third button and my collar and underarms were dripping with perspiration. I was parched and hot, and the oppressive humidity made me feel vastly more exhausted than I should have been. It was in this condition that I staggered into town.

The steading had been established at the center of a collection of small farms, which seemed to be quite prosperous. A neat row of three modest longhouses stood across from a pair of more modern two story farm houses, with a wide, well kept green in between them. It was quite idyllic, really.

Then I noticed something was missing. There was no church. This happy little hamlet hosted what had been described to me as a near fanatical cult, and there was no twice damned church, no chapel, no mosque, no synagogue, or no temple. There was not even the kind of motley collection of sticks, skulls and rocks that passes for a shrine in most native Skrealing villages.

Well bollocks, I though, as I planted my hands on my hips and let the frustration sink in properly. I was completely on my back with my legs in the air. I had no idea what to do next, when what, at the time, looked like my salvation appeared. From one of the pair of modern homes a woman emerged. I have seen few more striking. A cascade of golden hair framed a face that was close to angelic. Over a perfect nose a pair of eyes the color of the sky appraised me, all warmth and welcome. This remarkable head crowned a slender neck which flowed perfectly into a straight and shapely pair of shoulders, a perfectly proportioned bosom, and

YERSEY FRESH

hips which flared just enough to emphasize her femininity. There was a slight bulge at her middle which I guessed indicated she was a few months into a pregnancy. She was an absolute vision of a particular agrarian womanhood. She hid the work of art that was her form beneath a perfectly modest dress, but all her attire did was serve to make her more alluring, allowing the imagination to run riot.

"Well, hello there stranger."

Her voice was like the choirs of heaven. Against my own wishes and better judgment, I could feel myself grinning like a schoolboy.

"Why don't you come on in and tell me what brought you to our little town today?"

How, dear reader, could I possibly say no to that voice and that face? Invariably, I ended up in her parlor, sitting on a plain but well made couch and guzzling cool water as she catered to my needs, as perfect a hostess as she was a beauty.

As I recovered from the slog to this place, she made pleasant small talk, laughing freely, flashing pearly teeth and the smooth white skin of her neck as she tossed her head about. It was after such a bout of laughter that she asked, once more, why I was here.

Now, reflecting on it, my answer embarrassed me. I feel like an complete simpleton for uttering these words and even thinking that I could trick anyone into believing me. But I was desperate, I was tired, I was out of options, and I'll be damned but she was making me feel like everything I said was funny and intriguing so I wagered that it couldn't hurt and told her my lie.

"Well, madam, truth be told I'm a student of theology from Harrisfyrd University. Herman Blackfeather is my name and in my studies of the beliefs of the eastern coast of Amerika, I had heard, albeit secondhand, of your church. Now, I've learned of many religions, from the elephant gods of the Hindus to the Mohammedans of Arabia, but I have never been struck by the truth of any of them, until I read of your beliefs. So I have come as a simple pilgrim. Please, madam, teach me. Let me bathe in the wisdom of your faith."

To this she smiled again, an easy movement of the mouth, which could have sent nations to war. She gazed at me guilelessly, all warmth and welcome, and placed a delicate hand lightly on my knee.

"Well Mr. Blackfeather, I am delighted that you want to learn more about our Lord. My name is Marguerite Pennywell, and my husband is our minister. He's out in the fields right now, but he'll be back for lunch in just a few hours and he'll be happy to tell you more, if you'd be so kind as to wait."

"Mrs. Pennywell, I would be overjoyed. I cannot express how happy I am to finally be on the path to true wisdom."

"Oh that's wonderful Mr. Blackfeather. I hope you do not mind that I can offer you no diversion other than my company. I hope that is not too dull for someone from such a place Harrisfyrd. We must seem terribly dull in our little town to you," she said as she batted her eyes at me and let her lips slip into a pout for a brief moment.

"I would be delighted if you were to keep me company Mrs. Pennywell."

The next few hours passed too quickly, with her fawning over me and bringing me water and finger sandwiches. I was in the middle of regaling her with a concocted story about three sociology professors at a tea party, when Mr. Pennywell arrived.

The man was as intimidating as his wife was stunning. Now, this country, thank the Gods above, has never seen much in the way of Puritans, but I've been to England, and the English do have their share, and I could tell immediately that this man was a archetypal example of the breed. He was tall, wore a long but neat beard, and was dressed almost entirely in black. His face was severe, and he wore a scowl as he strode into the house.

"Lord be with you, Marguerite. And Lord be with you, stranger," he growled, as if the need to speak was physically uncomfortable to him, "Will you explain why you are in my home with my wife?"

Before I could stammer some inadequate, awkward reply, Mrs. Pennywell jumped to my rescue.

"Oh Jacob, this is Mr. Herman Blackfeather. He's from Harrisfyrd. He wants to know more about the Lord," she put a heavy accent on the word 'Lord' that should have sent me scrambling out of town, it was so telling, but at the time I was looking at her blue eyes and was somewhere past the point where alarm was possible.

"Did he now?"

"He did, and he was kindly waiting for you to come and preach the good word to him."

The big Puritan turned to me.

"So you'd like to learn about the Lord, Mr. Blackfeather?"

The emphasis was much more disconcerting when it was put in place by the column of black that was Mr. Pennywell. However, Marguerite was still smiling gaily at me, so my alarm was more muted than it aught to have been.

"Why yes sir, I am eager to learn about the Lord. I read a great deal about your faith back in Harrisfyrd and I have found truth in what small amount I have learned that is lacking in other faiths. I wish to be taught and learn the divine revelations of the Lord."

He smiled at me. It was an unpleasant, predatory smile that unnerved me entirely. The only thing that prevented me from flight was the fact that I had dug myself in so deep that I reckoned I had gone past the point of no return. So instead of following my instincts, I stayed put and kept digging.

"Well Mr. Blackfeather, it so happens that we're planning a special ceremony at the next full moon. You'd be welcome to attend, to learn the true power and face of the Lord. Once the ceremony is complete, we will all be enlightened, and our attachment to this place will be severed."

"This place? You mean you'd leave this lovely little village?"

He chuckled knowingly, "Oh, yes, I suppose you could put it that way. We only need one more thing for our ceremony, but we've been unable to find it?"

Ah, an opening, I thought, "Really? Perhaps you could tell me what that is. I have many connections in academia, and perhaps through one of them I might lend aid to you."

"I need Black Lotus. Stygian, specifically."

Black Lotus? And he wants Stygian? What the hell kind of Church is this?

Stygian Black Lotus is the province of the most jaded opium sots. It was not amongst my usual vices, but I knew where to get it, "Why, Mr. Pennywell, you're in luck. I know a botanist in Harrisfyrd who grows the stuff. I can have it and be back in plenty of time for your ceremony."

Mr. and Mrs. Pennywell smiled at each other, exchanging knowing looks. The preacher looked at me warmly for the first time. "That would be wonderful, Mr. Blackfeather."

"If you could provide me with a ride back to Elizabethtown, I can take the train to Harrisfyrd first thing in the morning."

Mr. Pennywell promised me that was possible, and in less than an hour I was in the back of a buggy, traveling the dirt road back to civilization.

"He wants what?" said Mr. Lenape, annoyed and shocked at the same time.

"Black Lotus, and not the cheap stuff either. Do not fret- I know a Chinaman who can provide the stuff. I just need enough money to pay for it, and I think your problem will be gone by the next full moon."

He merely narrowed his eyes and warned me that this had better not be a scam.

"Oh hello, Mistah Thornton. You come to buy?"

"Yeah, I need some Stygian, Chang, and a lot of it."

"Oh, most regrettable, boat get caught coming out of skylock. No Stygian for some time. You want buy Ethiopian Hagga? Almost as good, and I give you good price."

I thought about it for a moment, weighing my options. *There was no chance that some farmer in a cult could know the difference, right?* I told myself. And the difference would allow me to pad my bank account. And it's not like Lenape would be able to tell either. *To hell with all of them,* I thought.

"Sure Chang, give me the Hagga. Just do the characters for Stygian on the wrapping."

"Oh yes, oh yes, I do that," nodded my favorite Chinaman.

I found myself back on the outskirts of the village on the evening of the full moon. I had ridden there, but I tied my borrowed horse to a tree outside the village and came in on foot. I did not expect trouble, but I have always found those little touches of caution to be exceptionally useful if crisis does come.

It was abuzz with activity, men and women wearing black robes bustling to and fro, torches everywhere, and a growing bonfire in the town square. I personally had dressed in a simple black suit. I had a pistol in a shoulder holster on my breast and there was a slim knife inside my boot. I wasn't exactly expecting violence, but having had nearly a week to cool off from the proximity of Ms. Pennywell, I decided that caution was the better part of valour, so there was no way I would be going unarmed tonight. Carrying my poor-man's lotus in a package under my arm, I made my way to the Pennywell home. This time, Mr. Pennywell greeted me at the door.

"Ah, come in Mr. Blackfeather. We had been expecting you."

The home had been transformed into a sinister parody of what it was. A strange sigil had been traced on the floor in some black substance and candles burned all around, giving off a foul and oily smoke. Ms. Pennywell was still there, smiling at me. But the dim bit of comfort her presence provided was stripped away as I noticed that she no longer looked newly pregnant, but now looked as if her stomach was set to burst, distended and straining against the fabric of the robes that she too wore. I blinked a few times to clear my head.

Regaining my composure, I handed the package to Mr. Pennywell.

"Sir, here are your goods."

He opened the package and sniffed it. This was the moment of truth. A true fiend would have smelled my ruse in an instant, but he did not have that look about him, and I had gambled on my intuition. He considered a moment, and then smiled.

"Mr. Blackfeather, you have done us a great service. You are welcome to be our guest for this evening."

As he spoke, more black robed men and women filed into the room. Their faces grim as they quietly intoned a prayer in a language I had never heard. I started to cast about for excuses the leave.

"Ah, um, uh, I'd love to, but you see I've left the, uh, cat, um, in the oven and..."

"Mr. Blackfeather, I know who sent you, and I really do insist you stay for our Sabbath."

As he spoke, I reached for my pistol. I was not quick enough, and a blow to the back of my head sent me to my knees. I mouthed a protest, but no sound came, then a second blow brought darkness.

When I came to my wits again the sound of chanting in a language that was painful to hear filled my ears. The villagers rocked and swayed and prayed in a language that was alluring and sickening to the ear, sounding entirely unnatural in human throats. They had taken positions around the sigil, with Mr. and Mrs. Pennywell in the center, her prostrate before him while he intoned more words that I could not understand but that I guessed were some sort of spell or prayer. For my part, I found myself bound hand and foot, slightly outside of the circle.

I took in the situation for a moment before I settled on a plan of action. There were a lot of villagers cum cultists in the room. There was no way I was fighting my way out of this. I settled on a path of quiet escape.

I had a stroke of minor luck- the cultists had tied my hands in front of me rather than behind me. I set to work loosening the ropes immediately. I knew if I could get to my knife, I had a chance to make a break for freedom. While I was planning my escape, the cultists had continued to chant, their voices growing ever more feverish and louder. Suddenly, just as I had loosened the bonds enough to try and reach my blade, the chanting stopped, and Mr. Pennywell spoke in English.

"Oh ancient spirit of this land, we call upon you to come to this unworthy host," he said as he gestured at his wife, "and possess her womb and be born to us! We call upon you to bring your mighty rule upon this world and grant us your humble servants mastery over all who dwell here in the shadow of your dark glory!"

He lit a brazer and I could smell immediately that it was full of the Hagga I had given him. As the smoke wafted over the cultists, they began to undulate where they stood. I had managed to work the blade out of my boot.

"Come to us oh lord, we have opened the path, we have lit the way, now cross the threshold to rule this world! Empower your servants and raise us as masters!"

From outside I heard a howling wind and the crash of lightning. A sickly glow began to emanate from Mrs. Pennywell's very body. I had just finished freeing my feet and had positioned the blade to cut the bonds holding my hands.

"Baptize us in nomine diaboli! Bath us in your dark light and cleanse this land for all time!"

My hands were free, and I rose to my knees, making ready to dash towards the door, when there was a flash of light from the center of the sigil. A sound like the roar of one hundred locomotives split the night air, and I was thrown into the wall. The world went black for a second time that night.

I awoke to a horrid, plaintive mewing sound, like someone had tried to dunk a colicky kitten. Ignoring that for the moment, I took a quick inventory. I was sore, but it seemed that I had both hands and feet and a quick check down my trousers indicated that everything important was safe. Thank the gods. As luck would have it, whatever knocked me back had also shoved my knife towards the wall as well as my pistol. I grabbed both, putting the knife into my belt and preparing the pistol for action.

The room was a wreck and the air smelled like burnt sausage, but what immediately drew the eye was the red ruin in the center of the sigil. I assumed this had once been the beautiful Mrs. Marguerite Pennywell, and this foul puddle of gore was also the source of the pitiful noise. Inside the mass of blood and viscera that was once a beautiful woman, I saw a spasm of movement. A thing flopped out of what had once been a shapely abdomen, squawked once weakly at the assembled masses and then tripped and toppled to the floor.

The thing had the look of something half formed, like someone had started to create a fearsome demon, but had gotten lazy and drunk before he had finished the work. The creature's head was overly large and looked like that of a draft horse with fangs. It was far too big for the rest of the body. The sorry creature continued to try, and fail, to right itself.

It had spindly wings, which it had broken on its initial flop from Mrs. Pennywell's remains. The torso looked like that of a fawn, but with two worthless fore claws which were curled up against its feeble chest. The back legs were no better, a pair of useless stork legs mounted on hooves that were nearly too heavy for it to lift. It also had a long, forked tail which twitched weakly. It managed to raise its head at last and as its eyes met mine it opened its horsey mouth and squawked again.

I watched the poor thing for a time, entranced by this utter abortion of a creature. I must have been still dazed from my repeated trips into unconsciousness that evening, for I found myself wondering, in a rare philosophical bent, what kind of being would create such a pathetic creature. What kind of idiot god would spawn such a joke of a beast? All the while it continued to flop around as it was able, frequently exhausting itself. Then it would rest, wheezing and making blood bubbles from its nose.

It was then that Mr. Pennywell woke up. He groaned and rolled over, much worse for wear than I was, and tried to sit up. I leveled my pistol at him, but I don't think he noticed, as he gazed forlornly at the hideous creature.

"W..Where is the Destroyer of Worlds? Where is he who will make us the masters of this land and bend the wills of the unbelievers to our whims?"

The creature seemed to sense it was being addressed and lifted its swollen head to squawk at its high priest. This seemed to take every last bit of effort the little horror had left and it dropped its head and promptly fell asleep.

"I think maybe you might need to make an appointment with your world devourer after his nap," I said smugly.

"W..what happened? We followed the ritual to the letter. Everything was perfect."

"Might have had something to do with the Ethiopian Hagga I gave you. You really shouldn't skimp on ingredients when fixing fancy dishes," I added.

Before he had a chance to process this, I shot him.

The gunshot woke the bigheaded hellspawn snoring peacefully in the pile of ichor and gore. With a decidedly stronger squawk it clumsily bolted to its oversized feet and scrambled across the floor. Before my trigger finger could decide whether to work again the gangly little creature dove through a window and staggered out into the night.

As I looked about the room, I could see the rest of the cult slowly stirring. I decided it was time to leave, but I did the world a favor and made sure to set a few candles down on a rug near the door. You know, as a going away present for the people who tried to murder me. I watched the fire from the treeline, just to make sure the building caught well and good, and from deeper in the forest I heard a plaintive squawk. I briefly considered entering the woods to hunt down the pitiful thing summoned by the Pennywell cult, but after a moment I went to the stables instead, mounted up and headed back to Elizabethtown.

"How?" demanded Mr. Lenape when I showed up in his office the following morning.

"Well, it turns out they were all dope fiends. I made the delivery and I guess one of them kicked over a lantern while they were chasing the dragon, and the whole lot must have burned. I tried to get in there and save them, but the conflagration was too much, and I was forced to retreat. It does solve your problem though."

He clearly didn't believe me, but he also was obviously weighing how much trouble he really wanted to go through to investigate my story. But if he wanted to think I really was capable of murdering a few dozen people in cold blood, that was fine with me. He had hired me, and I was confident that no evidence to the fact would be found, so I was not worried about Marshals coming knocking. Besides, whatever he believed had happened, he was now legally clear to build his factory, and from what I know about businessmen, that is usually enough.

"I'm not sure what exactly you did Thornton, but we are damned grateful that it was done quickly. You can expect us to contact you again in the future, and if you are ever looking for a permanent place, you contact me directly."

He weighed and filled a sack with enough specie to cover my promised fee. I had to suppress gleeful giggles as I mentally began to spend the money. The first thing I needed to buy was a new hat. I had no intention of staying around either. The thing that I had allowed to go free in the pine lands of Yersey was a pitiful little devil barely strong enough to live through a Yersey winter, but I didn't want to stick around to see what might happen if that little devil got the chance to grow up.

YERSEY FRESH

LADY CITIZEN

By Brian D. Thomas

Captain O'Mally gripped the ship's wheel in a white knuckled death grip and let the boom of thunder drown out the screams of his dying crew. His burning eyes strained to see through the rain soaked windscreen and searched in vain across the glowing instrument panel for any sign of the skylock. "Where the bloody hell is it?" roared the airship captain in frustration. The seething storm roared back, though not quite loud enough to hide the blasts of shotguns and the shouts of fighting men out on the airship's deck.

The slam of the cabin door almost stopped Captain O'Mally's heart as his first mate rushed into the tiny pilothouse. The airman's chalk white face was soaking wet and his clothing was splashed with more than just rainwater.

"Mr. Feebs has blocked the door to the engine room and he swears he'll keep the boilers going until the devil himself says otherwise," gasped the first mate. "The crew got to the arms locker in time and they are pushing...them...back toward the bow" he continued in a strained voice.

"Get that fire axe and use it to bar the pilothouse door. That lock won't hold on it's own," commanded the captain in a tone he hoped hide his own terror.

The hurricane had blown up just as they'd crossed from Venus to the Macapa' Amazon lock and had been chasing them all the way to Caracas. At first the crew of the Imperial air merchantman *IAM Reliable* thought the tropical storm a blessing since it kept the unfriendly French airships of Guiana tucked in their berths while the *Reliable* ran north with the wind to the next skylock. A day later though the storm had picked up speed and power and slammed the *Reliable* in the tail, battering and driving her with gale force winds, threatening to smash her into the tropical jungle below. The *IAM Reliable* had a veteran captain and a seasoned crew and it wouldn't be the first storm they'd flown, but then...

Something slammed into the pilothouse door hard enough to splinter wood and O'Malley's first mate shrieked and fired his shotgun into the door, further weakening the barrier. Multiple shotgun blasts sounded from the other side, and O'Malley could hear someone outside praying loudly over the sound of the storm. The first mate fumbled with his weapon as he hurried to reload.

"There it is!" shouted Captain O'Malley as his eyes finally caught the sodium glow of the marker warning on the instrument panel of his skylock locator. The airship captain turned tired but hopeful eyes to his first mate, but instead of seeing relief he read pure terror in the downcast eyes of his crewman. The captain followed the mate's gaze down to base of the pilothouse door and saw the steady flow of blood and rainwater that was pouring in under the warped and buckled door.

Captain O'Malley snapped his eyes to his windscreen, straining to see the shimmering whirlpool that should be hanging in the sky just off the starboard side. There, hanging in the dark black night was the skylock, its light cutting trough the storm like a swirling heavenly beacon. O'Malley cut his wheel hard to starboard and aimed his dying airship toward the skylock and home. If he could just cross the lock he'd be in the Empire, away from this storm and only a signal flare away from help against these…

The pilothouse door exploded off its hinges and knocked the screaming mate to the floor. Captain O'Malley threw on the steering lock and drawing his pistol turned to defend his beloved Reliable.

Wilhelmina met the new morning with a yawn, a stretch and a smile. As much as she'd like to spend the day in her featherbed she knew she had duties to perform. She was after all a Lady Citizen of the Amerikan Empire and it just would not do to set such a bad example. Instead, the five foot, one and a quarter inch tall model of Imperial feminine citizenship rose from her bed and began her morning ritual.

Wilhelmina threw open her blackout shutters and allowed the morning sun to flood her spacious bedroom. She fairly danced over to her dresser and gazed with fondness on the collection of framed photographs displayed across it's oiled top. Arranged along the dresser were four gilt framed photos of what at first glanced appeared to be Wilhelmina herself. Indeed their own father often had a hard time telling the five identical sisters apart, though each photo definitely captured a different spirit if not a different person.

Wilhelmina greeted each day by kissing the photos of her four sisters and she brought an image of a short buxom woman in a military uniform to her lips in a ritual of familial affection. Next she kissed an image of an identically cherubic little woman wearing a welder's apron and goggles, posing with an enormous wrench and a bright smile. She replaced the photo and picked up two more. In her left hand was the seemingly same buxom cherub wearing a stern grey suit and an even sterner expression while Wilhelmina's right hand held the photo that looked like the same tiny woman in a bright stripped jacket carrying an enormous tuba. Wilhelmina kissed each in turn and then replaced them on the dresser.

Lastly she opened an ornate hinged frame and brought it close to her face. Instead of another mirror-like image it held a photo of a heavy browed young man in an Imperial Air Corp Uniform. Wilhelmina gazed wistfully at the image of her betrothed, Ensign Rawlmond Witt late of Her Imperial Warluft The *Irascible Wind*, and crushed it to her admittedly ample bosom before giving it a quick kiss and replacing it on the dresser. She couldn't just stand here all morning swooning like some free resident housemaid over her far off love.

Wilhelmina was the oldest of a set of identical quintuplets by a full seven minutes and was therefore the eldest child in the Wigglebottom clan. When her mother passed away both her citizenship and authority transferred to her eldest child, Wilhelmina. Her father had never remarried. While each of the Wigglebottom girls was a model imperial citizen, Wilhelmina was tasked with maintaining the family home and interests while her father traveled, and she took her duties very seriously.

Lady Citizen Wilhelmina Wigglebottom, mistress of Wigglebottom Manor and chairwoman of the Harrisfyord Imperial Ladies Auxiliary had things, important things to do today.

Wilhelmina dressed quickly...then redressed two more times until she was satisfied with the day's outfit choice before descending to the main floor of Wigglebottom manor. The little blonde woman bounced down the spiral staircase and waved a greeting to the various house staff already busy about their day's business. She crossed the huge kitchen and fought the urge to stop and sample the heavenly baked things that sat cooling on the counter. Aside from the fact that she was trying to avoid anything that might make her wedding gown fit anymore snuggly than it already threatened to, she knew the first rule of being mistress of the house was business first.

Wilhelmina skipped to the heavy oak door that led to the center of the Wigglebottom estate and the focus of her manor duties-The Glasshouse.

Technically the Wigglebottoms were farmers. Wilhelmina's father was a noted botanist, famous for his highly successful vegetable hybrids. The Amerikan Empire was in a constant state of food shortage and rationing and Gunter Wigglebottom had created several food preservatives and flavor enhancers that made even the basest fare both tasty and lasting. The sprawling two-acre greenhouse affectionately and appropriately named The Glasshouse was botanist Citizen Wigglebottom's laboratory and year-round hothouse farm. Of course the Wigglebottoms also had farmland in Wilhelmina's departed mother's homeland of Venezuela, and the bulk of their Imperial crops were raised there but the important work was always done in the Glasshouse.

Wilhelmina grimaced as the heat and humidity of the immense greenhouse hit her. Miles of copper pipe ran along the ceiling and floor of the Glasshouse carrying hot water. Two boilers worked round the clock to create the tropical jungle environment required to grow the peculiar Wigglebottom flora. Larger pipes pierced with holes provided a constant misting rain that fell on garden and gardener alike, and the entire atmosphere of the Glasshouse was a hot misty rainforest complete with colorful birds and even more colorful plants.

Wilhelmina stood on tiptoe to gaze over blazing red chili apple trees, and then stooped to glance down at the brilliant orange and yellow magma melons. Volcano peppers lay in vibrant rows down the length of one wing of the Glasshouse and jalapeno squash grew down from suspended planters overhead. The Empire loved its spicy food and the Wigglebottoms were the imperial suppliers of some of the hottest produce to ever burn a palette. Indeed few foreigners could even stomach some of the spicier botanical hybrids created in the famous Glasshouse. Imperials however relied on such spice to flavor their otherwise bland and even questionable foodstuffs that rationing and shortages provided.

Dozens of gardeners tended the plants and flowers that populated the Glasshouse. Most of the staff was Warao/Spanish blooded natives who had emigrated to the empire from Venezuela specifically to work for the Wigglebottoms, and most of them were also at least distantly related to the late Mrs. Wigglebottom.

The Warao Caribs were adept at coaxing tropical plants to grow in difficult conditions and so Gunter Wigglebottom relied on their skills and talents to keep his hothouse running and producing. They were also comfortable working long hours in the tropical hothouse while locally hired workers tended to collapse from the heat, crushing valuable plants, and sweating all over the produce.

After quickly confirming with her foreman Antonio that all was in order with the Glasshouse staff, Wilhelmina went to the main gazebo to care for her special staff. At the center of the Glasshouse was a three story glass domed gazebo that housed a gurgling fountain, flowering fruit trees and an elaborate decorative iron dinning set and wet bar. Wilhelmina opened a cupboard door under the bar and took out two cans of Greeble. She smiled as she held up the tinned meat staple of the Amerikan Empire.

As Wilhelmina opened the first can, the little lady citizen began to sing, "If it flies or swims or moves around on limbs, it could be, should be Greeble. If it's savory and sweet and nearly tastes like meat it could be, should be Greeble!"

As Wilhelmina sang the familiar jingle several throaty meows sounded from the undergrowth. Five big tawny Coon cats padded out from the mini jungle of the gazebo and closed on Wilhelmina like a pride of hungry lions. They purred like idling steam engines and head butted Wilhelmina's legs hard enough to make her stumble as she scooped tinned meat onto faded plates and placed them on the table. The big cats jumped onto the expensive iron table and greedily devoured the mysterious canned meat as their mistress petted their flanks and cooed at them as if they were furry children.

The beasts were barely pets. In a garden as vast as the Glasshouse there was always a problem with pests. Mice and rabbits snuck in under loose panels and moles tunneled up from outside to escape the cold of winter or to snack on the worms kept to loosen the garden soil. Short-pronged jackalopes had even forced their way in during winter snows to enjoy a tropical feast.

Wilhelmina's five feral cats kept the various pests in check though the tropical bird nests had to be hung from the ceiling to keep them intact and even the two Glasshouse beehives weren't safe from prying cat paws. The Glasshouse was not just a vast garden, it was a complete ecosystem and the Coon pride was the top of the food chain…along with a steady supply of Greeble tins. All Imperial subjects were expected to eat Greeble as a meat ration and Wilhelmina liked that her babies were doing their part too.

As she left her feral children to their breakfast Wilhelmina called to Antonio, "I'm going to town to arrange for the monthly Ladies Auxiliary good works luncheon. Be a dear and have my putterputt brought around and make sure the coal bin is filled."

Wilhelmina loved her little steam powered, three wheeled, saddle seated cart.

Many of the ladies of Harrisfyord enjoyed the feel of the vibrating saddle of a putterputt throbbing and bouncing between their thighs as they raced about town on their imperial chores. Some said that running chores on their putterputts made their tensions melt away. Sometimes those chores took all day and were often followed by a bottle of wine and a nap.

Lady citizen Wigglebottom chose a modest fur coat to fight the November chill and straddled her putterputt, coaxing the boiler and bringing up a healthy head of steam before engaging the main drive and rocketing out onto the main road to town. The three miles to town seemed to come and go in the blink of an eye, and it wasn't until she bounced into the center of town that she realized something was very wrong.

Her first clue that something was amiss was the sirens. Air raid sirens were howling out warning and Wilhelmina could see spotlights panning the sky. The fact that it was a bright sunny morning did little to quell the diligence of the town spotlight crews as they swept the sky for signs of aerial invaders and Wilhelmina smiled with civic pride to see her fellow Harrisfyordians refuse to let a little sunlight interrupt their duty. She couldn't actually hear anything over the sounds of the sirens but she was sure whatever had aroused the fury of the Harrisfyord Town Militia must be important.

Harrisfyord was not just any Imperial town it was a skylock town. Nearly one hundred years ago a skylock had opened just outside the town off the beach of the Susquehanna River with it's other end opening out over the city of Caracas Venezuela. Overnight, sleepy little Harrisfyord was turned into a booming trade link with South Atlanitcus and Spanish trade airships flew the lock as a shortcut to bring Hispania goods to the eastern shore of Amerika. The lock also meant foreign militaries and sky pirates could now strike the heart of the Empire and so Caracas was seized as an Imperial city to secure the passage. This didn't stop pirate raids or military incursions though. French strikes on Caracas threatened to spill over into the Imperial district of Pennysltucky through the Harrisfyord skylock and Carib skypirates had struck the town numerous times.

While the Imperial Air Corp provided the first line of defense against skylock incursions the real defense against aerial assaults fell to the city militias. Block wardens directed citizen manned gun emplacements, and neighbors competed with each other to shoot down the most invaders in a friendly competition of civic defense. Militia crewed patrol boats enforced air berth and harbor rules and provided constant air cover over Imperial skylock towns throughout the Empire.

The roofs that lined the main street of Harrisfyord were bustling with activity. Militia balloons and air corps fliers surrounded the massive elevator air berth towers that marked the center of town. As Wilhelmina watched several patrol lufts scooting overhead, a pack of young boys cut across the road carrying shells for the anti-luft guns stationed on the roof of the general mercantile air berth. Wilhelmina was forced to swerve aside to avoid running over the ordinance urchins and slammed her putterputt to a screeching hissing stop in front of the trade house building.

"Sorry Missus Citizen," called a chubby faced boy as he tried to both bow and catch a rolling eight-inch shell that he'd dropped in the street. With a gap-toothed smile the youth recaptured the escaped high explosive round and ran to catch up with his fellow ordinance gophers.

Wilhelmina was straightening her hat and collecting her composure when the air berth master exited the general mercantile building. "Oh, Lady citizen Wigglebottom, your arrival is perfect," called Berthmaster Williams as he trotted over to her hissing putterputt. "We've been very busy with this…occurrence but I was just going to send a runner out to the manor to fetch you," he continued breathlessly.

Wilhelmina puffed with pride. Whatever the emergency was, obviously the city official required the assistance of an important lady citizen and she was flattered that he had sought her out first. She was of course one of the leading town...

"Could you tell me Miss if your father has returned to town?" The Berth master's question deflated Wilhelmina instantly and left her confused.

"My father is still on Venus to best of my knowledge," she answered through a frosty smile.

"It's just that some of the cargo we were able to recover was addressed to your father, and I was hoping..." continued Berthmaster Williams with a strained official calm he obviously didn't feel. The man was fidgeting with his holster flap and kept glancing up at the sky as if a piece of it were about to fall on his head. It took a moment for the Berthmaster's statement to push past Wilhelmina's disappointment and sink in.

"What do you mean you recovered father's cargo? From whom?" Wilhelmina asked, her smile converted to a worried frown.

Citizen Williams pointed to the west of town and explained. " The night watch spotted the airship *Reliable* early this morning hanging dead just past the skylock, and sent patrol lufts up to see if there was a problem. The problem was the Reliable was crewless." The Berthmaster's face grew pale as he continued.

"We found signs of a struggle," he stammered. "There were bullet holes everywhere and the decks were covered in... well it was quite a mess I can tell you, Lady Citizen, and we've been looking for survivors all morning without any success. The cargo hold is a shambles and there is a gaping hole in her hull at the main hold and the cargo itelf is a wreck. The cargo that's not smashed is leaking out all across the river or the beach, but we did recover a few crates. In particular three big ones tagged for delivery to your father at Wigglebottom Manor."

The Berthmaster seemed to regain some of his composure as he took a more official tone. "We were hoping we could speak to your father and find out more about the *Reliable* and her ports of call. We sent a luft back through to Caracas but they said there was a storm and..."

"I'm afraid I can't help you, Citizen Williams," interrupted Wilhelmina in a similar official tone. "My father is away on business and I am the mistress of the manor. I'll take custody of these crates and see to it that my father is informed of this situation at my earliest convenience."

Wilhelmina's tone did not suggest that contradiction was an option, and she stuck out her hand as if the Berthmaster should drop three shipping crates into her palm.

"If there are skypirates about..." she continued, "It would be best if you saw to your patrol teams and gun crews and let me get on with my own business."

Wilhelmina's smile was now firmly back in place and she aimed it up into the tall city official's face like a shining torch of social superiority. Her confidence was so overpowering the man didn't actually speak as he led her to a loading dock outside the main building.

Wilhelmina saw three coffin-sized shipping crates standing on end on the dock. She dialed her smile up several more degrees and flashed it full upon the berth master. "Now how will I EVER get those big things into my poor little putterputt?" she asked in girlish innocence, batting her great eyelashes and tapping her tiny foot.

Once the Berthmaster and his teamsters had securely loaded and strapped the three big crates to the Wigglebottom putterputt, Wilhelmina thanked them profusely and gave each of the freeman teamsters a silver penny. She pointedly did not tip the berthmaster.

The return trip home was noticeably slower and Wilhelmina had to concentrate on guiding the overloaded little steam cart back up the road. The cold November wind had picked up and kept tugging at the crates sticking up in the back seat

Once home Wilhelmina gave the putterputt's little horn several sharp squeezes honking for assistance. On cue Antonio arrived with several house hands and began unloading the big crates.

"What have you brought us mistress?" asked Antonio in measured curiosity. No one made a move to actually open the crates without their mistress's express order to do so.

"Actually, I'm not sure Antonio. Let's open one and see!" Wilhelmina stepped back and clasped her hands in front of her chest as she watched Antonio take a pry bar to the first crate. He struggled with the heavy nails holding the crate together and Wilhelmina grew excited, like a child on Wotan's day opening a present.

By the time Antonio had pried off the crate lid, Wilhelmina was hopping up and down and clapping her hands. When she realized everyone was watching her, Wilhelmina froze in place and tried to look stoic, but in seconds she was bouncing in place again and making little high pitched humming sounds in the back of her throat.

Antonio reached into the crate and pulled out…what looked like an enormous pea pod. Judging by the foreman's efforts the pod was extremely heavy and he placed it on the ground with an audible thud. Wilhelmina inched closed, approaching nose first like a little dog smelling a stranger.

Her years working in the Glasshouse had taught Wilhelmina to trust her nose and the big pod had a fresh green smell and not the dry spice smell of a dried seedpod. The pod was indeed green and firm and Wilhelmina thumped one of the pea-like bulges with her finger. It looked for all the world like a giant pea pod.

"It looks like someone sent Poppa a giant pea pod," declared Wilhelmina to her staff. With her families line of work in mind it certainly made sense, and the members of the Wigglebottom staff all nodded their heads in agreement. "Antonio, uncrate these please and put them in the Glasshouse in one of the potting wings until father returns home," instructed Wilhelmina.

She had already lost interest in the big peas and just now remembered she hadn't done any of the errands she had originally gone into town for. As her foreman and staff began unpacking the other two crates and carrying away the big pods, Wilhelmina quietly headed toward the coal shed to refill her putterputt bin for a return to town. Perhaps, she thought she should change her clothes first since everyone had now seen this particular outfit today. Then she frowned as duty replaced vanity.

A change in hats would suffice.

On her return to town Wilhelmina skirted the General Mercantile building thus avoiding another encounter with the air berth master and instead circled around towards the river and the naval docks. Aquatic vessels and water-docked air ships filled the Harrisfyord docks and Wilhelmina spied several foreign flags waving above some of the craft.

As she crossed the main thoroughfares Lady Citizen Wigglebottom could see that the morning's chaos had settled down to normal daily activity. She did notice an increase in the number of constables stationed on the streets and she even saw a patrol of Imperial cavalry troopers in their brown jackets and copper buttons trotting up Fishwife's Way from the river docks looking very intense and official.

The cavalry was escorting a large wagon loaded with broken crates and barrels, and Wilhelmina remembered hearing that the *Reliable* had dumped much of her cargo near the river. Wilhelmina honked at the troopers and flashed them her brightest imperial support smile as she waved them on in encouragement. A stern faced sergeant tipped his brown kepi in salute and waved his troopers on. Wilhelmina pulled her chugging putterputt in behind the line of cavalry troopers and followed them deeper into town.

As residents stopped to watch the passing troops, Wilhelmina waved at her fellow townsfolk and honked her horn. The procession took on the air of a mini parade with the chugging, honking putterputt acting as a one-women band, providing compliment to clopping horse hooves.

Soon children were running alongside Wilhelmina's steam cart singing rude

Imperial marching songs as passing residents and citizens waved and shouted support. Wilhelmina smiled and waved back.

Finally the little lady citizen pulled off from the cavalry procession and brought her putterputt to a stop in front of a brightly painted building, and under a sign depicting a lady's foot. The Bared Ankle was a ladies-only club and the headquarters of the Harrisfyord Imperial Ladies Auxiliary. As Wilhelmina checked her coat she could hear the loud buzz of conversations from the main salon. The town's ladies were still agitated from the morning's events. The fact that no one called out a greeting as she entered the floor of the salon was both troubling and disappointing.

Wilhelmina spied two of her fellow auxiliary members seated at a side table and joined their heated conversation. "My husband, Chief Inspector Snurlison says that there were body parts scattered everywhere!" Citizen Lady Rasputia Snurlison was wife to Citizen Snori Snurlison, Chief Inspector of the Harrisfyord constabulary and she was often the best source of town news and gossip.

"I heard that the garrison has troops of cavalry out looking for escaped skypirates and that the navy has a gunboat watching the river for anyone attempting to recover the cargo dumped from the *Reliable*," replied her companion Lady Citizen BesBettica.

"I saw cavalry troopers!" added Wilhelmina as she inserted herself into the conversation. The conversation came to an abrupt stop as all three ladies stood and exchanged hugs and kisses, complementing each other's daily outfit choice and welcoming Wilhelmina to the table.

"As I was saying," continued Rasputia "My husband the Chief Inspector says that he doesn't think the hole in the hull of the *Reliable* was caused by cannon fire. He says the hole was torn out, not blasted in and thinks the skypirates meant to use it to dump the cargo out the hole onto their horrid pirate luft."

Lady Citizen Snurlison loved to talk about her husband's job and often reminded her listeners of his important position in the community several times in a single sitting. She went on to confide in her lady friends all the details of the morning's strange events that her husband had relayed to her in strictest confidence, and she swore her confidants to secrecy, just as her husband had sworn her.

"My husband the Chief Inspector says that it looks like the hole was hacked open with the same bloody tools used to hack up that poor crew. He said that most of the cargo was smashed and hacked apart too."

Wilhelmina considered telling her friends about the crates that were found but was loath to interrupt Lady Citizen Snurlison's detailed accounts, and besides she doubted giant pea pods were important to anyone but her father.

"Well," commented Citizen BesBettica "they must not have been very good pirates. I mean, who goes to all that trouble just to smash the cargo?"

The conversation eventually turned to other matters and the tragedy of the *IAM Reliable* morning's news gave way to afternoon's business. The Harrisfyord Imperial Ladies Auxiliary had both a history and an obligation of social works and the three lady citizens began plotting their next campaign.

Their latest efforts in the cause of the city's child labor force had been a stunning success. After visiting several of the city factories and seeing the work conditions the children of the city were required to work under, the Harrisfyord Imperial Ladies Auxiliary had successfully petitioned the city Alderman to institute not one, but three, mandatory cigarette breaks per day for the city's juvenile work force. Supported by a cartel of Virginia tobacco growers the initiative had even spread to other Imperial cities. Both growing Imperial support, and the smiling faces of the cities child workers as they gathered under the sunny morning skies and filled their young lungs with reinvigorating tobacco smoke, encouraged the members of the ladies auxiliary. Indeed the sight of an eight year old, smudge-faced pipefitter enjoying an afternoon cigarette and a stiff black coffee brought a prideful tear to the eye of every Imperial Lady who made it possible.

Several new initiatives were on the table and the auxiliary was planning to meet for a ladies luncheon at the Wigglebottom Glasshouse to discuss their options. Wilhelmina needed a head count from chapter mistress Rasputia as well as an itinerary so that she could plan an appropriate menu- one did not serve croissants for example if extensive French-bashing was part of the planned conversations. She also knew everyone was anxious to taste the new crop of Glasshouse fire zucchini and was hoping to find a way to include some on the day's menu.

One of the initiatives was "Sunday Soup" sponsored by the Imperial Amerikan Aquatic Navy. The IAAN had suggested that the ladies gather the various hard drinkers and homeless reprobates that cluttered the streets on late weekend nights and bring them to the navy yard for hot soup and a warm bed. The IAAN promised to loan the ladies wagons to collect the inebriated men and to set up tents and beds so the poor souls could sleep off their night's festivities. The navy suggested that a short open water cruise would be just the thing to clear a drunken head and the city fathers were certainly in favor of decreasing the number of drunks using the city parks to sleep off their drinking binges. Wilhelmina thought that a brisk fire zucchini soup might be just the thing after a night of heavy drinking and hoped that her fellow ladies would be impressed with idea.

The rest of the day passed quickly as the members of the ladies auxiliary plotted and planned their next contribution to Imperial society. It was well after dusk when Wilhelmina remounted her trusty putterputt and made her way home. Her mind was full of details for the upcoming luncheon and the day's excitement had left her both mentally and physically exhausted. She made a quick to-do list for the kitchen and garden staff and left it for Antonio. Having dined at the club she went straight to bed vowing an early start in the morning. Tomorrow was likely to be a busy day.

When Wilhelmina woke Sunday morning she felt refreshed and invigorated.

She gazed out her window to see a dusting of snow carpeting the lawns. The sight sent a happy jolt of energy through her waking body. She flew through her morning rituals and rushed down the stairs to ensure her staff was prepared for the pending afternoon luncheon. She was surprised to find the kitchen empty.

"Maria must be picking vegetables from the garden," mused Wilhelmina as she stirred an unattended pot on the stove. After a quick taste she covered the pot and headed out to the Glasshouse to ensure that it was ready for the day's guests.

The glassed in breezeway lead straight to the high domed gazebo so Wilhelmina decided to make sure her cats were fed and that the elaborate iron table was set for guests. She was miffed to find that the table setting was in complete disarray and that no staff members were insight. As she stood with her hands on hips surveying the scattered place settings and wondering if it was a clumsy staff member or a hungry cat that had made the mess she felt a gentle cool breeze caress her cheek.

It took her brain a minute to switch from appreciation to the realization that she should certainly NOT be feeling a cool breeze in the gazebo. She turned to make sure that she had closed the heavy breezeway door behind her and then began scanning the gazebo.

She let her nose follow the scent of snow until she found the breach in the gazebo wall. Several glass panes were missing from a patch near the ground and the iron framework that held them was bent and broken.

"Someone has vandalized my gazebo!" shouted the enraged little woman. It wouldn't be the first time someone had tried to break into the Glasshouse to steal vegetables or botanical secrets, and Wilhelmina was now quite angry.

Just as she turned away from the breach she spied something on the other side of the broken glass. She stepped closer to the hole in the glass paned wall and looked out to see a shape partially covered by the new fallen snow. Was she seeing a dog or perhaps a deer?

The shape was hard to identify and as she peered closer she realized the broken spars of the gazebo were pointing out toward the concealed shape. Whatever it was it looked…damaged and Wilhelmina realized some kind of animal must have gotten into the Glasshouse and then tried to smash it's way out again. Her anger melted away as pity for the poor creature replaced it.

"Still, we can't have cold air blowing in all day," Wilhelmina said out loud. "Antonio is going to have to get this repaired immediately before my poor plants die and my babies…" Wilhelmina then realized she didn't hear her cats. "Oh dear, if they've gone out in this weather!" Wilhelmina cried, now thoroughly anxious and frantic to find assistance.

She checked to ensure the doors to breezeway of the Glasshouse were secured and as an afterthought locked both wing doors from the gazebo side. She entered the south wing and closed the heavy door behind her as she passed, so that no one could open it to the cold air blowing in from the breached gazebo. The door at the far end of the south wing was now the only way out of this wing of the Glasshouse, and Wilhelmina congratulated herself on her own quick thinking as she started down the main aisle to look for her staff.

It bothered her that she neither heard nor saw anyone working. Where was everyone this morning? Even on a Sunday there should be half a dozen staff members working on various projects. The collection of trees and high plants along with the hanging planters and tiered planning beds made it hard to see the hothouse interior, and Wilhelmina's calls for assistance were going unanswered. She continued walking toward the far exit, calling "Helloooooo" in her best Imperial lady voice.

A loud rustling came from a behind a section of boozeberry bushes and Wilhelmina crouched down to peer through the big purple berries. The bush exploded into squalling thrashing chaos as two of her feral cats came leaping out from the bush knocking Wilhelmina back on her rump. The poor little woman sat shocked and unmoving as something…else…followed the fleeing berry stained cats through the heavy bushes.

Wilhelmina had never seen anything like the thing that landed at her feet gazing down at her. A shiny dark green head with enormous bulging black eyes sat perched on an upright body covered in a bug-like carapace. Two sets of sickle-ended arms like those of a praying mantis were twitching and pawing at the air. The bug thing was crouched and hunched but would easily be as tall as a man if it was standing up straight.

As the creature turned towards Wilhelmina it opened a fanged mouth flanked by formidable looking mandibles. Hanging from this terrible mouth was a coon cat's tail and Wilhelmina watched in stunned horror as the creature tilted its head back and slurped up the tail like a furry noodle. The reality that she had just seen one of her favorite cats being eaten by a very large bug slammed home in Wilhelmina's brain and she opened her mouth in a scream that rivaled yesterday's air raid sirens.

The sickle-armed bug horror recoiled into the boozeberry bush from the siren-like scream and Wilhelmina scrambled to her feet. She took several running steps back towards the gazebo before remembering that she'd locked it from the other side and instead dove through a stand of chili apple trees. She headed towards the far exit and glanced over her shoulder hoping to bypass the big bug. She stumbled over something soft and squishy, and looked down to see that she had run through the remains of a man's torso. The bloody and torn brown skinned torso was covered in the bloody and torn remains of a white gardeners uniform, and Wilhelmina stifled a scream.

She stood frozen looking around the mini orchard and saw other bits and pieces of person littering the ground. Part of her brain registered that were not necessarily all parts of the same person. The chili apple orchard seemed to be sprinkled with feet, hands and various chewed parts of people.

Another smaller bug thing, this one just over three feet tall was crouched by a fruit tree busily gnawing on a man's head. Even as the creature ate it seemed to swell and puff and Wilhelmina could hear a cracking sound. Wilhelmina watched as the bug's skin split, and the creature grew another several inches tall as it fed on the dead gardener's head. Moving as quietly as she could Wilhelmina picked her way between the trees and body parts heading away from the growing monster.

Something thrashed back near the boozeberry bushes and a loud crash sounded off to Wilhelmina's right near a section of peppermato plant trays. She willed her legs to work faster and she started to move down the aisle towards the far door. Somewhere a mechanical timer clicked and steam powered gears engaged the overhead water pipes filling the air with a heavy misting rain. The mist suddenly hid everything, but Wilhelmina clearly heard the hissing pipes answered by several sinister throaty hisses.

Wilhelmina had never really minded the tropical atmosphere of the Glasshouse but now the air felt close and choking and the heat was sapping her strength minute by minute as she snuck down the length of the hothouse wing. The once familiar garden had become a terrifying tropical hell, and Wilhelmina almost screamed as she hurried for the exit.

Wilhelmina kept searching for a tool or a weapon she could use to defend herself. Her eyes snapped left and right looking for a shovel or trowel-anything that might dissuade one of the bug things from eating her head. The Glasshouse staff was meticulous though and never left tools lying around. Now those same meticulous gardeners were littering the hothouse floor in gory little piles. Wilhelmina realized that she would actually have to search the corpse of a dead gardener if she hoped to find any kind of weapon and she was horrified as she wondered who's corpse she'd find next. She didn't dare call out for help. She could hear a choir of throaty hisses calling back and forth behind her, and she imagined the big bug eyed monsters talking to each other and discussing whom they were planning on eating next.

Even as part of her mind was looking for a way out another part was analyzing what was happening. There were giant bugs in the Glasshouse eating her gardeners and her beloved cats. There certainly had been other incidents where strange and exotic bugs had hitched a ride on some tropical plant to cause problems in the hothouse but never ones of this magnitude. The realization of just how… inconvenient…these things actually were was keeping Wilhelmina from losing her mind to terror. As horrible as it was that some of her staff and pets were dead, these big nasty bugs were really ruining her day, and this was making Lady Citizen Wigglebottom madder by the minute.

Her anger kept her from panicking and instead she moved as quickly as she could without blundering into the various pots and planters that crowed the hothouse floor. She passed a potting station, a long low table covered in sacks of dirt and rows of small clay pots. In the center of the table were several of the big pea pods she had found in the mysterious crates addressed to her father. The pods were split and empty, the big pea shaped bulges now missing from each pod. The only clue that something …bad.. had occurred was the severed arm holding a small potting trowel that lay draped across the empty pods. It only took a moment for Wilhelmina's brain to make the connection between the dark green pod and the dark green bug she'd seen eating her cat.

She pulled the trowel from the dead hand and clutched it to her chest. A sharp "snap" sounded somewhere on the other side of a row of low hanging planters, and Wilhelmina crouched low to see under them.

She could see something …several somethings actually, pushing their way through a section of tall cane plants in the center of the Glasshouse causing the tall stalks to thrash and sway.

The big bugs were pacing her as she hurried toward the farthest glass wall of the long hothouse wing. The panes of glass were only a foot square and the framework was steel, but perhaps she could knock out a couple panes and bend the frame to make a hole like the one in the gazebo…

he was so focused on this new line of thought, that the sudden bang on the outside glass made her shriek despite her caution. A terrified brown-skinned face pressed against the outside glass and a dirty fist began rapidly knocking on the pane trying to get her attention.

Wilhelmina could see blood on the gardener's face as his eyes locked on hers and he tried to yell something through the heavy glass. "Well at least someone made it to safety," Wilhelmina said out loud, and then immediately regretted having made any noise that might attract the hunting bugs. She glanced fearfully over her shoulder then hurried to the glass wall. She pressed her face against the pane across from her gardener and spoke in a voice as loud as she dared, "Get Antonio and bring guns!"

The bloody faced gardener was obviously distraught and he kept banging on the glass with his fist and yelling to her in Waro-spanish. Wilhelmina repeated herself several times, trying to pitch her voice loud enough to be heard over his knocking but not loud enough to carry deeper into the Glasshouse. She also wished he'd stop making so much noise. She was afraid his knocking and shouting would draw deadly attention. Wilhelmina brought her finger to her lips to shush her frightened employee as she tried again to instruct him to bring help. She was only partially successful. The mans eyes finally showed recognition and he started nodding his head in understanding when a loud warbling hiss sounded immediately behind Wilhelmina.

The frightened man began shouting and slamming the glass again in warning and Wilhelmina didn't even bother to turn around before plunging down the aisle away from the noise. She heard something hit the glass wall behind her in a shrieking, hissing bang but she did not hear the tell tale sound of breaking glass. Unlike the panes of the gazebo the main hothouse walls were inches thick, and she was now glad she hadn't wasted time trying to break her way out. A sound like a huge glass cutter screeched behind her and she could imagine one of the big mantis-like arms clawing at the glass, but she still didn't waste time turning around to look. Instead she moved quickly and steadily along the aisle toward the far end of the Glasshouse and the south wing door.

The little Imperial lady ducked under a row of planters into the next aisle. She then cut though a plot of tall cane plants as she tried to conceal herself but she could hear at least two of the hissing creatures now following her as she fled. A small wooden table sat at the end of the cane plot and lying on the table was a broad bladed cane knife. Willhemina swapped the planting trowel with the arm-long cane knife and gave the flat bladed machete a couple tentative swings. Again, the thought that these…things…had killed her people in her home drove down the terror of being hunted by giant man-eating bugs from... whereever.

Wilhelmina could see the door that led out of the Glasshouse now. From the edge of the cane plot the glasshouse floor opened onto several yards of flat wooden tables. This was where the picked produce was kept before being shipped out to imperial shops and kitchens, and Wilhelmina realized there was nowhere to hide once she stepped out amongst the tables. Except maybe under the tables.

The mistress of Wigglebottom Manor dropped to her hands and knees and scooted under the first row of produce tables as fast as she could. The tables were fairly low and it was only the fact that Wilhelmina was not particularly tall herself that allowed her to keep her head up while she crawled her way toward freedom. She had to navigate around bushel baskets, storage pots and sacks of fertilizer, and her still holding the cane knife wasn't helping. She was debating dropping the big blade when something thumped on the table above her.

Wilhelmina shrieked. She hadn't meant to shriek. She tried not to shriek, but the shriek just came out on its own. The table above her splintered and split as two huge, green sickles plunged through the wood just over her head. She shrieked again. The two mantis arms pulled back and struck again and again hacking their way through the heavy table like a pair of woodsmen's axes.

Sacks and pots blocked her path and Wilhelmina was forced to roll out from under the disintegrating table. She popped up like a cork and came face to face with a bug-eyed nightmare. The huge man-bug was crouched on the table with all four sickle arms buried into the wood and it leaned out towards Wilhelmina's face opening it's dripping jaws and razor sharp mandibles wide in a long slow hiss. Wilhelmina let out her third terrified shriek and buried the cane knife in the creature's head.

Both Wilhelmina and the creature stayed frozen for several seconds as dark ichor spurted from the thing's ruptured head, then with a loud sucking sound the big bug-man fell off the blade and slumped dead onto the table. Wilhelmina stood transfixed, the dripping blade still in her hands as she stared at the sickle-armed horror that was now leaking all over her produce table.

"Ha!" shouted the little woman.

HISSSSSS! Another man-bug from the other side of the ruined table hissed like a ruptured boiler as it crouched and readied to leap.

"Crap!" shouted Wilhelmina and she turned and sprinted toward the Glasshouse door. The bug thing was faster though and it leapt over a long table of fire zucchinis to land between Wilhelmina and the exit. Citizen Lady Wigglebottom charged and with all her strength she swung the dripping cane knife at the creature's head. With an almost casual flick one big sickle arm swatted the knife away and then the creature craned its long neck forward and hissed.

Wilhelmina scrambled backward, groping blindly behind her for something to protect herself. Her hand closed on the long club-like shape of a fire zucchini and she swung the heavy vegetable in front of her like a sword. The bug swatted at the nearly three foot vegetable, but Wilhelmina sidestepped the sickle arm and with a high pitched shout clubbed the creature in the eye. The bug gave a warbling hiss and shot it's head forward, biting the end off Wilhelmina's zucchini club. Wilhelmina swung again and this time the creature bit the rest of her club in half.

The deadly man-bug advanced on the mistress of Wigglebottom Manor with its four arms thrown out wide and its head craned forward. Wilhelmina threw the zucchini stump at the creature's face and then snatched at the various pieces of produce arrayed on the table beside her. As the beast advanced, Wilhelmina grabbed and threw whatever her hands found. She hurled a peppermato at the beast's eye and a handful of volcano peppers in its face. The sickle armed horror swatted and snapped at the vegetable projectiles biting some right out of the air. The beast took a hopping step closer to Wilhelmina. And then it stopped.

Lady Citizen Wigglebottom had reached the end of the table and the last piece of produce. Her small hand fell on the hard rind of a magma melon and she pulled the heavy fruit to her chest. She raised the magma melon over her head and prepared to hurl it at the bug thing when she realized the creature was standing still and rapidly blinking it's big bug eyes. The man-bug straightened from its looming crouch, it's eyes blinking faster and faster and then doubled over onto the ground.

The now familiar hiss came out as a pathetic wheeze as the creature rolled itself into a ball on the ground. Wilhelmina, the magma melon still raised above her head stepped closer to the stricken creature. The beast gave another wheeze and began coughing up dark red fluid. Its body began to convulse and then it laid still, its mouth wide and eyes closed. Wilhelmina nudged the still creature with her toe and then lowered the heavy melon. The bug thing was dead.

"Stupid foreign bug can't stomach good ole' Imperial spice!" shouted Wilhelmina triumphantly. Obviously the mix of Glasshouse vegetables had proven lethal the giant bugs from…wherever. Wilhelmina calmly walked the distance to the south wing door, the magma melon tucked under her arm. Just as she reached it the door flew open and Antonio shoved the twin barrels of a shotgun into the Glasshouse.

"Oh mistress, we are so happy you are safe. When Inigo told me what was in here…" The relief in Antonio's voice touched Wilhelmina and behind him she could see the relieved faces of several other staff members gathered and armed with a collection of guns and farm tools ready to charge into the hothouse. She shooed them back with a casual wave of her hand.

"I think everything is going to be fine, we just need…OOF!" Wilhelmina was cut off as something slammed into her back and sent her sprawling out into the yard to land face first in the snow.

"Don't shoot! You will hit the mistress," yelled Antonio as the army of armed house staff scattered backward from the Glasshouse door. The big Waro-Spaniard reversed the shotgun and slammed the butt down on the four-foot bug that had leapt upon his mistress' back swatting it off into the snow.

Wilhelmina scrambled to her feet, cursing like a dockworker, scooped up the fallen melon and raised it over her head again. Her house staff swarmed around her protectively and aimed every weapon they had at the bug thing in the snow. The bug thing didn't move.

It tried to move, but it seemed that even as the staff of Wigglebottom Manor watched the bug thing seized up, unable to rise out of the snowdrift. "So you don't like spicy food and you don't like the cold," sneered Wilhelmina. "Welcome to Harrisfyord you big creepy…creeper!"

Another of the bug things stuck it's head out of the Glasshouse door, gave a long sibilant hiss and then retreated from the cold November air back into the hothouse. Two of the manor's gardeners rushed through the door and Wilhelmina heard the loud crash of shotgun blasts before the two men reemerged, smiling.

"I want this to be organized before we just go charging in," said Willhemina in her best authoritative voice. She had come out alive and successful from her first real battle and the Viking blood of her ancestors was singing in her veins. Now she would lead her troops to cleanse the family holdings of these disgusting invaders. Wilhelmina wondered triumphantly what would be the proper hat for such an occasion as she snugged her melon firmly under her arm.

"What should we do with those?" asked a shaken staffer. Wilhelmina followed the man's shaking finger. Lying beside the Glasshouse wall was a stack of giant green pea pods. The shaking gardener turned worried eyes on his mistress and continued. "The Berthmaster say they find these scattered all over the beach from the empty airship. He say the broken crates have your father's name on them so he bring them here this morning." The mob of armed gardeners turned their weapons on the pile of big peas.

No invading creatures were going to gain a foothold in her empire while Lady Citizen Wilhelmina Wigglebottom was on duty. "First we clear out the Glasshouse boys, then we make pea soup!"

End

CITIZEN DEFEATS ALIEN MENACE WITH ZUCCHINI!

Miss Wilhemina Wigglebottom defends here garden against an invading horde of Venusian Blatt Bugs armed only with her annual harvest of prize winning vegitables.

Once again the spirit of the imperial citizen shines forth to burn away the shadowy menace of foreign influence. This time the evils of malevolence come not from the depraved shores of France or the pirate coves of the decedent Carib, but from the fetid jungle of the green hell of Venus! Venus, a hundred shades of green and a thousand ways to die! The ministry of agriculture and preferential trade announced that a brood of horrific Venutian blatt bugs apparently stowed away on Her Majesty's Imperial trade blimp the "Lady Bertha", and disgorged directly over the lovely gardens of Miss Wilhelmina Wigglebottom of 12 Buckle St, Harrisfyord, Pennsyltucky. Rightfully dismayed at the wanton destruction of her prized gourd harvest, Miss Wigglebottom took up arms against these foreign interlopers, and showed them just what a proper lady of the Empire can accomplish with courage, grit and a Pennsyltucky Zucchini. Wearing only... (cont.)

Cavalcade of Fancy Ladies

CAVALCADE OF FANCY LADIES

By Brian D. Thomas

It's strange that an empire that so hates foreigners, guards its borders with jingoistic zeal and restricts even basic rights exclusively to its free residents and full citizens should offer even temporary hospitality to gypsies. Wandering travelers and foreign merchants are subject to official scrutiny and general mistrust, but dress them in colorful clothes and let them entertain with exotic music and dance and any town in Imperial Amerika will freely open its gates to them for five days. Five days for any band of Romani dancers and fortunetellers to ply their trade. Five days for any band of Chinese Boxer acrobats and musicians to dazzle their audience. Five days for a circus of exotic and alien animals to thrill the crowds. Five days for any caravan or airship of peddlers, tinkers, entertainers or mystics to distract the imperial citizenry with their exotic ways.

On the sixth day a squadron of Imperial pony soldiers rode in with sabers drawn and that hospitality would end, but for five days any band of travelers was safe…assuming they put on a good show.

The Cavalcade Of Fancy Ladies was known throughout the Empire for putting on a very "good" show. The dancers of The Cavalcade rivaled Romani dancers, outperformed Boxer acrobats and sold goods…and secrets… that other traveling merchants only dreamed of. The Cavalcade Of Fancy Ladies were not Gypsy, nor Boxer nor members of any other culture…that they ever admitted to, and they had connections not only in Imperial Amerika, but across the other continents of the world that allowed them to travel roads and cross skylocks with a freedom that others envied.

The Cavalcade performed for royalty and commoner alike, and many a young girl dreamed of running away with The Cavalcade to live with the beautiful, mysterious "Sisters" to live a life of adored performance and adventure.

Little did they know...

The Cavalcade of Fancy Ladies airship arrived in the night. The Cavalcade set up its elaborate tents and stages in the central town park without ever waking the sleeping community, and in the morning the Imperial town of Bjornston woke like Yule morning to find that a gift had arrived. Citizens and residents lined up outside the high, thick canvas walls of the encampment waiting for a peak at the mysteries inside. Once the Cavalcade opened its gates the folk of Bjornston were not disappointed.

Dozens of beautiful women in fantastic costumes drifted throughout the camp, dancing, signing, juggling and basically being fabulous. Some women sat by open stalls selling spices, exotic oils and scented herbs while others displayed bolts of gossamer silks or delicate jewelry of enticing, alien design. The giant and silent robe-shrouded guards in their elaborate masks, arms and weapons hidden in the folds of their clothing did nothing to dispel the magic of the camp, and the few who noticed them only briefly wondered what dwelt under the seven foot tall visage before some more pleasant sight or smell called their attention away.

While the women of the Bjornston town marveled over the goods of the Cavalcade the menfolk marveled over the performers. The Cavalcade Of Fancy Ladies oozed an erotic perfume that called to the men and kept them riveted in their seats inside the main performer's tent, whispering to their deepest desires even as it called for them to empty their wallets at the feet of the swaying, swirling dancers. As night fell the town's children were hustled away from the cages of fantastic beasts and back to their beds as casks and kegs of potent spirits were opened and served at candle lit tables and in shadowed corners.

Night time was the true time of The Cavalcade Of Fancy Ladies and when they conducted their true business.

Sister Lillette gazed out from the park and considered the large stone home of one Dr. Homer Malphurgis. It was a solidly built three story stone affair overlooking the far end of the park where the Cavalcade had set up shop. The house boasted an ivy covered low wall, a cobbled walkway, trellised gardens… and barred windows.

This last feature was the one that most caught the sultry dancer's eye, as it was the one feature that was likely to make this job that much more taxing. On the other hand, the low wall would provide splendid cover from watchful eyes, and the park provided deep shadows from the gas streetlights. The Cavalcade's newest employer had also provided a detailed floor plan of the house so perhaps the bars would only be a slight inconvenience after all.

Sister Lillette generally favored jewel toned silks and low cut necklines to draw appreciative eyes where she wanted them drawn but tonight she was wearing a deep blue short caftan and a hooded cloak specifically meant not to draw unwelcomed eyes. Gone was the glittering array of jewelry and rings. The belt of coins and baubles that usually encircled her slender waist was also gone, and a many-pocketed sash now replaced it. High soft boots replaced her brightly colored dance slippers and the total effect transformed her normal appearance of an exotic, enticing dancer into one of, in most respects…a thief…which tonight was a fairly accurate representation.

"Are you sure you don't want a few more of the sisters?" Sister Lillette turned her head to regard her companion even as she considered the question.

"No," she replied. "This should only take the two of us, and besides he's just one old man. If you just blink those big blue eyes at him a few times he'll probably tell us everything our employer wants to know." Lillette pulled her caftan open a bit exposing a glimpse of ample cleavage and whispered in a husky tone, "…look into my eyes!"

Sister Dolcina giggled into her hand as she crept closer to her fellow Cavalcade Lady. Though she was taller and "fuller" than her caravan sister Dolcina moved more quietly than her companion as she stepped closer to get a better look at their target. Sister Dolcina wore an outfit similar to her partner's and both women pulled veils up over their faces, as they quickly crossed from the edge of the park to mansion's wall.

It was late, much later than the women had intended, but people had been lingering along the street well past dusk. A gaggle of pram-pushing young mothers had stood gossiping in front of the house for hours. A little Asian girl wearing shiny shoes and a big pink bow had spent the evening admiring an old man's cart of brightly colored rubber balloons while scolding a kitten, keeping both the old man and the kitten out on the street well past the time when little girls, old men and kittens should be home enjoying supper.

Cavalcade watchers had notified Sister Lillette when the street had finally cleared and the two women glided through the deep shadows of the park like a pair of graceful dark spirits while the rest of the Cavalcade camp distracted any lingering nightlife. Now Sister Lillette and Sister Dolcina of The Cavalcade Of Fancy Ladies danced around the pools of light cast by the streetlights and flowed up and over the ivy covered wall like wraiths.

The two women stealthily circled the house, examining the windows on all three floors. It was close to eleven pm now and the only lights visible in the house were on the third floor, where according to the provided floor plan, Dr. Malphurgis kept his study.

The Cavalcade's instructions were rather straightforward: Abduct Dr. Malphurgis, and recover his research materials. If neither of these were possible the Fancy Ladies was instructed to destroy the doctor and all records of his current work. The sisters of the Cavalcade didn't know what that work was, but they were not paid to know. They were paid to perform.

At the back of the house, tucked between the trellises, Sister Lillette found what she wanted- a pair of storm doors to the basement. The doors were wood and a quick peek through a barred basement window showed the single bolt on the inside face of the doors. Lillette shut her piercing blue eyes as the location of the bolt was burned onto her mind's eye. With the location of the bolt now fixed in her head, she moved to the door and set out her tools.

Lillette pulled what looked like a constable's baton from the folds of her caftan. The wand was dark and seemed to be made of heavy rubber. She then drew a small but complex looking device from a pocket inside her sash. Light from the moon winked off the teeth of a tiny saw blade. Lillette held the wand, and flicked open a cap at the base of the handle with one well manicured thumb. She checked the tiny gauge there and then plugged the clever little omni tool's cord into the exposed socket. She gave the wand two gentle shakes. There came the familiar scent of ozone and the omni tool hummed to life.

Purring saw blade met wooden door and purring saw blade won the contest. Midway through cutting the hole the blade seemed to slow it's progress, and Lillette gave the black wand a sharp tap. The tool's power surged, and a section of the door fell into the darkness.

"You know smacking it like that just makes it angry," commented Dolcina dryly.

"That's pretty much the point," replied Lillette smugly as she unplugged the omni tool and placed it back into her sash. Without further comment she reached into the hole and threw the bolt, then lifted the storm door and the two Fancy Ladies quietly entered the doctor's basement.

The basement of Dr. Malphurgis' house was a cavernous space. The basement was not completely dark. Stacks of boxes and crates were everywhere and numerous machines crowded the huge room. The various pieces of machinery quietly hummed and glowed softly. Lillette spotted one big crate was full of bullets.

As Sister Dolcina's eyes adjusted to the low light she stopped short, grabbed her companion's arm and gave a little gasp.

A giant was hanging from the ceiling of the basement.

As the two shapely burglars crept closer they could see it wasn't a giant man, it was a giant suit. It had a round blunt head and oversized thick limbs. It looked vaguely like a deep-sea diving suit, though both women doubted there was much call for deep sea diving in Bjornston Harbor. The enormous suit was hanging from chains with its arms forward, and it reminded Sister Dolcina of a giant discarded puppet. She shuddered. Sister Dolcina hated puppets.

Lillette moved around behind the dangling metal suit and saw a tangle of pipes and wires all terminating at a point on its back.

"Something's missing," she whispered.

The various pipes and wires looked like they were meant to plug into something, and a space for that something was now obvious in the center of the suit's back. Lillette glanced around. Although the basement was scattered with crates and equipment nothing looked like it fit the puzzle. Any further investigation was cut short as the basement gaslights were suddenly dialed up.

Like performers in a choreographed dance the two women simultaneously dropped to the floor behind a large machine that periodically went meep. From this beeping hiding spot they watched a young man descend the basement steps. The lad was totally absorbed with the bulky camera he was carrying, and didn't look up until he was well into the basement workshop. Lillette nudged her companion as she considered the young man's details.

Dark hair peeked out past pale skin from under a knit cap, and a bulky wool coat hid his clothing. Sister Lillette could easily detect the scent of hair palmate as well as a smoky fish smell. *Herring and hair oil,* thought the Fancy Lady, *a Russian.*

The young Russian photographer moved around to the back of the suit, his camera flash strobing as he recorded the details of the hanging metal giant. When the young Russian's back was to her, Lillette rose from her crouch, drew her baton and flicked a catch on the handle. The outer black rubber sheath fell to the floor exposing the core of the wand.

If the young Russian had turned around he would have seen that Lillette now held a black rubber handle fitted to a sixteen-inch brass and metal cage. If the young Russian had looked even closer he would have seen the creature that resided within the brass and metal cage. He would have seen the green and blue-pebbled skin, the snake like body, and the strangely intelligent yet wholly evil eyes.

If the young Russian had turned around he would have seen an actual Venusian Tesla Adder trapped in an Adder Wand, but unfortunately for him he never turned around. Lillette gave the wand a sharp snap of her wrist, then stepped forward and rapped the wand against the base of the young Russian's skull. This time the scent of ozone was followed by a loud POP and the smell of cooking bacon as the young Russian fell soundlessly into Dolcina's waiting arms.

The Tesla Adder was just one of the many deadly creatures of Venus. What was the saying- 'Venus, a thousand shades of green and a million ways to die.' This was hardly the only native of Venus that lived in the Cavalcade nor was it arguably the most dangerous, but it was one of the more useful ones.

The Tesla Adder produced an electrical discharge whenever it was annoyed.

The best way to really annoy one was to flick its fourteen-inch body down a sixteen-inch tube and slam it snoot first into the tip. The problem was, the more annoyed a Tesla Adder became the stronger the discharge.

On a really bad day an angry adult Tesla Adder could electrocute an elephant.

"I told you it was going to get angry," scolded Dolcina., "Instead of shocking him you fried the poor boy's brain."

Lillette gave a little shrug as she patted the dead man's pockets. The man represented a complication. She highly doubted Dr Malphurgis made a habit of having Russian houseguests, especially since the Czar had declared war on 'Amerikan Imperial aggressors.' She also doubted the good doctor had given permission for photographs of his large metal basement puppet, so unfortunately this meant there was probably a second performance troupe trying to take the stage.

Dolcina dragged the dead photographer behind a palette of boxes, as Lillette slid the black rubber sheath over the now sleeping alien eel's cage.

"You know it's just going to sleep for hours now after a jolt that strong," complained Dolcina as she rather effortlessly dragged the dead weight of the dead man. "You really should be nicer to it."

"Well I can't exactly pet it now can I!" hissed Lillette in response.

With the lights now dialed up The Fancy Ladies could see more of the basement's interior. Tables were arrayed with half built devices, and schematics and blueprints cluttered every surface. Crates of ammunition lay open and spilled onto the floor, and tools lay everywhere. Overall it looked like an army of people had recently been working in the space. The sisters even spied empty cups and discarded Greeble tins.

Lillette hated clutter and her opinion of Dr. Malphurgis dipped significantly. It was one of the many reasons she did not allow men to stay with the Caravan. Men meant clutter.

The women carefully crossed the basement floor avoiding the mess and had almost reached the flight of stairs heading up when they heard another set of footsteps descending the stone steps.

Lillette shoved the now dormant adder wand back into her jacket as Dolcina stepped around her and pulled a small silver pipe from her sleeve. Dolcina waited until she was sure it was just a single person coming down the stairs, then brought the puff pipe up in a straight-armed stance and squeezed the trigger.

The small fluted needle in the puff pipe benefited from another strange creature, though this one was from dear old Earth. The venom that lay in the grooves of the dart came from a sea urchin of the South Seas, and the little compressed-air dart thrower could also play a merry tune if you knew where to put, and not put, your lips.

The second Russian had just enough time to look confused before the venom clamped an iron fist on his muscles and then his lungs. The man teetered for a moment then fell onto his back-his body locked in a frozen pose like a cigar store skrealing.

Dolcina looked down into his frozen face and gave a little sigh. The man's mouth was open but no air was going in and his wide opened eyes began to roll back into his head. Dolcina tilted her head to the side considering the dying man then reached into her sash and drew out small needle. Lillette gave a disgusted little huff as Dolcina pricked the side of the man's neck with the needle. She waited a moment then pressed firmly on the man's chest in three sharp pushes. The man gave a loud gasp of air and then passed out.

"See, nobody died," said Dolcina as she smiled and stood.

"It's early, and there's probably more of them," replied Lillette curtly. "Check his shoes."

Dolcina looked at the man's shoes, then his jacket and his hands. He had a heavy coat, callused hands and gum-soled shoes. She glared up the stairs. "We need to move sister," the curvy woman growled, and together they hurried up the stairs.

The first floor was dark but the Sisters could see light and hear voices and music coming from the third floor. There was a gorgeous maple spiral staircase leading to the upper floors, and the two women wasted no time in ascending. As Lillette wound around and up, she pulled a cloth patch from another of her many sash pockets and let her hand trail up the stair rail. The patch left a light grey film on the rail as the two quietly climbed the stairs. Dolcina dipped into her own sash and paused every so often to drop something on the step.

Two huge oak doors dominated the third floor, and Lillette knew this must be the doctor's study. The doors were slightly open and somewhere inside a victrola was playing something classical and French. Moving in a dance-like glide the two crossed the third floor landing, crept to the open doors and listened. They could both hear voices speaking Russian, and a strong draft of cool night air was blowing on their faces from the study.

Lillette eased around the door just as a man shouted happily in Russian, "I've found it cousins!"

She saw three men in long wool coats and knit caps. One man was excitedly waving around a small leather book. Another was holding a bulging knapsack, obviously filled with books and rolled papers, and was trying to undo the buckles to stuff this new find inside.

"We may not have found the Doctor but we have his personal journal. That should mean something!" said one of the burly Russians. All three men clustered around the small leather book.

The night breeze grew stronger and Dolcina poked her head over Lillette's shoulder, looked around, and then up. "That's what I was afraid of," she muttered as her eyes registered the gaping hole in the ceiling of the study.

They could both see the night sky through the hole. They could also see the doubled rope leading down from the hole to the large metal pulley anchored to the study floor. The other ends of the double rope disappeared through the hole and into the night sky.

A series of straps and belts were attached to one of the ropes, and the third Russian began undoing buckles and gesturing to his companion with the knapsack.

The two sisters exchanged a silent glance and then nodded in unison. The adder wand would be useless for a few hours yet, and the heavy coats would seriously reduce the effectiveness of a puff pipe. The Fancy Ladies reached into their caftans and each withdrew an elaborate clockwork pistol.

Each pistol had an oversized cylinder and a long narrow barrel. The weapons were covered in silver chasing and had pearl inlay handle grips, making the delicate Vickers Clockwork Defender very much a "ladies" gun.

"We need them to stay grouped together," whispered Lillette. "There's too much cover in there for us to get them all on the first volley if they scatter," she added hastily.

Hiding by the door Dolcina lifted the little silver handle that ran atop the gun's barrel and gave the crank three full turns. Now properly wound, she replaced the lever and turned to look at her sister.

"Stay behind me," whispered Dolcina and without waiting for a response she straightened up and walked boldly into the library. Lillette gave a little squawk and rush in behind her caravan sister.

One of the Russians was cramming another book into the knapsack, now rigged to the hoist, when he spotted Dolcina. He shouted something and pointed as the Fancy Lady threw off her cloak and ripped open her caftan.

"Hello boys! Look into my eyes!"

Dolcina was not wearing anything under her caftan and every set of male eyes in the room was now glued exactly where Dolcina wanted them. It took Lillette a moment to understand what had happened before she scooted under her sister's out flung arms and opened fire on the stunned Russians. Dolcina shot the third man- who never looked up from her exposed chest even as he died. Dolcina was slightly flattered by that.

As Dolcina closed her top and scooped up her cloak Lillette hurried into the library. The heavy coats, caps and the gum soled boots on the dead men all meant one thing- these men were Russian Airmen. That also meant the rope attached to the pulley in the floor didn't just go to the roof. It went to a black painted airship hovering somewhere above the house that in any minute would send more men down to investigate the gunfire. The Vickers pistols were not exactly quiet weapons, and the Fancy Ladies had little time to act.

Sister Lillette crossed the room and opened the daggling knapsack. She quickly pulled out the books and papers and dumped them on a table. She then pulled a bulky satchel from the small of her back and ripped open the flap. She and Dolcina had flipped a coin to see who would be the one to carry the satchel and Lillette was glad to finally have the thing off her back.

Lillette pulled the bomb from the satchel.

She grabbed the dull black cap and gave the screw a full turn, then quickly stuffed the lethal bundle into the now empty knapsack. She grabbed a few random books from a nearby shelf, placed them....carefully...on top of the now armed bomb and tied the knapsack closed.

Lillette paused for a moment then gave the dangling rope three sharp tugs. She had no idea what signal the Russians used on the rope lift, but in her experience if you tugged on anything hanging three good times something usually happened. A few heartbeats later the pulley began to rattle as the rope was reeled up into the night sky.

Dolcina took the empty bomb satchel and stuffed the books and papers into it then slung it over her shoulder. Lillette bent over one of the dead Russians and pried the little leather journal he had been so happy find out of his stiff dead hands. She stuffed it into the small of her back where the bomb had been and was happy to replace that lethal thing with the little book.

She patted the dead Russian on the cheek, "Sorry you missed your appointment with the good doctor. I think you are a little to far gone for his medical advice, but I will give him your regards when I catch up to him." Dolcina gave her sister a stern look as they bolted from the room.

As they crossed the threshold into the hall the smell of hair cream filled Lillette's nose causing her to turn her last step into a forward tumble. The hatchet that was aimed at her head missed, and buried itself into the doorframe rather than her delicate skull.

Dolcina slammed her open palm into the nose of the man - yet another Russian in a wool coat, who was desperately trying to pull his hatchet from the doorframe, and he stumbled backward bleeding and cursing. Lillette came out of her tumble and threw a spinning kick into the small of his back as Dolcina threw a front kick into his stomach.

The kicks drove the air from the Russian's lungs, but the big Slav refused to go down. Abandoning his hatchet the Airman pulled a knife from his belt and took a swipe at Dolcina.

"We don't have time to play sister," shouted Lillette. "Just kill him and let's go!"

Dolcina brought her leg straight up over her head and then down on the man's knife hand, knocking the weapon away before slamming him again in the face with a palm strike. As the man finally went down, Dolcina leapt past her sister and like a cowgirl vaulting onto her horse she straddled the stair rail.

"Then lets go sister," and Dolcina began a fast slide down and around the spiral stair rail towards the ground floor.

Lillette mounted the stair rail and the graphite powder she'd spread on the railing on the way up now sped her all the faster back down. The two women screamed like little girls as they flew.

The bleeding big Russian staggered to his feet and tried to follow down the stairs, stepped on the glass marbles Dolcina had seeded on the steps on her way up and began his own speedy descent down the staircase. He also screamed like a little girl.

The two dancers landed like, well, dancers, when they hit the ground floor and turned to watch the battered Russian tumble down the last few steps. Even Lillette winced in sympathy for the man. Neither woman moved to cause him further pain. Bleeding and broken he was no longer a complication.

Lillette turned and carefully opened the front door. Seeing that the way to the street was clear she motioned to her sister and the two women exited the house.

Caution gave way to speed as the two sprinted down the cobbled walkway heading for the street and the safety of the park. Dolcina tucked the knapsack full of books and papers they'd taken from the Russians under one arm and glanced back at the house. She saw a puzzled look cross her caravan sister's face and swung her head forward in time to see the huge bunch of colorful balloons blocking the gate to the street. Neither woman stopped running, and Lillette crouched low as she ran intending to go under the balloons but Dolcina gave a little shriek and lashed out at the colorful globes as she crashed through them. Dolcina hated balloons more than she hated puppets.

The balloons burst and the two women were engulfed in a cloud of billowing green gas. All coordination went out of their bodies and the women crashed to the ground. The two Fancy Ladies slipped into blackness.

Dolcina's next conscious moment was the feeling of someone tugging on her arms. She tried to push herself up but her arms had no strength, and her nose was filled with a flower smell like lavender. Little hands patted at her and rolled her onto her back. She could hear singing- a child's singing in an oriental language- and she could feel small hands prying open her grip on the knapsack full of books.

A tiny face with angled eyes and porcelain skin swam into Dolcina's view. Her vision was clearing as a tiny hand stroked her check and a little voice said, "Such pretty ladies. Thank you pretty ladies. Thank you very much."

Lillette was lying on her face and so she could only see shoes…shiny little-girl-shoes. She raised her head just enough to see a little girl with shiny shoes and a big pink bow standing from her sister holding the satchel of Dr. Malphurgis's books and papers. The little girl from the afternoon still held her balloon in one hand, and clutched the satchel in the other. The Nipponese child was singing sweetly as she skipped away with the Fancy Ladies prize. She turned and gave a friendly little wave then continued across the street toward the park.

Lillette struggled with her Vicker. She needed to load it. She needed to wind it.

She threw up instead.

Dolcina pulled herself to her knees and watched as the vendor cart emerged from the park. The way the little man, also Nipponese, was straining and puffing the cart he was pushing must weight far more than it looked.

Dolcina didn't think balloon carts were supposed to be all that heavy. A massive bunch of balloons was tied to the frame of the brightly painted cart. Realization began to fight its way through her foggy brain as the little man bowed to the child and then began to help her into some kind of harness.

She was just able to stand when the little man pulled a lever and the entire balloon bunch shot into the sky. The little girl blew a parting kiss and then her harness was jerked up into the night sky. Waving, the child and the knapsack disappeared into the dark. Without looking back the little man abandoned his empty cart and melted back into the park.

"Well," mused Dolcina as she turned to help her sister. "At least the damn balloons are all gone."

The two Fancy Ladies were just getting their bearings when they heard the air raid sirens start to wail. That would be the Russians ship. The bomb they'd sent up to the Russian Airship should have gone off by now- which was why the women had been in a hurry to leave. The burning airship had probably been spotted by some sharp-eyed block warden, and any minute now one of the neighborhood guns would blow it out of the sky. These Bjornston neighborhood watch groups were vicious. What was the Amerikan slogan-"The security of the Empire starts in the home!" Which was all the more reason for the Fancy Ladies to be moving along.

"I'm going to strangle that child with her own damn bow," growled Lillette. The smell of sick was blending with the residue of the gas and together with the fact that two professionals had just been beaten by a child, made Lillette understandably cranky.

Dolcina was about to reply when something bumped her foot. Looking down she found a small black kitten nuzzling his leg. It was the animal the little girl had been scolding this afternoon. Without a word she scooped up the kitten and held it up toward Lillette. Lillette's rage boiled away, just as Dolcina knew it would.

"Mommys got a new baby!" cooed Lillette as she nuzzled the kitten's fur with her nose. The kitten nuzzled back ignoring the smell of her recently sick new mommy. Dolcina smiled indulgently as she watched her sister before nudging her with a scraped and bleeding elbow. Realization struck that they were both now standing in the middle of the street dressed like ninjas and holding a kitten. The two women crossed back into the park giving the empty balloon cart a wide berth.

As they neared The Cavalcade camp Lillette had a thought. Cradling the kitten to her chest with one arm she felt at her back with the other. It was still there. The little oriental gas-tossing demon had not found the journal in her waistband. As she carried the kitten toward camp she opened the journal.

On a back page written in small letters was an address, a date and a phrase.

" Now what would you be doing there?" mused Lillette, and showed the page to Dolcina who raise one perfectly plucked eyebrow in response.

"Tell the others we are leaving," ordered Lillette as they entered the camp.

"It looks like our employer might get her performance after all." Smiling, the two Fancy Ladies petted the kitten and planned their next show.

CHARITY WORK

CHARITY WORK
By Raymond J. Witte

It was summer and once again I was broke. I had sunk most of my money into a string of investments that went belly up and the rest of it...well, a man has appetites and mine are more expensive than most. So I found myself holed up at a boarding house in questionable, or at least as questionable as my social standing would allow, neighborhood, with the rent due in two days and nothing to my name other than a handful of coin, a half bottle of brandy and a tin of Greeble, wondering what I was going to do to make some money when there was a knock on the door.

"Mr. Thornton, Mr. Thornton are you in there?"

Oh for god's sake, I thought to myself, *What can that imbecile of a doorman want now?* I still had two days to find the rent for next week. I needed to get rid of this cretin and quickly. I still had half a bottle of brandy left and I wanted to enjoy it in quiet.

"Yes, what is it?"

"Letter for you."

"From whom?"

"The carrier didn't say, Mr. Thornton."

"Well then enough chatter, give it here man!"

The letter slid under the door and I snatched it up, tearing the expensive looking, ornately addressed envelope open immediately. The paper within was just as pricey as the envelope and was covered in the neat, distinctly feminine, florid handwriting. It read:

Dear Mr. Thornton,

Your presence is most humbly requested for dinner in the Imperial room at Olafson Plaza. My backers and I have a task which we believe is well matched for your not inconsiderable skills. I pray that you will grace me with your company so that we may discuss the matter further and in person. If you would care to join me, I will send a carriage for you at a quarter to eight this evening.

Most sincerely,

N. Torresdale

It was certainly an interesting proposition. And a supper at Olafson Plaza beat the hell out of the half tin of Greeble that I was planning on eating for dinner. And with a woman! Suddenly, my evening was looking a lot brighter. I opened the door, planning to head to the water closet to freshen up, nearly running into the doorman, a cretin named Smith, in the process.

"What are you still doing here, Smith?"

"Mr. Thorton, I need to talk to you about the rent..."

"Which is not due for another two days."

"Not next week's rent, this week's rent Mr. Thorton, which you still haven't pai..."

"TWO DAYS SMITH, AND NOT AN INSTANT BEFORE!"

I slammed the door in his face. He wouldn't wait outside forever, and I still had another four hours. Which was good because I certainly couldn't go to Olafson Plaza like this.

Maybe Reynold's Habberdashery will give me credit for a new Thylacine fur hat, I thought to myself, *and if I can talk Sophia's into extending my line for another suit...*

Suddenly my prospects were looking up again. I spent the afternoon primping. I was able to get the hat, but Sophia's would only give me last season's style on credit. I swear the depths of my poverty in those days knew no bounds. But the hours flew by, and before I knew it there was the clack of hooves and the clattering of wheels on the cobbles in the street. I rushed out to meet the carriage, stiff-arming the protesting Smith nearly over the banister at the bottom of the stairs when he tried to stop me. I paused briefly at the door to ensure I was still neatly dressed and tidy, then stepped out calmly to meet the driver.

"Mr. Thorton, I presume?"

"I am he."

"Well, good sir, Ms. Torresdale sent me. If you are ready, shall we be off?"

"Of course my good man. Horace P. Thornton never keeps a lady waiting."

I climbed into the carriage and we were off. The contraption just screamed wealth. The seats were Martian Banth leather and covered with gold monogramming. The Door handles could only have been made from Pleiso-leviathan ivory.

Would they notice if I broke one off? I thought, *I bet Chang would pay a small fortune for it. By the gods, this carriage is worth more than that whole ratty boarding house I'm staying in. There's money to be had with this woman or I'm a love sick Frenchman.*

I became engrossed in mentally cataloging and pricing every lavish detail of the carriage. The driver interrupted me while I was contemplating what the filigree would fetch on Fleet Street.

"Here we are sir, Olafson Plaza."

Before I could react, a valet had sprung up and opened the carriage door. Now, I've moved through the circles of high society for long enough that I rarely look like a gawking yokel, but the Olafson Plaza was making it hard. The first thing I noticed was an automata string quartet, smoothly playing their instruments, their steam-lines discretely running to what I assumed to be a power plant hidden somewhere underground. Though most of the guests arrived in horse carriages as I had, there were a handful of newfangled electro-coal oil motorized carriages sputtering and churning along. The signs of opulence and power were everywhere. I thought to myself, *Horace old boy, now you're moving in the right circles,* as I made my way to the concierge.

"Yes sir, may I help you?" said the concierge. He was dressed in a suit that would cost most free residents a year's pay and his Eagle was proudly displayed on his chest. He probably pulled down a small fortune every year in tips alone. From the haughtiness of his face, I could tell he took great pleasure in ensuring that only the finest members of Imperial Society were welcome at Olafson Plaza. I also guessed he was positively eager to send me packing.

"My name is Horace P. Thornton and I am here to meet Ms. Torresdale."

That tidbit got his attention. Apparently Ms. Torresdale had some cache here. His attitude shifted almost immediately and I allowed myself a smile. Coming here had been a wonderful idea.

"Of course Mr. Thornton. If you'll follow me, the Imperial room is right this way."

He lead me through a set of massive ornately carved double doors and down a hallway lined with more tastefully displayed signs of unimaginable wealth. Fine art, priceless antiquities, and furniture made from the rarest and most exotic hardwoods were placed every few feet for the length of the passage. It was daunting.

"Here we are, Mr. Thornton, the Imperial room. Ms. Torresdale's table is right here."

If I had thought the hallway was impressive, it had nothing on the Imperial Room. I ordered a brandy and took in the splendor. More art, pulled from every corner of not just this world but Mars and Venus as well, and trophy heads, taken from animals I didn't even know existed lined the wall. There wasn't a single surface that wasn't gilded or inlaid with platinum and gems. And it all dimmed when she walked into the room.

"Why hello there, Mr. Thornton. What a pleasure it is to finally meet you."

If someone called this woman gorgeous I would have to slap them for damning her beauty with faint praise. Her dress was slim and sleek, not the usual bustled monstrosity, and it showed off her long, lithe legs to devastating effect before swelling to hint and tease with the graceful, sensuous curve of her hips and bottom. She was tightly corseted about her petite waist and the corset was cut low to show off a truly magnificent bosom. Her face was equally stunning, with a full set of lips cast into a mischievous smile, a tiny nose, and a large eyes the color of a spring sky, all framed by long curls of golden hair lightly streaked with red. It's amazing I managed to say anything.

"Ms. Torresdale I presume?"

"Please Mr. Thornton, call me Teresa."

"Well Teresa, it is a pleasure to meet you. And please, do call me Horace."

"I take it the accommodations have been to your liking Horace?"

"I doubted I could be more pleased Teresa, until you walked through those doors and showed me what was absent."

She laughed flirtatiously at this, "So it's true, you are the relentless flatterer that you are reputed to be."

"Please Teresa, you do me a disservice, flattery implies that I'm not being honest, and you have my word, you outshine every jewel in the room."

Oh, I could have sat there and complimented her all day and night just to see her smile. We continued to make small talk and eventually ordered our meals. I couldn't take my eyes off of her. Everything she did was alluring. Somewhere, in the back of my mind, there was a voice screaming that, once again, a nice set of legs and some curvy hips were going to convince me to put myself into mortal danger for some paltry sum, but then she would move just so and a flash of cleavage would make that voice shut up. We ordered our meals, made small talk, and as the meal wound down, this lovely vixen finally made her pitch.

"Now Horace, my dear man, I'm sure you're wondering why I called on you tonight."

"Actually my dear lady, I was certain it was purely for the pleasure of my company."

That brought more flirtatious giggles.

"While you're company is enchanting, my dear Horace, my pleasure isn't valuable enough to cause my patrons to spring for two diners in the Imperial

Room at Olafson Plaza. You see, my dear Horace, that my patrons run most of the orphanages and houses for wayward children in this city and that's why I have come calling on you. Some of our children have gone missing."

"Gone missing?"

I gave her a devil of a look.

Why would I want anything to do with a piece of charity work, hunting down some filthy, squalling pack of children? I don't even like children. I thought.

Now, don't get me wrong, the bottom on Ms. Torresdale was pert enough to stir a dead man, but charity won't pay my rent and keep me in bourbon. As tempting as it was to do it just to gain her approval, apparently my wits hadn't fled that thoroughly.

"Oh, I know I can't ask you to work gratis Mr. Thornton. My patrons know that there are considerations to be taken," as she spoke, she produced one heavy purse which clinked as she placed it on the table, "This should cover your expenses, and as we know a man of your station must have a volume of pressing work this will be for your time," a second purse joined the first. "should you successfully complete this assignment."

"Well, well Ms. Torresdale, with such generous considerations in mind I would be happy to help in this matter. Can you tell me more?"

"Well it seems that three days ago, six of our children went missing."

"And you suspect foul play?"

"I don't know what to suspect Mr. Thornton, that's why we've retained you. We do have reason to believe that they may be in the tunnels beneath the city. There is a maintenance passage near their dormitory and the grate was found ajar the following morning."

"Then the tunnels seem like a reasonable place to look. I can start tomorrow Ms. Torresdale."

"Oh that would be most splendid Mr. Thornton!"

"Well, anything to make a lady happy."

"Find those children and I'll be very happy indeed."

And I wanted to make this fine piece of Imperial womanhood to be quite happy indeed.

"Happy enough to indulge me with another dinner?"

She smiled, and once again, there was that wonderful giggle.

"Bring those children back and you'll find out."

We spent the rest of the meal discussing the particulars of our arrangement and setting a rudimentary timetable. I went home that night feeling better than I had in a long while. Which was a bit shocking because I needed to take the steam ferry to Yersey in the morning.

Now, you don't go into the tunnels without a guide, and I knew just the character. I just had to find him. Well, finding where he was staying was the easy part. After all, if you know a tramp isn't staying under a bridge you'll find him in a dump. And Yersey is primarily composed of dumps, at least the parts that aren't swamps and factories. Retrieving him on the other hand, might be an issue. I had to bribe my way into the particular dump where I thought he would be, only to have the one-eyed proprietor inform me that it would not be his problem 'if you get shived.'

The place was worse than I remembered. Even for Yersey it smelled bad, the odor of dead fish and industrial waste mixing with the rotting stench of swamp typical of Yersey. I was busy trying to keep from retching when I found my path blocked by a quartet of hostile looking tramps.

"Hey! You! Pretty man! What you doin' in our dump?" said the first tramp, a filthy, hunched over figure in a long coat with one eye swollen shut and leaking puss.

"Huh huh huh. Yeah pretty man, this our dump!" said the second. This one was naked except for a sandwich board depicting a mechanical duck. His eyes rolled about randomly, and he twitched spasmodically every few seconds.

"Look at them pretty man shoes he got!" chimed in a third hobo, this one a rotund woman with wild hair dragging a string of dead cats.

"I smell jerky! You got jerky, don't ya pretty man! Gives it over!" added a fourth. He was completely toothless and wore nothing but filthy long johns and a beard that came to his waist.

"Now, now my good fellows, I'm looking for One Tooth Lenny," I replied, thinking that dropping the name might save me some trouble.

"And I'm looking for some shoes pretty man!" said the woman, as she gathered her feline corpses up into her massive arms.

"You do not even need to talk, just gesture in the right directio..."

"WHERE'S MY JERKY!" shrieked the one in the long johns.

This was not going well.

"GIMME THOSE SHOES!" added the cat lady, as she began to whirl one of the cats like it were a flail.

"You know what boys, I think I'm gonna stab him. I think I'm gonna stab him."

Adding deed to word, the one with the swollen eye produced a switchblade.

"And I'm gonna beat him with my club!"

The one wearing the sandwich board brandished a table leg.

"And I'm gonna make his face into jerky and his brain into soup!"

"I just want them shoes!"

They began to close on me. It was time for drastic measures.

"We got a knife and a club pretty man, what you got?"

"I have dynamite."

I love having an expense fund. Half a pound of high explosive and a handful of penny nails do wonders to clear out hostile hobos.

As the smoke cleared a nervous voice called out, "Mr. Horace, is that you?"

"Ah, One Tooth Lenny. One of your greatest qualities is knowing when to duck and cover."

"You got some work for me Mr. Horace? That tin can you paid me with last time's almost wore out."

"Oh I do Lenny. And what treasures I have for you this time. Look, two cans of Greeble and a jug of kerosene!"

"Ooooh, and that's good drinkin' kerosene too Mr. Horace. So what we doing this time?"

"Well Lenny, we are going into the tunnels under the city."

"But Mr. Horace, don't you know there's sewer gators down there?"

"Don't be foolish, that is just a legend. And I know you want this kerosene."

"Oh I do Mr. Horace. Between that and the Greeble I'll live like a king! Oh alright, I'll do it."

"Good man. Meet me tomorrow morning by the access ditch on the north side of Central Park."

"You got it Mr. Horace!"

Once I was able to return to civilization, I made a few more detours to pick up things I might need, before spending an enjoyable evening about town celebrating my luck. The next morning I found One Tooth rooting through a garbage can near the access ditch.

"Looky here Mr. Horace! I found some chicken bones and half of a day old sandwich! You city folk know how to live! Care to join me for breakfast?"

"Erm, no thank you Lenny. I've already eaten."

"Alright then, suit yourself."

I watched as Lenny scarfed refuse while I prepared myself for a sojourn into the sewers, briefly wondering if I should have stayed in law school and committed myself to making an honest living. But my guide quickly finished his breakfast, I thought about how much I would get paid for what would hopefully only be a day's work, and it passed.

"Are you ready Lenny? I'd like you to go first to scout ahead."

"Ok. Mr. Horace, I'll make sure the coast is clear."

I opened the gate for him, spinning the heavy wheel to retract the bars that held the gate in place. Lenny seemed almost eager as he scrambled into the sewer and made his was down the ladder. I heard him splashing too and fro at the base of the thing as he scouted ahead.

"Looks OK to me, Mr. Horace!" he called up.

As I climbed down the ladder, the smell coming from the tunnels made One Tooth's usual stench of rotten leather and halitosis a spring day in comparison. I nearly wretched as my boots hit the ankle deep water. I was still trying to compose myself when One Tooth, apparently wholly at home in such an utterly rank environment, piped up.

"Lookee here Mr. Horace! Pictures! What do you think they are, Mr. Horace? Is that Skraeling writing?"

"No Lenny, I've seen something like this before, but it was not Skraelings that wrote it."

I had to think back. Part of the graffiti had obviously been drawn by children. The pictures were stick figures, mostly happy, which boded well for my assignment, engaged in what I assumed to be play. No worries there. But the other parts...

I had seen something that was broadly similar. Once. Those are some memories I don't like to bring up. There are some dark, old things in this world and there are dangerous, desperate men who truck with their secrets. I prayed to every god I could name that this was not the case, and that those symbols were old, written by someone long gone. If it were otherwise, I most likely wouldn't make it to get the second half of that reward.

It was then that Lenny piped up again.

"You hear something Mr. Horace? I think I hear some scratchin' in the walls."

" I don't hear anything at all Lenny. Must be your imagination. Have you been sniffing turpentine again?"

"Well, not this morning anyway. There it goes again Mr. Horace!"

"You're just suffering from the delirium tremens, Lenny."

"Maybe Mr. Horace, maybe."

I took then opportunity to have a slug brandy. After seeing those glyphs, and knowing what they might mean, I needed it.

"Say Mr. Horace, could I maybe have some of your brandy?"

"Absolutely not, this is emergency brandy and I have a condition. You'll just have to tough it out. Now onward!"

Lenny trudged on sullenly, slogging though the sewer muck and grime and I followed him through several more filthy tunnels until we reached another spot of scrawled figures on the wall. Just like the first set, some looked like they were drawn by children. These seemed to indicate that there was some path downward. There was other writing as well. Similar to the glyphs we had seen at the entrance to the tunnel and even more ominous, this time depicting something hulking and clawed and decidedly not human.

I started feeling even worse about this job. I even thought about backing out and making up some story about the children all being dead. But what if they tried to get the bodies? Or worse, what if the brats showed up alive somewhere? My reputation would be ruined and the prospects of coasting off of it for the rest of my days would be gone forever. Once again, I was stuck.

"Say, Lenny, this seems to indicate that there's a way down. Can you see anything?"

"Nope Mr. Horace, I don't see anything. Oh look, a tin can!"

He ran off like a child on Founding Day, eager to get to his treasure. I called for him to wait, but there was no stopping his headlong rush. Well, at least there wasn't until the floor collapsed beneath his feet and he disappeared from my sight.

"Lenny, are you hurt?" I called down to him. I wasn't terrible concerned about his well being, but if he had broken a leg or had gotten himself impaled on a pipe, I'd need to waste another day finding a new tramp.

"I think I'm OK, Mr. Horace," I heard him stand and brush himself off, "Seems like we found a way... Oh lord, Mr. Horace, it's that scratchin' again and it's louder than hell this time!"

This time I heard the scratching, desperate and wild, coming from a dark area further down the tunnel. I was about to start to lower a rope down, when Lenny screamed.

"Help me Mr. Horace! Rats! Good lord giant rats!"

I looked over the edge and there were at least a dozen that I could see, each the size of a bloodhound but obviously heavier, bodies low and skulking, all mange and dirty fur and enormous, yellowed teeth. I abandoned the rope and began desperately rooting around in my pack. I had brought something for this situation.

"Hold on Lenny, just one second!"

He didn't answer. I could hear him shouting 'Get away!' and I heard a clatter, which I assumed to be him throwing stones. I found what I was looking for. The stock settled nicely into my shoulder and a few quick cranks had the device primed.

"Lenny, you might want to cover your ears..."

I stepped to the edge and discharged. Even with the aperture pointed away from me, the emanations were painful, a raw and grating hum just beyond what I could hear, both too high and too low for humans to process. The waves were invisible, but I could judge my aim by the effect and I played the broad copper bell over the unusually sized rodents as the generation box vibrated in my hand. The weapon's discharge might not be visible, the effects where dramatic. Everywhere I pointed the weapon, I was rewarded with frantic squeaks quickly followed by a wet bursting sound. All too soon, the weapon wound down, but it had been enough. The rats were in full retreat under my breath I muttered, "Thank you, Mr. Edison."

For his part, Lenny seemed to be shocked that he hadn't been eaten. He was bent over and vomiting, from what I've read that's the usual side effect of exposure, but once he had recovered, and I had climbed down to join him, he was practically bursting with gratitude.

"Oh lord Mr. Horace I thought I was a goner, then you called out, and the giant rats, they just exploded. How'd you do that Mr. Horace?"

"Well Lenny, when you've got an Edison Electro-Sonic Disrupter, things like giant rats or mutant wild boars or angry snow pygmies aren't much of a problem, though the damned thing seems to have burned out on me."

"Say, didn't that Tesla feller invent that?"

"Oh Lenny, of course Tesla didn't invent it. Mr. Edison holds the patent! How would he have the patent if he wasn't the inventor?"

"Whatever you say Mr. Horace."

"Come on, let's get going."

"Sure thing Mr. Horace, but first I wanna put some of that rat meat in my bindle. It's gonna make a great soup!"

Lenny busied himself picking up gobs of rat for his supper while I quietly readied another little toy, cranking up the rotator gear and making sure everything was in order with the cartridge box. When I was satisfied, I slung the machine over my back. Before long, we were on our way again, with Lenny leading.

We were walking for maybe a half an hour when we came across more of the drawings we had seen before. Once again, it was the same pattern. Children, but something else, something that should be threatening, but in this case...

"Well I'll be, Mr. Horace, those kids in them pictures look happy!"

And he was right. Not a single face was drawn in anything other than a smile. Even the giant mutants seemed to somehow look cheerful. It was disconcerting. But at least, it seems, we were on the right course. We pressed on.

As we rounded a bend in the tunnels, Lenny suddenly stopped.

"Mr. Horace," he whispered, "Look!"

As I neared the corner I could here voices. Some were obviously those of children, even as distorted as they were by the strange acoustics of the sewers and the burbling of an underground river nearby. There were other voices as well.

Unsettling, inhuman voices which sounded too high pitched. When I reached Lenny's perch on the corner, I could see shadows. There were the shadows of children, yes, but there were other shadows as well. Hulking, clawed shadows. Shadows that matched the monsters from the drawings we had seen on the walls. I leaned in close to hear what the voices were saying but they were still too muffled, the old brick causing distortions and echoes. I whispered to Lenny, "You need to check what's on the other side."

Then I gave him a friendly shove around the corner for encouragement.

Immediately, I heard a grating, high-pitched shout of "Intruder!" and then Lenny was screaming.

I fumbled in my coat, trying to bring my weapon to bear, as I watched Lenny pull a knife on something the size of a gorilla. It had tiny eyes and a small, pointed snout. And it had foot long claws on each hand. It advanced on him, screeching "Intruder!" once more. Lenny was panicked.

"Stay away you! I got a knife! Get away from me or I'll cut you!"

It kept advancing, and Lenny made the mistake of making a wild jab at its face with the knife.

The thing moved its right claw with alarming speed and took poor Lenny's arm off at the elbow. He didn't have time to scream before the things other arm came up and ripped his belly open. The monster casually tossed him to the side, and turned its attention to me. Three more of the things closed in on the first one from behind, and they were all getting closer. Looks like it was time for action.

"You ripped him clean open! Do you know how hard it is to find a good tramp these days? That's it, I'm gonna..."

"Wait, stop!" one of the children, a girl of no more than ten years old, had interposed herself between the things and me. "They thought you were going to hurt us!"

"Huh? What is this? You've been with these things? That one just ripped a man in two!" I looked around. The rest of the children were slowly emerging from their hiding places, looking at me with a mix of curiosity and fear.

"It's not their fault. They were protecting us. They're the Mole People. They're our friends. He scared all of us when he burst in here. He shouldn't have tried to stab Big Henry," she gestured to the creature whose claws still dripped with bits of Lenny. To my surprise, it spoke.

"Yes, yes, love the children," the Mole Person said in its bizarrely high-pitched voice, "Want to nurture and care in every way. They grow and learn with us, away from horrors and evils of the surface world."

I have seen a lot of things in my time. I've seen sights on Venus, Mars, and Ultima Thule that would boggle most men's minds. I've seen tentacled horrors from beyond the stars, aliens of every size and shape, animals that ought to have been extinct for millions of years, and some that should not, by rights exist in the first place. But watching this seven foot tall beast pontificate about childcare while its foot long claws were still dripping blood was a remarkably strange event, even for me. I needed to put this whole experience past me so I could have a much deserved brandy.

"Well, yes, that's all quite nice. But it's time for the children to go home with me now."

"But we like it here. The Mole People are kind to us. They give us nice clothes and good food."

"That's great. But you need to come with me. Now."

"We won't! This is a good place and you can't make us!"

"Look, I really need you to come with me. Just a quick trip to the surface and I'm sure everything will be sorted out. I'm sure your parents or matrons or what have you are worried sick about you and it will be naught but sunshine and rum cakes when you get there."

"But we're orphans! We don't have parents! We won't go back! It's horrible there! They feed us gruel and make us work in the foundry all day and beat us with sticks if we don't! I'm staying in the sewers!"

The mole man spoke up again, in the unnerving high-pitched voice, "Won't let you take children!" the rest of the beast joined in a chorus of 'Yes, Yes!' and 'The children.' It continued, "Before they came to us they live in awful place with cruel people."

"Yeah! The Mole People are good to us! We won't go back to the foundry! I don't wanna pull the cart any more!"

"That's wonderful, but I must insist you do come with me."

"We won't let you take them!"

The creatures were getting more and more agitated. They started to fan out, forming a circle around me, a circle that started to close. I stammered for a bit, "Look, you, just let the children come with me... I mean it... stay back... I warned you..."

They kept pressing in. I tried to do this the nice way. Now it was time to do things the easy way. I brought the gun up to my hip and the ten barrels came up to speed in a gratifyingly brief interval, then my Colt Peacekeeper Gatling pistol began to chatter.

Now, the Colt Peacekeeper hand-held Gatling pistol is not the most efficient weapon in the three worlds. The shells are hellaciously expensive and the weapon's chief selling point, its prodigious rate of fire, makes it an inefficient tool for dealing with more modest numbers of foes. But when you are staring down a horde of blood crazed cultists, Shanghai corsairs, or even seven foot tall mole monsters, it is no small comfort to have Mr. Colt's 10 barreled, steam driven, high caliber angel at your side. I played the weapon back and forth, hosing bullets with abandon, until it spun down with a click, all 450 shells gone in about 35 seconds. Now it was just me and the children, in a sewer covered in bits of mole people.

"They're all dead! You killed them all!"

I smiled. I was about to get my way and it was a pleasant feeling, "Why yes, they are, and you all need to come with me now. There are people waiting for you."

CHARITY WORK

"We still won't go! We'd rather stay here alone than ever go back!" this time a boy, of about six or so, was the one who piped up. As he spoke, he inched backwards, getting closer to the subterranean river. He seemed like he was preparing himself for a spectacular tantrum with his lips quivering and his face turning red. As he took in an enormous breath to start his bawling, a massive set of reptilian jaws burst from the fetid water and clamped around his middle. Before he could scream, the sewer gator pulled him backwards and disappeared bellow the surface. This set the rest of the children to panicked screaming, as they tried to get as far away from the water as possible.

For my part, I was briefly stunned, and for a moment could only think, *Well, what do you know, poor Lenny was right. There are gators down here.* But this situation I could work with.

"Ok, kids, you can either stay with the gators or get in the sack."

As bad as working in a foundry was, it beat ending up as gator chow. Soon, the children were safely, if not quite comfortably, contained in burlap and on their way back to their hot and smoke filled 'home.' As I back tracked towards the surface, I began to contemplate all the wonderful things I could spend my money on, and just how much of it I would need to spend to find my way into the lovely Ms. Torresdale's boudoir.

Valkr's Wing

VALKR'S WING

By Raymond J. Witte

Crew of the *Valkr's Wing* brought the converted frigate to pursuit speed and she settled out at about 700 feet up. The ship had trailed the Plesioleviathan at a distance for most of the morning as it wove its way through the Marsh Sea, closing the only gradually to avoid startling the creature. The beast had only just noticed the airship looming above it, and now the chase had begun in earnest.

Captain Anton Grey stood at the bridge, watching the water rush by below and waiting for the minute hand on his pocket watch to tick forward. Grey felt impatient. He went over the calculations in his head for the hundredth time since they had sighted the great, serpentine beast.

The chase lufts had the legs to see the chase through from this range. Letting them loose now could shave hours from the hunt. The nimble little airships would pace the creature long before their mothership could close. Since the killing itself would take a while and the chase lufts carried enough gear to get a head start on the rendering process, launching them now was almost guaranteed to end the chase in good time. However, the nimble little craft had a hellacious appetite for fuel, and the coal oil that powered their propellers and kept them aloft was expensive. A launch from too far out could actually pitch the morning's operation well into the red. So Grey waited.

It was a balancing act. In a perfect world, Grey could have held off launching the luftskiffs until he was almost on top of his quarry. That's how things had been three years earlier, when the *Valkr's Wing* had first been refitted as a whaler.

But things had changed after the second and third Sky Lock to Ultima Thule had been discovered. What had once only been open to Amerikan vessels was suddenly accessible to the French and Chinese from the Indo-China skylock and from anyone who could run the Russian guns to reach the Caspian skylock.

Though transport hulks and traders had been first through, warships followed soon enough and it wasn't long before a simmering shooting war had developed, a conflict of all against all, with each side taking its shots every time they thought they could get away with it.

No nation had yet been willing to push through enough air power to attempt to establish complete air superiority and even if they had the requisite muscle, every indication was that no one was willing to pay the butcher's bill that the all out war for supremacy would entail.

So the would be belligerents contented themselves with nibbling around the edges of each other's territory and whatever harassment each individual captain thought they could get away with, which essentially meant making life miserable for those merchant men trying to make a living above the Marsh Sea.

Privateering became a fact of life. Before the new skylocks had opened up, there had been a few air pirates, generally desperate men and traders who had fallen on hard times who had managed to bootleg enough Liftium to get a ship into the air. They had contented themselves picking on short haul tugs and pleasure craft.

A whaling frigate like the *Valkr's Wing* was too well manned and well armed to be an easy score.

Now far too many airship captains from every nation had gotten themselves Letters of Marque. The old pirates found themselves out of business in a hurry, as the commanders of modern war-built corvettes, sky frigates, and even the odd destroyer luft took up piracy, all notarized and perfectly legal under international law, so long as they were a least a bit picky about their targets.

Any of those ships could likely outfight the *Wing*, her guns had been replaced by the heavy and expensive specialized processing tools of the whaling trade, and most could outfly her as well, as burdened as she was by those same tools.

Neither of those things mattered much while the *Wing* was at cruising height. Above the cloud cover, sight range was essentially only limited by the range of the eyepieces of a given crew. With that much warning, trying to chase down any but the slowest of airships was a fool's game and even in this modern age aerial battle still consisted of comparatively close combat.

But that was not where the *Valkr's Wing* was now. The ship was flying low and beneath the cloud layer visibility dropped to a fraction of what it was at cruising height. That sharp decline in warning time opened up an entire suite of tactical options for an enterprising commander.

Suddenly, pursuits weren't so pointless, and it was even possible for to attempt a sort of ambush, if the conditions were right. That meant commercial captains tried to spend as little time as possible below the deck.

Unfortunately for Grey, he needed to be beneath the cloud layer for his crew to hunt, and that was the cause of his dilemma. He needed to limit the exposure of his ship and his crew, but if he were to launch the luftskiffs too far out, the expedition's profits would flow straight into their fuel canisters. But every minute he held them back was another minute of vulnerability.

Taking up his field glasses, Grey sighted the Plesioleviathan again, measuring it against the small marks etched into his lenses. It still was over two miles out, cutting through the water and moving at speed. The serpentine leviathans could swim at a good clip, propelling themselves through the brackish water with their powerful tail flukes. They were nearly as fast as a slow airship and could easily outpace most wind-powered surface vessels. He decided he would launch when they had closed to a mile. If his math was right, that would limit the fuel expenditures of the luft skiffs enough to make this the break even kill for this trip, with enough profit left over to justify a return to port.

The primary profit of any whaling expedition came from the fluid stored in chambers along the spine of the Plesioleviathan, giving them a distinctive humped appearance. Grey had heard that the beasts used it to help them stay afloat in the freshwater sea, but that might have just been scuttlebutt. Whatever nature's purpose for the substance was, it could be refined into top quality Liftium, comparable to that found in the purest strata of blood-coal, and that made it wildly valuable for use in airships, second only to the wondrous Phlogistern in terms of lift potential. The processing cartels back in Port Venture paid well enough per cask to make the risks of piracy and privateering worth it, provided, of course, you didn't eat up all of your profits filling your hold.

Once again, Grey was forced to reflect on what a profitable business this had been when he had first refitted his ship. Not only could a crew turn a profit selling the spinal fluid, but the ships could afford to have a floating Greeble cannery following them to process the carcass once the more valuable parts of the carcass had been was harvested. That didn't pay much per unit, but 65 tons of anything, even Greeble, added up to a hefty pile of Geld. But that took time and the cannery barges were slow.

Now they would be easy meat for any marauder worth the name. The barges still operated, of course, but now they were a government operation with dedicated escorts and they rarely strayed this far out into the Marsh Sea.

These days, hunting crews harvested the fluid, cut enough slabs of meat to provide fresh rations, then left the vast bulk of the carcass to the penguinopods, those vicious, ever ravenous bundles of teeth, beaks, fins and tentacles that inevitably swarmed over every kill.

It seemed like a lot of wasted effort to Grey- a day spent hunting and carving up a hundred ton animal for nothing more than a few casks of the spinal fluid and some steaks- but it kept the *Valkr's Wing* in the air and his crew paid, so he did it gladly.

Grey's ruminations were interrupted by his second, LaGrasso.

"Captain Grey, shall I order the chase crews to their balloons?"

Joshua LaGrasso had been one of the first crewmen that Grey had hired and had proven himself to be invaluable time and again. He had been fishing the Marsh Sea as long as anyone in Port Venture and had almost infallible instincts. If he thought it was time to prep the luft skiffs for launch, he was probably right.

Still, Grey felt compelled to check the distance once again. He wanted this to be the final kill of the expedition. Launching early would scuttle that hope, so Grey raised his field glasses once more and quickly worked through the sums in his head. They had gained a bit more than a half-mile on the Plesioleviathan.

Yes, it's near time to launch.

He nodded to LaGrasso.

"You may order the crews to ready for the chase."

"Aye, aye, Captain."

LaGrasso began to bark orders to the deck hands who ran steam lines out to each of the four skiffs. The luftskiffs were built off the same chassis, a small hunting platform flanked by a set of lift tanks with a coal oil engine attached to an oversized propeller in the rear and a central steam tank to service the skiff's weapons, but each one invariably evolved to reflect the preferences of its chief harpooneer.

As the steam lines began to charge the tanks on each skiff, the harpooneers attached their weapons to the hunting platform of each craft. The weapons were an assortment of lances, barbed spears and explosive charges, some long and narrow with spade shaped tips, designed to finish a kill cleanly on a disabled Plesioleviathan. Others had explosive heads, intended to cause horrific wounds should the prey attempt to dive before it could be killed. Still other harpoons sported broad heads with stars of wicked points to slow the beasts as they sliced through muscle, tendon and fins. Two of the luftskiffs sported weighted barrels of powder to stun the animals and to force them to surface.

Grey, like most captains, left the loadouts of the skiffs to their crews. The harpooneers knew they needed to work as a team to score a kill, and smart captains knew better than to try and micromanage them.

The chase ground onward as Grey's men swarmed over the little airships, making them ready for launch. For the most part, Grey kept his eyes on their prey, obsessively measuring the slowly closing distance, though he would cast his eyes about the deck occasionally. It was always good for the deck hands to see that their captain was interested, even if it was LaGrasso who did the real work of making sure each harpoon crew was ready when the launch order came.

"The crews are ready, Captain."

Grey put down his field glasses for a moment to inspect his crew. Each harpoon team stood at attention in front of their luft skiff, ready to launch on his order, less than ten minutes after the order had gone out. His crew was a good one and they were getting better each day. Grey hoped that this kill would be a quick one. He was nervous. He had already been beneath the deck for longer than he would have preferred, and he had no idea what other vessels might be in the area.

He was tempted to climb above the clouds to make sure the *Valkr's Wing* had the skies to herself, but that risked losing their quarry. The creature might reach a trench and dive or shelter in one of the dense reed islands that dotted the Marsh Sea before they sighted it again. Grey would have to chance a launch without any additional reconnaissance.

"Alright boys, you know your business so I'll not waste breath telling it to you. Make it quick one and we'll back in port three mornings hence and the first round's on me."

That brought knowing smiles and even a few chuckles to the faces of the crew. Port Venture meant cashing their shares, then women, drink, gambling, and a few weeks of safety on dry land until they had spent everything and needed to risk another hunt. They knew the dangers as well as their Captain did, and they were just as eager to top off the holds and head home.

"Luftskiffs away, Mr. LaGrasso."

"Aye Captain. You heard the man, cast off and good hunting!"

The deck crew of the *Valkr's Wing* first hauled in the steam lines then began to manipulate the lifts and hoists cradling each luftskiff, swinging the light craft so they were well away from their mother ship. Once the booms were at full extension, the crew sparked the coal oil engines, bringing the propellers up to speed as each skiff's engineer manipulated the Liftium tanks until the little craft achieved neutral buoyancy.

Then they were away, darting off in pursuit of their quarry like a pack of angry hornets. As the skiffs launched in staggered succession, first port fore, then starboard fore, then port aft and finally starboard aft, Grey took the helm and let the *Valkr's Wing* come up to her full speed. It put too much strain on her coal fired boiler to fly at flank speed when she was hauling the skiffs, but with them away, the converted frigate could really spread her wings.

For a few glorious moments, Grey's concerns melted away as the ship's engines gently thrummed beneath his feet while the air began to rush by. He nudged the *Wing's* nose slightly down and began a slow dive, picking up more speed as he descended. He could never hope to keep pace with the skiffs, but his ship was still fast and fairly nimble and he reveled in her speed and with it the chance to recall the ship's glorious history.

The *Wing* hadn't always been a hunting ship. Once, years ago, Grey had used her to run guns on Mars and as burdened as she was by the necessary tools of industry, beneath it all she was still built to be a pure blockade runner.

Even now she looked it. Her hull was long and sleek, coming to a sharp prow, designed to cut through the air and offer no purchase for drag. A single tank of Liftium stretched her length, secured closely to her deck to keep her profile small. At the rear of the ship was Grey's parapet, a two-tiered structure that allowed the captain to either supervise the deck or scan the skies around the ship.

In the aft were the ship's four squat smoke stacks, belching black fumes as the engines churned in her belly. She was a beautiful ship and fast, much faster than almost anything her size, when she was properly outfitted.

A shrill whistle from the fore interrupted Grey's reminiscing. Already knowing what it meant, he raised his field glasses anyway. The whistle from the lookout signaled that the skiffs were making their attack runs on the massive sea creature.

Grey's crew had been lucky. This particular beast had not tried to dive nor did it change course as the creatures sometimes did, it merely tried to outrun its pursuers, the Plesioleviathan's enormous tail churning the water as it endeavored to gain speed.

But it was a futile effort. The skiffs had closed the distance and now mates on each vessel would use semaphore to coordinate their strikes. The colorful flags flashed quickly, far too quickly for Grey to keep up with their message and moments later the kill began.

The lead skiff dove steeply, and through his glasses Grey watched one of the crewmen aiming a harpoon launcher fixed to the bow of the little vessel. In a puff of pressurized steam, the lance was away and Grey could tell well before it struck that it would be a good hit.

It was a broad headed lance and it cut savagely into the tail of the beast. The Plesioleviathan's toothy head reared up as the creature bellowed in pain. It tried to swim more quickly, but the lance had sliced muscle and tendon and the strokes of it's tail grew sluggish and truncated. Meanwhile, the crew of the luftskiff busied themselves reloading their weapon.

Two more of the luft skiffs swooped down to make their strikes; this time each one fired a thin harpoon into the bulk of the creature's back. As crippled as it was by the first strike, the kill was effectively assured.

But the Plesioleviathan was not yet dead and the hardy animals could linger near death for a long time before they finally expired. A long kill meant more time vulnerable to pirates, so now the crews of the skiffs had to finish the kill.

Unlike the lance of the first skiff, the harpoons of the second and third boat were tethered to the hulls of the craft that launched them. As they sunk deep into the animal's flesh and found purchase, the crews of those skiffs would cut power to their propellers, forcing the whale to tire itself by dragging the small craft behind it. As soon as their steam launcher was charged, the crew of the lead boat sunk a harpoon into the serpentine beast as well, adding their luft skiff's weight to the effort.

The final luft skiff darted in front of the Plesioleviathan and held position.

This would be the kill boat, its launcher loaded with an explosive tipped harpoon designed to finish the job, if it got a good hit.

However, quickly killing something as large as a Plesioleviathan even with an explosive harpoon, if you didn't want to blast it to a mountain of chum, required a hit on something vital. And each of the explosive charges was frightfully expensive. Needing to shoot a second shot would cost a good chunk of the profit from this kill.

Even though the entire crew constantly worried about privateers, no one wanted to cost their comrades money by being too hasty so they were forced to wait until the whale was exhausted from the chase. Only then, when they were guaranteed a clean shot, would they make the kill.

As the luft skiffs made their assault, the *Valkr's Wing* closed on the creature, faster now, as the animal was slowed from injury and dragging the hunting skiffs behind it. Meanwhile, the crew that remained on the *Wing's* deck began to set up the works to process the Plesioleviathan's oil.

The oil was stored in spongy tissue and in its natural state was quite dilute. The engine crew was in the process of stoking the *Wing's* engines to keep up speed while a portion of the heat was directed to the enormous vats of the try works where pools of the spinal fluid from the creature would be concentrated so it could be stored for travel and later use. This would run the boiler hotter than was technically safe, but as long as the try works were in operation, the excess heat would have a safe outlet.

After ten more minutes, the kill boat was in position, low and just behind the head of the Plesioleviathan. By now, the beast was hardly moving. It bled from a half dozen wounds and already the penguinopods had gathered around the creature, waiting for it to expire so they could move in and feed. With a puff of steam, the harpooneer launched the explosive shot.

It was a good strike, hitting just behind the Plesioleviathan's skull and sinking deep. A moment later that was a muffled thump and the animal jerked suddenly, its head drooping nervelessly and beginning to loll at an unnatural angle.

A cheer went up from the crews of the skiffs and spread to those still on the *Valkr's Wing*. It was a good kill, neat and professionally done. Now all that remained was to process the beast and make best speed for Port Venture.

The luft skiff crews began work almost immediately. The pilots maneuvered their craft low and close, bringing them as near to the carcass as they dared, while other crewman hung over the gantries, wielding long handled flensing spades to slice into the flesh of the Plesioleviathan, casting slabs of muscle and fat into the sea to clear it out of the way. As they worked, the sea reddened with blood and began to churn as the viscous penguinopods worked themselves into a frenzy over the scraps.

Once more, the sheer scale of the waste involved struck Grey. But meat didn't bring in enough geld to haul it back to port, and it needed to be out of the way before the crew could siphon the precious spinal fluid, so it went into the brine.

As the *Wing* continued her decent, the luft skiffs slid out of her path, making room for their mother ship and her more extensive butchering equipment. Thick lines attached to flesh anchors were cast overboard and sank into the Plesioleviathan's flesh, allowing the *Wing* to take the whale's weight from the skiffs.

Relieved of the burden of supporting the weight of the beast, the skiffs rose once more, their crews now serving as scouts, keeping watch for pirates. It wasn't a great solution. The skiffs didn't have the lift ceiling that the larger ship did and it was still possible for a privateer to approach undetected by taking cover above the clouds, but it was better than being completely blind.

Grey felt himself relax as the *Wing* settled into position and the crew started processing the animal. The hard part was nearly over, and soon he would be above the clouds once more, heading for port with a full hold and an intact crew. He allowed himself a small grin, while the crew set to their task, lowering the long, hollow iron tubes which they would use to tap into the Plesioleviathan's bones to extract the precious fluid.

Suddenly, the furthest luftskiff bucked wildly as a spray of splinters erupted from her deck. Before he could react, Grey saw the small craft buck again and this time he heard the sharp report of a naval rifle. Then a third round hit, but this time, instead of bucking, the skiff sagged at midship, her back broken by the shot, and began to lose altitude and list, spilling injured and dying crewmen into the sea. Grey turned to raise the alarm, but LaGrasso was ahead of him, ringing the ship's bell wildly and calling out "ENEMY CONTACT! ALL HANDS MAKE READY!"

"Order the skiffs to cut lines and run at best speed. Give us all power to the engines," Grey barked his orders, his ensigns signaling wildly with semaphore flags or shouting down the speaking tubes into the engine room.

As the lines were cut and the crew scrambled back aboard their skiffs, the Wing's assailant broke cloud cover. She was a corvette and bore French markings on her sides. She was half the size of the *Wing*, but she was built for war and fully armed, with a trio of fixed heavy guns in an armoured housing on her prow. Those pieces were silent for the moment, but the pair of Hotchkiss guns mounted to the underside of her forehull barked again, this time in tandem. The 42 millimeter cannons dismantled a second skiff with a string of well placed shots, their cylinders rotating to feed round after round into their breaches, sending another boat full of men to their deaths.

Looking horrified, LaGrasso asked, "Why are they shooting up the skiffs Captain? Aren't they worth enough to take?"

"The *Wing* is the prize they're after, Mr. LaGrasso," Grey answered with as little emotion as he could, "These are French Privateers, not mere pirates. I'd bet you anything they're under orders to take only heavy shipping, so the luft skiffs aren't worth their time. Murdering the men on the skiffs just means fewer for them to deal with when they board us. I doubt they plan on taking us alive either. No Letter of Marque provides compensation for taking prisoners, so we're not worth their time. In fact, I expect to see their Oriflamme any moment now."

As if on cue, the French ship unfurled a long, red three tailed banner with a prominent gold sun, the ancestral Frankish signal that no quarter would be asked or given.

And there it is, Grey thought morosely.

"Crew's accounted for captain!" The shout came up from the Chief Deckmate.

"Take us about and all speed to the engines! Dump everything you can overboard and tell the crew to arm and make ready to repel boarders."

The *Valkr's Wing* banked into a turn and began to slowly pick up speed as casks, tools, and even the precious spinal fluid all went over the sides. The two remaining skiffs dashed out well ahead of the converted frigate. The privateer was a much more immediate threat to them, and they could try to link up with the Wing later, if the larger ship were able to escape.

Despite jettisoning most everything that was not permanently bolted to the deck, the Wing was not gaining speed fast enough. Slowly but inexorably, the French corvette was gaining ground. Grey peered through his field glasses at the approaching ship. Other than the occasional wild shot at the pair of fleeing skiffs from the Hotchkiss guns, the corvette's heavy weapons were silent. However, her decks were crawling with men taking up firing positions with an assortment of small arms, taking aim for the moment their prey came within rifle range.

Grey's crew were arming themselves as well. The *Valkr's Wing* carried rifles enough for her officers and many of the crewmen had scatter guns or pistols amongst their personal effects, but the majority had simply grabbed whatever tools were at hand, improvising a motley assortment of melee weapons.

"LaGrasso get everyone to cover," Grey barked, "I don't want to lose people to those riflemen."

As if to emphasize his point, one of the deck hands spun to the deck clutching his shoulder and cursing. The air began to grow thick with thuds and whines as sharpshooters from the privateer began to crack away with their long guns.

Grey's crew scurried to whatever cover they could find, while Grey crouched at the wheel, doing his best to keep from exposing himself to sniper fire as he steered the ship.

The Frenchman closed and the fire intensified, now returned by some of Grey's men. Risking a quick glance back at the privateer, Grey saw what her captain intended. She was maneuvering to board. She would pull abreast of the *Valkr's Wing* and a bit above her. Then her crew would probably drop bombs first to clear the deck and then rope lines, the greater altitude of the French ship allowing her crew to attack from a position of advantage. The situation was grim. Grey looked to what would be his last resort.

One of the safety mechanisms common to most modern airships was a set of kill switches on the steam lines leading to the engine nacelles and other machinery on deck. Designed to stop the flow of steam in case of a line breach, they were safe if a captain vented the main steam tanks, but if tripped simultaneously and without venting, they would cause the boiler to build up pressure until it burst. The explosion would certainly doom his ship and kill everyone aboard her, but at least Grey would go to the next life knowing that there was a good chance that he would mortally wound the privateer.

The French ship was pulling into position and her crew was deploying steam grapples on her railings. The *Valkr's Wing* shuddered as a dozen heavy irons sunk into her deck planking, locking the ships together and trailing thick ropes, ropes that would be swarming with marines in a moment.

"Boarders!"

The cry came from a dozen throats. Thinking quickly, Grey settled on a plan. One set of barked orders later and his crew was in position. Grey knew two ways to repel boarders. The first was to meet them head on. That was the way of marines and warships and the way the French apparently expected Grey's crew to meet them. They began their assault by casting grenades and nail bombs. Moments after the bombs burst, Grey heard the sound of heavy boot falls on the ship's deck.

"Let them have it boys!"

Grey burst from his hiding spot, his revolver blazing away as the rest of the crew followed suit with shotguns and pistols, sending half the boarding party tumbling to the deck. When his pistol clicked empty, Grey holstered it and hefted an ax normally used for cracking bones as thick as a man's waist, then launched himself at the boarders with a hoarse shout.

"Come on, get stuck in!"

Grey had opted for the second method of dealing with boarders: let them come aboard then come at them all at once. If you hit them hard enough and took out enough of their first wave, their crewmates might be convinced to look for easier prey. It seemed like his plan might just work. Though the Frenchmen were wearing body armour, they had been caught off balance by the initial fusillade and were shaken.

Grey charged the confused knot of French marines, taking off the top of a man's head with the first blow of his ax. Most had not had the opportunity to draw their swords and were trying to fight off his crew with knives and hatchets, overmatched by the improvised clubs, hooks, and spades wielded by his crew.

Grey brought his ax around and swung it in a great overhand arc at the man standing closest to him. That man sidestepped the blow and jabbed at Grey with a knife. Grey leaped back from the wild thrust and lashed out with his own weapon, the axe sailing harmlessly through the spot where the Frenchman's arm had been.

As Grey recovered, there was enough time for his enemy to draw his saber and swing. Grey caught the blow, an artless downward slash, near the head of his ax and used the momentum of the strike to swing the butt of his weapon around and land a viscous blow in his foe's stomach. The man doubled over with a grunt. Grey punched out with the head of his ax, connecting with the temple of his enemy with a sickening crunch, and the Frenchman went down with a groan.

Next to Grey one of his crewmen struggled for control of a cutlass with a French marine. Grey reversed his ax and smashed the heavy socket into the

Frenchman's back. The Frenchman's grip slacked as he gritted his teeth in pain and that was all the opening Grey's crewman needed to wrest the blade out of the hands of his foe and hack it into the man's neck.

Grey risked a quick glance around. By some miracle of fortune, his men were actually winning the fight. Most of the boarders were down and the handful still standing were cornered against the rail, the vengeful crew of the *Valkr's Wing* closing in. Those that had them had reclaimed their firearms and were loading them. Those who only had a weapon suited for hand to hand snarled and shouted curses at the French, who huddled into a tight knot and snarled and cursed right back. Grey began to reload his pistol, managing to fill the chambers despite the relentless shaking of his hands, when he noticed movement on the underside of the privateer.

He began to call out a warning, then was thrown from his feet as the corvette's Hotchkiss guns swiveled to aim down at the *Valkr's Wing* and opened up with a load of canister, intent on sweeping the decks clear of men. The shrapnel shells burst as they struck the planks of the deck, sending jagged iron shards and rough metal balls scything through the Frenchmen and Grey's crew indiscriminately.

Grey lurched to his feet and began to scramble for cover when another shell burst nearby. Grey felt a sharp pain on his forehead then the world went white.

The first thing Grey felt was a trickle of warmth running down his forehead and a larger patch on his left arm. The second was the wave of agony that washed over him. He groaned in pain, his legs curling involuntarily as every muscle in his body screamed in agony. That was enough to convince him that he wasn't dead. Grey slowly opened his eyes.

Another wave of French boarders was thudding on to his ship's deck. Grey's eyes scanned the ship, looking for any of his crew who might be able to put up a fight, but none of his people were standing. Some, like his deck chief, were bloody and broken, limbs splayed at unnatural angles and bodies perforated by iron shot from the canister rounds. Others yet lived, but were stunned or dazed like their captain, their movements weak and clumsy as they tried to gather their wits.

Slowly, cautiously, the Frenchmen began to fan out from where they had alighted, wary of the chance of another ambush. As they advanced, their cutlasses and sabers flashed down occasionally, finishing off those wounded they found, and making sure those that seemed dead were.

This is it, Grey thought, *This is how it ends.*

He looked about. There was still one option left to him. Trip the kill switches and let the tanks blow. If he and his crew were goners anyway, he thought it was best to try and take as many of those frog-eating bastards to hell with him as he could.

Grey spied the controls for the safety valves. They were a good ten or fifteen feet out of reach and he had to get to them without catching the eye of any of the enemy crew prowling the deck. He slowly began to crawl towards the safeties. For a long moment he froze as one of his men began to scream horribly until the sound was abruptly choked off. Inch by inch he crawled towards the switches, expecting to be pinned to the deck with a French saber at any moment. Twice more he froze in place. Once as another of his crew died screaming and a second time as a man in the dark blue of an French officer's jacket passed by far too close for comfort.

Slowly, his muscles screaming in pain every inch of the way, Grey advanced to the controls. Checking one final time that he had not been seen, Grey looked over the controls, quickly flipping the four safeties, blocking the main steamlines to the engines.

Unnoticed by the French, the propellers slowed and stopped. Immediately, the gauges scattered across the instrument panel began to climb, the pressure of the steam quickly building to dangerous levels.

All that was left was for Grey to shut the emergency vents and watch the pressure mount until his ship blew. Hand on the fateful lever that would doom his ship and everyone aboard it, Grey took a slow and deep breath, steeling himself to do what was necessary. His fingers tightened on the lever and he tensed his arm. He felt the heavy pull of the switch, the pressure of the steam fighting against the closing of the valve. His muscles tensed as he prepared to put his back into it when there was a blinding flash of blue light and a crack like a wooden beam breaking.

A scorched and smoking spot marked the deck where a French officer had been standing moments before. The rest of the boarders looked up from hunting Grey's remaining crew as arcs of blue-white electricity flashed across the deck, reducing another handful of Frenchmen to their component parts in a string of thunderclaps.

There was a loud, evil sounding hiss and a set of thuds that Grey felt through the deck plank, then the sharp bark of gunfire. Grey forced down an urge to break his cover to learn who else had landed on his ship.

Judging by the rate of pistol fire, whoever the new belligerents were there were a lot of them and they weren't being picky about their targets. The Frenchmen scattered, trying to find cover so their could return fire at their new assailants.

Another loud hiss drew Grey's attention and he watched as something soared over the deck on twin plumes of white smoke, bulky and bulbous. Grey marveled at it in stunned shock and it took him a moment to realize that the thing was a actually man.

He wore what looked like a whiskey still on his back, from which sprouted a pair of comically small and flimsy looking wings and a pair of nozzles, the sources of the white smoke. The man wore thick pauldrons on each shoulder and on his chest was another heavy plate on which was mounted some technological marvel that crackled and flashed with electrical energy. On his head was a strangely elongated helmet, mounted with both goggles and a rebreather.

Even as he flew the man shouldered a rifle and fired, loosing a bolt of lightning. The bolt cracked into a man trying to turn one of the French deck guns and blasted him into atoms. The man wearing the flying machine swooped towards the deck of the French corvette and was followed by a half dozen of his comrades.

The air around Grey was filled with the cracks from lightning rifles and the deeper roar of pistol fire. With a sickening crunch of bone and flesh, a Frenchman landed in a heap in a few feet from Grey.

He heard a harsh voice barking something in English then saw more of the French learning to fly the hard way, hurled bodily over the side of their own ship. Risking a quick look about, Grey saw the shape of another ship, substantially larger than both of the Frenchman and his vessel.

Whoever the hell this new ship is, her skipper has a set of brass ones if he's attacking two ships at once.

Another set of man-made lightning bolts flashed overhead as Grey heard the sound of boots advancing at double quick, coming towards him. Fear ran through Grey. He could still shut the vents and force his ship to self destruct, but whoever these new boarders were, they offered he and his crew a chance for life. He decided that he had to risk it and opened the steam lines again, watching the pressure bleed off from the tanks.

The tramping boots came closer and closer. Grey suppressed a gasp as one of their wearers can into view. If the troopers looked disconcerting in the air, they were the essence of intimidation at these close quarters. The weird, oblong helmet, the bulky winged flight pack, and the heavy, sloped armor covering the shoulders and chest, all worn by a tall, broad shouldered figure, conspired to give the trooper a hulking outline that made him look more like a heavily armed flying ape than a man. As he took in the trooper, Grey noticed the man's cog and eagle insignia on top of a tricolor flag. It was the Imperial Amerikan Air Corps.

Well, it could be worse.

Technically, Grey's ship was flagged to the Amerikan Empire, but as an auxiliary. Grey was not a citizen and thus could not have legally owned the ship if it were flagged to the Amerikan Merchant Marine. However, he could expect the IAAC to wring out every piece of geld they could legally get from him for the rescue.

As long as you weren't flagged to one of their constantly shifting list of enemies, the IAAC rarely resorted to direct violence, preferring to subtly threaten and to fall back on a Byzantine set of laws governing shipping to do their robbery.

At least the Amerikans didn't share the endless bloodlust of the French and Russians. They wouldn't enslave his crew like a Turkish or a Chinese vessel would. They wouldn't even impress half the crew into their ship's black gang like a British flagged ship would.

No, they'll just rob us blind, patting themselves on the back for doing it under the cover of law.

The fight was ending. The IAAC troopers continued their relentless advance across the deck, casually butchering the French before them. Some of the French tried to surrender, only to be beaten to the deck with rifle butts or cut down with sabers. Once the French were finished, the IAAC began to lend aid to Grey's crew, doing rough triage on the decks. One of the troopers addressed Grey as he came to his feet.

"Are you injured reside..oh," the trooper stopped as he realized that Grey was the captain of this vessel. "Captain, if you're not injured, our Captain will see you."

"I am fine. I will be glad to meet with your captain."

Grey did not have to wait long. The IAAC captain came down the same line her crew had used to board the *Valkr's Wing*. The woman was of medium height. She had broad shoulders and carried herself in a way that spoke of ample physical strength. Her skin was a dark olive color. Her hair and eyes were dark as well, indicating Mediterranean or North African blood.

Not much lighter than me, thought Grey. Though it was not exactly common to see someone with her skin tone in IAAC drab, it was not surprising either given the Empire's loudly and frequently expressed, and utterly sincere, lack of regard for all characteristics save loyalty and obedience when it came to recruiting.

While the woman did not wear the full boarding armor of an IAAC marine, she was not in the cropped jacket and skirt of her dress uniform either. Her attire was mostly functional with enough formal elements to satisfy decorum if need called for it. The skirt was still there, though slashed to the front and back to allow for freer movement. Under it she wore leather trousers and knee high boots. Her jacket still sported the braids and shoulder bars expected of an Imperial officer but the cut was longer than usual, closer to that of a male officer's uniform.

Probably, Grey reckoned, *for warmth and the modicum of protection the heavy canvas offered.* He also noted that she wore the heavy leather gauntlet and bracer that marked an Imperial Air Corps sword master.

Those marines not seeing to the wounded snapped to the attention as she confidently strode across the deck. She stopped in front of Grey, appraising him briefly and removed her rebreather. It was obvious to Grey that she had once been quite pretty. As it was, her visage remained striking, though weathered by her long term of service in the skies and sporting a ragged horizontal scar that had cost her a portion of her nose.

"I am Captain Asha Tsemblenko of the Warluft *Raven's Daughter.* May I assume you are the captain of this vessel?"

"Yes ma'am. Anton Grey at your service."

"Well, the Air Corps is always happy to lend a hand to a properly chartered merchant shipping. Your charter please?"

Grey retrieved the documents from the case on his belt. He had been dreading the question. He was a free resident of the Amerikan Empire but his ship was flagged as a Dutch East India Company trader and, though the Dutch East Idea company had maintained a decades long policy of neutrality towards conflicts on worlds other than Earth, the IAAC was notoriously possessive towards what they considered their skies. With some trepidation, he handed the documents to the officer, who leafed through them.

"So, Resident Grey, care to tell me why your ship is not flagged to your mother country?"

Grey grimaced to himself. The Captain had to realize that a free resident couldn't register a vessel with the Empire. The right to own real property, ships, and businesses was reserved for full citizens and the Empire never missed a chance to remind the world of that fact, to the point that one would need to be a simpleton to not know it. But idiots didn't generally keep IAAC commands. The competition for the helm of a Warluft was far too cutthroat. She was just playing with him.

"As the Captain knows, free residents can't legally own ships in the Empire, so I had no choice."

"You did have a choice, Resident Grey. You could have sold a controlling share to a Citizen. It would have saved you a lot of geld today. Fuel costs geld, training men costs geld, Blitzencasters cost geld, everything that saved your ship today cost the Empire a great deal of geld, Resident Grey, and I remind you that all must pay their share, and if you don't pay in blood, you will pay in geld."

The Imperial officer was handed a leather bound book by one of her troopers. Her eyes scanned the page and she made several 'hrmph' noises.

"Resident Grey, you owe the Empire forty three thousand, five hundred and thirty seven geld, the total sum due immediately. Will you be paying in specie, bill, or trade goods?"

Grey's eyes bulged. That was a fortune. Even if he had not dumped the ship's cargo, there was no way he could have paid that much money.

"Captain Tsemblenko, I just don't have that much money on hand. If you can let me get back to port, I might..."

"Resident, I said the sum was due immediately. May I assume you don't have the necessary funds to pay?"

"Yes, Ma'am. I just don't have it."

"Ensign, what's the value of this vessel?" she turned to one of the troopers.

The man replied immediately. It was obvious that Tsemblenko's crew expected this exchange and was practiced at it. "Captain, she's got a good set of try works and a basic refinery and she's a solid ship all around, so despite the damage I'd say she'd fetch fifty four thousand geld."

"Then under Article 232 of the Privateer and Shipping Code of Imperial Amerika, I hereby seize this vessel and all her cargo and accoutrements. Resident Grey, you will be issued a voucher that can be redeemed in our home port for what value remains after your debt is paid."

Grey's mouth dropped open. They were going to take the *Valkr's Wing*. They were going to steal his ship out from under him. "You can't do that Ma'am, how will my crew get back to port? How will I make a living?"

"Resident Grey, what you do when you get back to port is not the Empire's problem. I suggest in future ventures; you consider the value of acquiring citizenship yourself, or at least bringing a citizen in as a part owner, so that you may enjoy all of the protection and privileges thereof. As for your passage, you and your crew can pay for it with labor in kind, or I can take it out of your voucher, the choice is yours," as she finished, she handed Grey the voucher, drawn from a bank on Harrisfyrd, back on Earth, several long, and very expensive, trips distant.

"But I was attacked ma'am!"

"So you were, and that gives you a claim against the French government under Section A Clause 2C of the Conference of Civilized Conflict. I suppose you could press a claim against the French vessel, under Section D Clause 9, if you wanted to."

Tsemblenko turned her head to look at the French ship and Grey followed her eyes. The corvette was in worse shape than the *Valkr's Wing*. Blood was running freely from her scuppers and she had taken on a small, but noticeable, list. A column of smoke rose from her deck. Something was, or had been, burning but apparently it wasn't a serious danger as there were still IAAC troopers on her, systematically stripping out anything of value.

Tsemblenko turned from the ship and looked back at Grey, "Like I said, she's yours, if you want her. You might want to make sure you've got enough men left to get her back to port. It will take my crew an hour or so to rig this ship for towing, you've got that time to reach your final decision."

"We'll fly her. Don't you worry about us Captain."

Tsemblenko gave Grey a smile with the corner of her mouth that told him that she didn't think he would be able to manage the corvette with his surviving crew and if he couldn't Tsemblenko wouldn't be losing sleep over it.

' Ia'am, with your permission?"

"Of course, Resident Grey. Don't let me detain you."

Grey and LaGrasso watched the IAAC ship as she towed the *Valkr's Wing* back to her home port. Grey was filled with the distinct feeling that this would be the last he saw of his ship for a very long while. She was quite a prize and as he was not a citizen. He had no way to reclaim to her. The French vessel was poor consolation for the ship Grey had lost. The IAAC had not been gentle during the fight. She had been swept with grapeshot, canister and small arms fire. Her planking was scorched in two places from minor fires, her wheel was a wreck, and Grey suspected that the bloodstains on the deck would never be scrubbed out. But her guns were intact, both the big rifles in the fore and the under-slung Hotchkiss guns, she was still buoyant and her engine worked. That was enough for Grey.

The *Valkr's Wing* had been the child of half a lifetime's worth of work and now she was being stolen, because Grey hadn't been willing to shed and spill twenty years worth of blood to earn a thrice damned Amerikan Citizen's Eagle. Throughout his life, he had paid his taxes and fees and levies and now an Imperial ship and crew that those taxes had helped fund had just stripped him of his ship, in which was invested all of his Earthly wealth. They had left him with an under-crewed ship that still dripped blood from her decks and a voucher that he would have to travel across a continent and two worlds to redeem.

"So what now Captain?"

"Hunting serpents seems to have lost it's promise, wouldn't you agree Mr. LaGrasso?"

"That it has sir. Do you think we should go back to smugglin'? This ship might be fast enough for it."

"No Mr. LaGrasso, I had something else in mind. Those Hotchkiss guns still work and the trio on the fore are still in good shape. We still have two of the skiffs. I'm tired of being a chicken amidst the foxes. This ship has some teeth. I think we best make used of them. It's time to take our turn as a hunter. Those bastards stole my ship. They stole it and patted themselves on the back the whole time!"

"Are you suggestin' we turn pirate Captain? We might make a living for a while that way, but what are the odds you'll run into the *Wing* again?"

"I'll find her Mr. LaGrasso. The *Wing* is a hunter, and there are but a few places where she can ply her trade. They'll have her back out Mr. LaGrasso. You can count on that. There's too much money to be made to keep a ship like that in drydock somewhere," Grey stared at the *Valkr's Wing*, his precious ship, his treasure, the single thing he valued most in the world, being dragged away from him. "I've heard that the Turks are granting letters of marque. I have it in mind to go to New Aleppo look into those rumors. Then I don't know about you, Mr. LaGrasso, but I have a lot of scores to settle after today."

I have lot of dead friends and a lost ship that need to be reclaimed then reckoned for, Grey thought, *I'll have my revenge, if I have to carve it out of everything that flies over this world.*

LaGrasso nodded his agreement, "It gets old always being the one who's scared."

"Then take us high and set course for New Aleppo. After those Imperial bastards are out of sight, hoist a black flag. We have work to do."

THERE'S ONE BORN EVERY...

THERE'S ONE BORN EVERY...

By Brian D. Thomas & Raymond J. Witte

Every eye in town gazed upward in hungry anticipation to watch a spectacle witnessed by a lucky few only once or twice in a decade. Hanging in the sky, visible by day or night, was a glowing cloudy ball that pulsed with a mystic inner life and a promise of affluence and trade. People traveled great distances to watch the birth of something great. And thousands waited for weeks as the glowing cloud mass grew more dense and swelled like the belly of a pregnant wife with its promise of a magical delivery. Even now, when its glow had grown bright enough to scorch the eye as if one were staring at the summer sun, still every face in town was turned towards the heavens to watch the birth of a skylock.

This birth would mean a world of difference for the sleepy little town of Oggsburg. The opening of a skylock would bring commerce flooding in to wash away the smell of fish, desperation and poverty that hung over the decrepit collection of hovels and fishing net stands that clung to the banks of the Patapsui river. Visitors would no longer focus on the sloped heads, wide mouths and slightly amphibian features of the locals…a certain "Innsmouth" look attributed to a rumored migration from up north. A skylock would turn the backward town into a focal point of cultural exchange and international, maybe interworldly, travel.

Depending, of course, on where the newborn skylock led.

That was part of the excitement. The learned men of the world still had not found a way to predict where a new skylock might open nor where it would lead once it opened. Skylocks always opened in pairs, forming a bridge from one location to the other, and to date no one had been able to identify another currently birthing skylock anywhere else in Imperial territory.

Betting parlors across the Empire were taking book on where the new celestial bridge might lead. With the recent discovery of Venus, good odds were that another path to that green jungle world was now opening over fishy little Oggsburg, while others were betting on a link to South Atlanticus and a short cut to Brazil or Peru.

Major Girth, commander of The *Irascible Wind* and newly appointed admiral of Task Fleet Oggsburg clasped his hands in nervous anticipation. A new skylock not only meant a new path leading out from his beloved Empire, it also meant a new path into his nation. Imperial Amerika couldn't just let foreigners and aliens go traipsing about as they pleased, and this uncharted new skylock created an unsecured border.

Imperial Amerika did not tolerate unsecured borders.

In recognition of some of his latest "achievements" Major Girth had been given command of an airship task force to secure this new skylock chain and to chart and hold its corresponding exit point. Task Force Oggsburg included not only the mighty warluft *Irascible Wind* but also two Gunhawk class battlelufts and the scout luft *Sky Snake*. The *Sky Snake* and her two escorts were poised to cross through the emerging skylock the moment it opened, and Girth smacked his lips in a hunger that had nothing to do with the plate of finger sandwiches his deck officer was holding. He squinted through the swirling glare and tried to see though to the mysteries on the other side.

On the ground below the *Irascible Wind* additional security safeguards were being put in place as dozens of "Oggsburg Militia" swarmed over their brand new aerial defense guns, placed into their care by a loving and paranoid empire. If Girth had looked down he might have seen the local gun crews drilling under their new artillery instructors, learning how to target incoming air ships, how to plot fire missions and how not to load the ordinance in backwards. The locals were so overjoyed with their new guns, air raid helmets and polarized glare shields that they didn't even complain that half their town had been leveled to make room for the massive artillery pieces.

Horace P. Thorton watched disinterestedly as the local gun crews waddled through their drills, and he smiled to himself with poorly hidden anticipation. The anti-warluft ordinance was only a part of the frenzied festival atmosphere that had descended upon the town as the moment the skylock would finally open drew near.

All day, Thornton had been dragooned into watching, with poorly hidden annoyance, as the children of Oggsburg clumsily performed pageants depicting key events of imperial history. The conquest of the Skraeling nations, the Battle of Plymouth Rock, and the Emperor Snorri Running Bear's crossing of the Mississippi had all been recreated by a pack of barefoot, stuttering, suspiciously similar looking children. After that, Thornton had been forced to choke down deep fried Greeble, cream chipped Greeble, Greeble balls and Greeblehash on toast as the locals went out of their way to share their new found affluence.

Then there was the tiresome barking of the Imperial officials, hawking preemptive war bonds and coaxing people into twenty year stints in the service. With the amount of hard cider her Imperial Majesty's representatives were pouring, it was far from surprising that the recruiters were having a great day. Oh what a roar rose from the crowd when a third of the children from the pageants signed on en mass to do their part!

Yes, so far, other than counting the piles of money he was bound to make, the highlight of the day had been when the townspeople had managed to wrangle a foreigner for a rousing game of "Kick the Frenchy". Thornton suspected the man was actually from Yersey, but decided it was best to let the locals think what they wanted to think. After all, Oggsburg was about to become very good to him.

The fish eyed yokels had been eager to sell their dank, stinky hovels and moldy piers to him for far more than they had considered the ramshackle structures to be worth. They were so pleased with their new guns and the status of the militia postings that few had taken the time to think about the financial implications of the skylock opening, beyond the possibility of adding the stray alien to their usual diet of grits, squirrel, and sickly little crabs. They had little idea that every inch of property for miles around would skyrocket in value once the new skylocks opened. But Horace knew.

Horace had sunk every penny he had, and more borrowed under the name of Franklin Unrah, the Imperial Citizen whose name was on all the deeds, into as much land as he could convince the locals to sell and then hired the fish eyed cretins to erect sky berths. The banks of the Patapsui River were now dotted with what he had modestly named "Thorton Towers."

Truth be told, at the moment the Thorton Towers were a haphazard collection of surplus fuel pumps, stitched together sacks of Liftium, jury rigged repair docks and pulley operated cargo hoists, all perched upon spires of drift wood and swamp pine, all prone to fire and collapse with a frequency that should have been distressing.

But Horace didn't care. Location was everything here. And once the Geld started flowing in, Horace was sure he would get around to replacing the current towers with something more suitable…eventually.

Still he smiled as he looked out over his small personal fiefdom of cheap lumber and rusted brackets rising into the summer sky. He had finally latched on to a scheme that just could not lose. Soon every airship traveling between these new locks would be renting dock space, paying cargo handling and repair fees and renting warehouse space from Thorton Towers, and frankly Horace didn't care where the new locks led. Wherever a skylock led, commerce flowed and Horace was poised like a pilot fish on the snout of the shark that was the Amerikan Empire, ready to gather up all the scraps he could catch.

He smiled as he contemplated the riches and the social opportunities that this

THERE'S ONE BORN EVERY...

venture would open up. He would make enough coin that Citizen families would be begging to adopt him. Then he would get his Eagle. No need for years of danger and toil in the Empress's service to win his citizenship, just a bit of luck and foresight. Then he wouldn't need people like Unrah to act as front men for his cunning business ventures. The name Horace P. Thorton would be spoken in glowing terms in the saloons and dining rooms of the rich and powerful across the nation.

Lady Citizen Wilhelmina Wigglebottom licked her lips as she inspected the trumpet section of the Harrisfyord Lady Patriots Marching Band. As bandleader it was her duty to ensure everything was in order. She and her sisters-in-arms had traveled via the new rail line from Pennsyltucky to Baltimoot to attend this auspicious event and lend their musical prowess to the pending celebration of Imperial expansion. Nothing stirred the patriotic blood of the residents and citizens of Imperial Amerika more than the thunderous sounds of a marching band and the sight of heaving bosoms as ladies blew into their instruments.

The diminutive little woman nearly glowed with authority as she politely pointed at a speck of discolored brass and tapped lightly on one of the great marching drums to test it's timbre. She wanted to ensure that everything was perfect for the moment she and her band mates sounded the fanfare that would announce the opening of the new skylock.

Seventy-two proud and patriotic women stood bedecked in uniform and ordered ranks, their musical instruments held at port arms with military precision. Each member of the marching band had practiced, worked and fought (quite literally…missing tufts of hair and powdered black eyes still showed as proof) to stand in these hallowed ranks to represent Harrisfyord society and Imperial pride. The Harrisfyord Lady Patriots Marching Band had been chosen from all the other Imperial Districts to play the fanfare and Lady Citizen Wigglebottom was going to be Loki-damned if she was going to let anything spoil her…and her sister's of course…moment.

Wilhelmina spared a glance up. She knew that somewhere inside the huge Imperial gunship that hung above the crowded street her beloved "Snuggle Bear," Ensign Rawlmond Witt- bridge officer of The *Irascible Wind*- was gazing out a porthole and looking down on her with loving, longing eyes. Or least he had better be. She hadn't been able to spend much time with her betrothed since arriving in town other than a few stolen hours in one of Oggsburg's less fishy smelling hotels, and they hadn't spent much of that time talking. Wilhelmina had been excited to show off her marching band uniform and to describe in detail the planned performance, but her fiance had attacked their short liason with typical military enthusiasm.

"If he shouts about 'taking the trenches' one more time I shall become quite cross with him," Wilhelmina muttered to herself. Then her frown melted into a smile as she recalled the rest of that short evening's campainge, and she blushed inspite of the fact that no one was looking. She looked back up at the floating gunship and sighed.

The short Imperial bandleader adjusted her dress sword and primped her bustle as she glanced up at the blooming skylock and the waiting airships. "Remember ladies," she shouted, "Play loud enough for them to hear us even in Valhalla and don't let a single sour note spoil Odin's mead!"

"It's a great day to be Imperial!"

High in the sky over the muddy Patapsui River the glow from the swirling ball of light intensified until most had to avert their eyes. Those experienced in these things knew that in time the intense glare of the new skylock would dull to a swirling glow like a harvest moon seen through a foggy night, but for now even eyes protected by goggles or glare shields would tear and water if they watched the infant celestial miracle for too long.

It was time.

Onboard the *Sky Snake* glare shields were raised in the pilothouse and airmen donned goggles as the scout luft slipped into the now fully opened sky lock. The Gunhawk lufts followed closely behind guns run out and ready to welcome a new territory into Imperial embrace.

Major Girth had to squint against the glare of the newborn skylock to watch the tail of the last gunhawk pass through the portal.

"Raise glare shields and ready main guns, Mr. Stout!" Girth excitedly shouted orders and his equally excited crew flew to obey. The entire crew hung in anticipation on the scouting fleet's report. The major turned to a buxom female sergeant and commented in a pleasantly lascivious tone, "You know I may name a mountain range after you."

"Something is coming through the lock," interrupted the ship's watch. Girth instantly forgot his sergeant's mountains and grabbed his monocular, straining through the glare to identify this intruder. Through watering eyes the major spotted the prow of an airship poking out from the skylock.

On the ground below the assembled crowd gasped as the dark silhouette of an airship slid out from the skylock. Horace P. Thorton gave a small sigh as he saw his first profits gliding out from the glowing portal.

The members of the Harrisfyord Lady Patriots Marching Band tensed and looked to their bandleader for the signal to sound the Imperial Fanfare. The entire waiting crowd was silent, then....BWAAAK! Mrs. Juniper Slowwaters, her trumpet still firmly placed against her lips blew out a scream of terror at the dark invader.

The Imperial crowd erupted into chaos, some cheering in welcome, some running for the air raid shelters while local militia whooped with joy, grabbed helmets and rushed to their defense guns.

"Give me an ID on that damn ship NOW Mr. Witt!" Major Girth slammed one meaty hand on his command lectern as he shouted at his bridge crew and snatched at his speaking tube.

"Main guns," Girth yelled into the speaking tube, "Track that foreign interloper as she exits. Main Watch, tell me the moment anyone spots a flag!"

"It's the lock glare sir," growled Ensign Witt. "We can't see anything clear enough to…"

The glare of the skylock suddenly had competition as the Oggsburg defense guns opened fire on the emerging airship. The dark shape of the intruding ship was sandwiched between the light of the lock and the flashes of heavy ordinance now erupting across its surface. The huge guns of the Oggsburg Air Defense Militia tore the invading airship out of the sky, just as another vessel emerged from the swirling skylock.

"Secondary target coming through sir," shouted one of the bridge crew. "This one is twice as big as the first," he hurriedly added.

The militia guns were still targeting the now falling first ship, blowing it to pieces even as it fell out of the sky. Major Girth opened his mouth to order his own guns to fire even as a thought snagged in his brain. He'd seen this new shape before…

"FIRE!"

The order leaped from Major Girth's mouth even before his brain knew he'd done it… which considering the number of times he'd shouted that particular order in his career without first consulting his brain wasn't really a surprise.

The *Irascible Winds*' entire compliment of heavy guns opened fire on the second silhouette even as Major Girth's brain finally kicked in. He suddenly knew why he recognized the shape of the airship poking out of the skylock. He'd just watched its tail as it entered the lock moments before.

THERE'S ONE BORN EVERY…

"HOLD FIRE!" Girth bellowed, trying to be heard over the thunder of his ship's guns.

"HOLD YER DAMN FIRE! HOLD FIRE! HOLD FIRE! HOLD FIRE!"

With each shouted order the Major was now smacking his ensign on the head with his dress gloves as if Ensign Witt's head was some kind of off switch for the barrage that was tearing the reemerging Imperial gun hawk into burning pieces. Below, the Oggsburg militia joyfully swung their heavy guns to bear on the second invading ship. Even as The *Irascible Wind* silenced its guns the second stricken airship of Task force Oggsburg began spiraling towards the ground. Below, the militia defense crews cheered. It was a great day for the Empire.

In the end everyone agreed it didn't make sense. Never before had a skylock been found that didn't actually lead…anywhere. The three airships of Task Force Oggsburg had flown through the new skylock only to come right back moments later. There had only been the briefest pause as they entered, then exited the glowing portal-just long enough for everyone to assume they were ships crossing from the other side, and long enough for two of them to be blown out of the air and come crashing down on the town. The learned men of the world would be pondering the peculiarity of the Oggsburg skylock for years.

Horace had watched in mute distress as a piece of flaming hull, hull from the Amerikan ship that had moments before sailed through the skylock, slammed into one of his towers, creating a domino effect as the flimsy structure toppled over into three of its mates. Horace fumed. It was as if the gods themselves were conspiring against him. What had he done to deserve this?

Ok, well, I have probably pissed off some gods, but those were always the weird little foreign ones. Not gods that actually counted, he thought, as his dreams of easy wealth and instant respectability burned like the scout ship the locals had so eagerly blown from the sky.

He turned to glower at the remaining Thorton Towers. The ruinously expensive and now entirely useless Thorton Towers. The Thorton Towers that had cost him every penny he had in the world to build, and now weren't even worth the cost of the scrap that had gone into their construction.

Skylocks meant commerce. It was a hard and fast rule that the entire world lived by. No one would ever go to places like Oggsburg if it weren't for the incredible trade opportunities that Skylocks offered.

No one ever came to fishy little Oggsburg before, and now the world, after it finished laughing at the stinky little town and all the suckers who had been waiting with baited breath for this moment, would forget about the hamlet and its slack jawed yokels as it slid back into obscurity. Certainly no one was going to need the towering air births or empty warehouses. Horace doubted anyone but the locals would even want the properties, certainly not at even half of what he had paid for it, and even if they did he knew for a fact that they'd already drunk through most of what he had paid them for the land in the first place.

Every penny he'd spent was wasted. Every penny he had was gone. Even worse, Thornton would now have Franklin Unrah, Imperial Citizen, whose name was one each deed and whose credit had financed more than half of the project, looking to make good on his investment. Horace had no idea how he was ever going to buy enough time to pay that particular debt. He frowned up at the cooling, swirling portal, cursing it, whatever sick twist of the universe had put it there, and everyone gathered to watch it open. Then he looked at his ridiculous towers and cursed those too, briefly considering simply lighting all of them on fire and collecting the insurance money before he remembered that he had spent so much on building them that he had not been able to afford that luxury.

Instead, Horace opened the celebratory bottle of brandy he had saved for the occasion and began to drink deeply, resolving to get horribly and utterly drunk. There would be a carriage that he had hired with the intention of driving up to

Baltimoot for a celebration of his success. Instead, as he gulped brandy, he found himself wondering just how far west the driver would take him before he realized that Horace had no means to pay him.

Horace put down the bottle and looked back out at Thorton Towers, the spindly symbols of his failure and the repository of all of his earthly wealth. Who the hell had ever heard of a one-way skylock before?

Lady Citizen Wilhelmina stomped her foot in anger. Her Imperial Citizen band uniform was ruined from crawling into the air raid shelter, several of the band's instruments were bent and broken from the stampede, and some fool militiaman had panicked and stabbed the huge bass drum with a bayonet.

Apparently there was to be no fanfare, which was just as well since most of the horn section was now buried under burning airship wreckage. Citizen Lady Bettica was shouting at a group of rescue workers to dig faster while she hungrily eyed a broken shop window and the scattered shoe display now exposed to the elements. Most of the sheet music had caught fire from the falling embers, the band's uniforms were freckled with burn holes and a bunch of frog faced little pageant girls had run off with the color team's flags.

Wilhelmina fumed. The Harrisfyord Lady Patriots Marching Band was in ruins... never mind the condition of the stupid town! She had worked months for this day and all she had to look forward to now was a long train ride home and weeks of searching for replacement tubas. Lady Citizen Willhemina looked up into the sky and wondered what had gone so horribly wrong. She narrowed her eyes at The Irasible Wind and wondered if it her hotheaded husband-to-be were in any way to blame for this fiasco. If she found out they were, Odin himself would not be able to protect them from her rightous fury. Tears were streaming down her chubby dirt-smudged cheeks as she surveyed the damage. This was supposed to be a great day for her... and her sisters of course.

Major Girth tapped his foot in agitation. There was simply no way he was taking the blame for this one. He was sure the Imperial Ministry of Commerce and Conflict would understand the confusion and subsequent destruction of two of the three airships of his scout fleet, not to mention the destruction of most of the fishy little town. He was sure they would recognize the rarity of a one-way skylock.

Yes, he was sure they would take into consideration the fact that the militia guns had been the first to fire and that he, a loyal defender of the realm had acted with reasonable promptness to the perceived threat of foreign invasion.

Yes, he was sure they would understand... Girth though to himself as he scanned the bridge crew for someone else to pin the entire mess on.

The folk of Oggsburg had no idea why everyone seemed so upset. Today had been so very exciting! The children still wearing their pageantry finest picked through the wreckage for choice bits while their mothers scraped off the worst of the dirt from the Greeble fritters.

The Oggsburg Militiamen croaked happily at each other as they waddled past stunned, soot covered Imperial Officials and weeping ladies with bent trumpets. The militiamen crawled over the ruins of their town and marveled at how much easier it was to see their new skylock without all those buildings in the way. They diligently cleaned and reloaded their lovely new defense guns then happily settled down to wait for the next foreign invader to appear in their sky.

It was a great day to be Imperial.

END

CPSIA information can be obtained at www.ICGtesting.com
Printed in the USA
LVOW13s2212090714

393593LV00028B/1117/P